I0582979

Sinister

PROTECTOR

H.L. PACKER

What happens when your walk home takes a turn for the worst?

When Ruby's solitary journey is interrupted, she should just walk away, but she's never been one to do what she's told. So, in the dark, she watches and waits, but will she find that this was a mistake?

Dex's sees the young woman being dragged from the ground and flung through the air, and he gets the first real look at the girl that will change his life. He can't walk away and leave her, not if he wants to live, anyway.

Two paths converge, and both lives will be irrevocably changed but this moment, but will it be for better, or worse?

Editor – Vicki at The Indie Hub

Cover Design& Formatting – LJDesigns

one
Ruby

It was the end of summer. The nights were still bright, and the air was still warm. My birthday was imminent, and the return to school was hovering on the periphery. My sixteenth, the final year at school, my exams, and a tentative reach for freedom were all so close, until they weren't.

One night changed everything. One moment flipped the world on its axis, and I would never be the same again. Lucky, I suppose, considering the things that followed.

But let's start at the beginning, with… the incident.

6 months ago

The can clatters across the desolate street, the sound of it echoing as it finds its way to the entrance of an alleyway just ahead. The dent in its side could be from where it bumps into the casters of an old, industrial-looking bin, with its red paint flaking, or it could have been from my boot, the contents long gone.

A neon sign at the takeaway over the road flashes twice and then goes off. Even they've had enough for the day, but at least they have a purpose. The team in there will no doubt be cleaning down, putting things away, prepping ingredients for the next day, then hitting the hay. Not me, though. I'm alone, traipsing through the streets in the middle of the night, and nobody gives a shit.

Reaching down, I pluck the can from its resting spot, preparing to throw it down the alley—maybe see if there's a box or bin I could aim for—when suddenly, voices interrupt my thoughts, my musings momentarily forgotten. Panicking, I duck behind the bin, hoping to wait them out.

"We all get our cut, man. Don't make this harder than it has to be," someone says from farther down the alley. His disinterested tone does nothing to ease the fright that courses through my veins as I press my back against the dank wall; a cold liquid seeping through to my skin as my heartbeat thunders in my ears.

If I get caught here, I'm dead.

There's nobody out on these streets up to any good. Not at this time of night, anyway. After pushing my breath out through pursed lips, I do my best to remain silent, inconspicuous, invisible. I'm no one, nothing, and it needs to stay that way.

"I just don't see why we're cutting you in, that's all," another voice replies while I edge along, peeking around the side as my curiosity gets the better of me.

Cautiously, I take in the scene at the end of the alleyway. There's one huge guy, with his hands shoved in his pockets as he loiters, clearly waiting for something while two others shuffle around nervously. It's pretty easy to work out that he's in charge of whatever the hell this is. Not that I need to know or remember anything about anything. Certainly not this. In fact, I very much need to shuffle back out, away. I should close my eyes, cover my ears, and pray to God that they're gone so it's safe for me to leave once I've counted to, say, a million or so. Yet I can't. I can't pull my gaze away from the twitchy movements of the two men closest to me, with the obviously most dangerous one being farther away.

There's something reassuring in that, at least.

It's dark, but he stands beneath a streetlight, his dark hair clipped short at the sides, his T-shirt hugging biceps that don't belong on any teenager I've ever seen. But it's the bored look on his face that captivates me. The way he looks straight through the two men in front of him who are clearly older, dangerous, thinking they're the ones running this... whatever it is.

But they don't. He does.

This teenager with the bulk of an adult and the presence of a hitman. At least that's what I think it would be like. You see it in the films; the dangerous guy with the dark eyes and looks that can kill. Yeah, he's got that look, and I can't turn away.

"Yeah," one of the edgy-looking guys adds as he adjusts the baseball cap on his head, hiding his face from this angle. "It's not like you're doing any of the wok here. So, why the hell am I giving you money, huh?"

Money? Fuck, I really shouldn't be here.

Baseball cap and his jittery buddy face off against the other guy, squaring their shoulders and preparing for...

something.

Holding my breath, my fists clench as tension coils through my body, and my guy chuckles.

Wait... my guy? And why does the sound of him echo down the alleyway so beautifully, like melting dark chocolate as it caresses your throat, warm and comforting, despite the bitter bite. There's a warning in that sound, and cunningness in the look that cuts their way. Something that says he knows exactly how to deal with these two idiots. The two tweakers who clearly don't see the danger they're in right now like I do.

"Your boss says, that's who." My guy pushes off the wall he was leaning against, squaring his shoulders and preparing for a fight.

I've seen it before: the shuffle. Adjusting the angle to your opponent, getting ready to strike or fend off an attack. This is the calm before the chaos, and looking at the size of the guy, it would be chaos. He's easily half as wide again as either of the men in front of him, the short sleeves of his T-shirt cut to showcase his bulging muscles as he plants his feet and crosses his arms over his chest.

He's big, scary, yet there's something immoveable and permanent about him. I've made those same moves myself when I've had to. You don't grow up where I do without learning a thing or two about looking after yourself.

Sliding one hand in my pocket while keeping an eye on the men in front of me, my fingers graze the pocketknife I keep there just in case. If this goes south, I need to be able to protect myself, because if there's one thing I've learned over the last few years, it's that nobody else is going to do it.

I wait out their altercation, knowing I'll safely be on my way soon as long as I keep quiet and out of sight, then it will all be over before it starts.

"Why don't you take it up with him, then?" baseball cap guy hisses, thrusting one finger into the big guy's chest.

Oh, shit.

My guy looks at the finger, which quickly disappears into the depths of baseball cap's torn up jeans, before pining the man himself with a look so full of hatred that even I snap my mouth closed and press myself farther into the wall.

Fuck, I hope no one ever looks at me like that.

Baseball caps' friend—the one who started this entire argument—pulls a wad of cash from his back pocket, doing his best to diffuse the quickly deteriorating situation which he created by thrusting it towards the now pissed off, huge guy.

"Here," he grumbles, letting go and stepping back as quickly as he can manage.

Great, now I'm witness to a fucking crime.

My stomach churns. The entrance to the alleyway is just... there. Dragging my gaze from the obvious threat farther in the alley, I peek over my shoulder, eyeing the distance with trepidation.

What kind of a person jumps behind a bin in the middle of the night when they hear voices, anyway? Me, apparently. Instead of doing the sensible thing, the normal thing, and bypassing it completely to go home, I stuff myself into the middle of it.

Stupid, stupid, girl.

I should be at home in the warmth, tucked up, sleeping

soundly... as if that was ever an option. I certainly shouldn't be trapped behind a smelly bin that's dripping something disgusting way too close to my foot while watching something illegal go down.

"Just fucking leave it, will you?" the argument creator grumbles, shoving baseball cap towards the entrance of the alley, right in my direction.

I hold my breath as they near, ducking behind the grimy metal and praying to anyone that can hear me that I make it out of this in one piece. Then one of them kicks the bin, forcing me back into the wall with an "oomph".

Before I have time to register what's happening, the bin is wrenched away and two pissed off guys are standing right in front of me.

"My, my, what have we got here?" the guy with the baseball cap sneers as his friend reaches for me.

My head pounds, and the two of them blur and merge before separating again. Then suddenly, I'm moving, in flight, being hauled from my scrunched-up position and thrust into the middle of the alleyway, my feet dragging along the ground.

"Looks like a sneaky little rat to me," one of them says, holding me at arm's length as the pleather of his jacket creaks and groans—my brain attempting to hold onto anything and everything in the here and now.

His beady eyes look me over with contempt, clearly seeing nothing worth saving. I'm just a kid, a teenager, a girl... and not even an overly pretty one. I don't have thick, luscious locks or huge tits, and there's no virginal innocence hidden in my eyes able to trick the man into letting me go.

The only thing in my eyes right now is pain and confusion.

Why didn't I keep walking?

"Rats that get caught end up dead," baseball cap guy sneers, getting in my face, his rancid breath causing a cough to splutter from my chest while my ears continue to ring, and I still can't see properly.

I completely miss the hand that flies towards me, slapping me across the face hard enough to make my brain rattle inside my aching head. But I have no words to get me out of this. No friends or family to call and plead to. Whatever retribution is about to come my way, well, there's fuck all I can do to stop it now.

"That's enough," a voice booms from the other end of the alleyway; a blurred shape in a dark shirt drawing closer and closer.

The guy holding me shakes me like a rag doll, clearly having said something or asked me something that I missed, too wrapped up in the man I thought had left—the one who currently sounds a whole lot like he may be my saviour here.

"I said that's enough," he repeats.

Before I have chance to get my weight underneath me, I'm tumbling, falling to the ground in a pathetic heap before a boot connects firmly with my stomach, knocking the air out of my lungs.

Soon, though, I'm not the only one losing their footing, and a growl echoes from damp wall to damp wall before the guy in the fake leather jacket lands with a serious thump against the wall opposite me. Black boots are planted in front of my body, shielding me from whoever it is that's left here. Baseball cap guy... I think?

"I suggest you fuck off," the man in front of me demands, his voice much calmer than you might expect for someone who just threw a person ten feet or more across an alleyway.

There's no reply from anyone, though, and I can't focus on anything past the boots ahead of me to work out what's going on. Nobody shares a name, a nickname, and I can barely breathe, never mind consider a description, but the creek of that fake leather soon comes from behind me, and before I even realise I've done it, I'm reaching for my knife, and swinging wildly in the direction it came from.

Then all hell breaks loose.

The huge guy with the bored tone and the dangerous stance explodes in front of me, dragging what must be the baseball cap guy from his feet and pounding him into a bloody pulp only a few feet away from me.

Not ready to let sleeping dogs lie, the one I swiped and apparently caught with my knife sidles in behind me, waiting, with his arm across my throat, until what little energy I have left dissipates only seconds later. He slaps the blade from my hand and unsuccessfully attempts to haul us both from the ground.

Panic threatens to take over, my supposed saviour busy with the other guy as I rake my fingers across the grimy ground, seeking out the smooth polish of the knife that's always kept me safe. My head pounds, my stomach throbs, and I'm reasonably sure the sticky substance that tickles the back of my neck is blood. Then I find it, and I stuff the handle between my fingers as my assailant calls out, "You might want to stop that..."

Not sure whether he means me or the other guy, I stop,

holding my breath as I wait for whatever happens next.

If crickets were present in England, this is the moment you'd have heard them, somewhere between the end of the wet thud, thud, thud of skin hitting skin and the scratching of my boots against the concrete slabs. Instead, there's this incredible moment of stillness. Nothing but four sets of heavy breaths echoing in the silence of the night while the rest of the world keeps turning, completely unaware.

"If you want her alive, I suggest you back away," the guy holding me hisses, the tension bouncing from one wall to another something I've never experienced before.

Sure, I've made mistakes. I found myself on the wrong side of the football captain before, and I called the drug dealer who waits at the kids park a paedo once, too, which didn't go down well. But I've never honestly thought my life could be over within a matter of moments—seconds, even— like I do right now.

I drag air into my bruised lungs, clutch my pocketknife, and wait to see what the man in front of me does—hopefully nothing that gets me killed—but there's nothing more than the narrowing of his eyes and the cock his head, apparently.

Why did I stop? Why did I hide? Why the hell didn't my stupid arse just keep walking down the street?

"I'll kill her," the guy holding me says, but his voice shakes, and his body quivers behind mine, whatever adrenaline he had left draining quickly now he has my weight to contend with as well as his own. "I will!"

The man opposite us allows his piercing gaze to catch mine before it drifts down to my hand as I adjust my grip on the knife before sneering at the waste of space behind me.

I'm barely holding on, the edges of my vision blurring, but I'm not going down without a fight.

I hear the snap that comes from the man opposite me, the final nail in both the man behind me and my coffin as my saviour ends the life of what used to be baseball cap. He's nothing more than a bloody blur at this point, but you never miss the sound of bones breaking, especially not in this weighted silence.

That's when I plunge the knife into the closest piece of flesh I can manage—his leg. The man in leather behind me screams and drops me, the knife dragging out as I fall and brace myself for whatever follows. Except the only thing that comes next is another snap, this time behind me, before warm blood seeps around my feet, soaking into the bottom of my jeans.

Darkness threatens to pull me under, but I'm not alone here, and there's no way I can consider myself safe yet. Not with everything I've just seen. Strong arms slide beneath me, then the huge guy picks me up, cradling me against his chest and whispering words of comfort in my ear, making sure my knife is with me before attempting to move away from whatever hell we're surely enclosed in.

The smell of cigar smoke and sandalwood surrounds me, his body heat pushing back the cold fear that had taken root. He strides us out of the alleyway, carefully crosses the road, then deposits me inside the back of a big, black car. There's nobody around to see it; not that he moves like he'd give a fuck if there was. Instead, he clips the seatbelt around me and presses a palm to the back of my head before inspecting the amount of blood with pursed lips and a shake of his head.

I have no idea why I don't open the door and run, why I don't take the opportunity presented and finally get myself as far away from this horrendous situation as I possibly can, but I don't. There's something about his calm silence that placates the chaos which is usually running rampant in my mind. That, and the fact that I'm suddenly so tired, I have no idea how I'm still awake.

An engine starts, a phone rings, and smoke fills the vehicle just seconds later.

"Hey, all good?" someone answers the call, the voice seemingly a million miles away as obscurity threatens to pull me under.

"Clean up needed at location, two for collection," my rescuer clips out, if that's even what I should call him.

Can someone who just took two lives and called it in like a takeaway really be considered a saviour?

The leather of the seat is supple against my skin as my consciousness begins to flicker, but I do my best to hold on, find out who this is, and what they're going to do with me. Have I just made it out of the frying pan and into the fire?

"Tell me it wasn't the sons," whoever is on the other end of the line asks, a resigned sigh tumbling following his question.

"No, it wasn't, and I'm sending Emmie an address. Tell her I need her help ASAP," he replies from the front seat, revving the engine.

I have no idea if their conversation continues, no idea who either of these people are, nor the ones who died in that alleyway. My mind is finally catching up with my body and shutting down, and then blissful unconsciousness finally pulls me under.

two
Dex

I don't know why I did it. I should have taken the money and left, but something about the dark hair and inquisitive eyes seemed familiar, and I couldn't walk away. When I finally got a good look at her, I knew exactly who she was and why I had to stay.

This girl is not one that can die on my watch.

So, I waded in, saved her as much as she saved me. I did everything I could afterwards to let her live her life, but I couldn't do it alone. Not without making sure she was safe, but who was going to protect her from me?

It's the middle of the night, and nobody should be awake, but when I drive down the shitty little street, more than one set of curtains slam closed. I guess the reputation that comes with this type of car does come in handy every now and again.

Peering over my shoulder, I see the girl is out cold, and there's no way in hell I'm risking waking her up whilst rifling through her clothes for the keys. That sounds like a good way to end up with a knife wound, so it seems like we're doing this the harder way.

After locking the car once I've climbed out, I try the front door, peeking under the mat and an overturned plant pot, just in case a spare key happens to be there. It's unlikely in this neighbourhood, but I suppose you never know.

Coming up short, I walk around the back, hoping for better luck there. The overgrown hedges scratch at my exposed arms, but I don't have time to bother with them. I need to get her inside, and quickly. The back door is locked, but a gentle shove with my shoulder has it giving way easier than it should to be classed as safe.

Well, at least we're in without alerting every neighbour in the vicinity. I do a quick double-take when I step inside, making sure we'll be alone before I bring her in; the couple of empty cups in the sink the least of the girl's problems.

One door hangs off, the kitchen cupboards are held up by nothing more than hopes and prayers, and there's a whole chunk of the banister railing completely missing in this place. It's like someone fell down the stairs, crashed right through it, and landed in the middle of the hallway. Fuck, this is worse than I expected, but at least there isn't anyone else here. Not yet, anyway.

Knowing I'm on a time crunch, I move quickly from room to room, finding the one that must be hers with ease. Grabbing a handful of towels, I throw them over the small mattress on the grubby floor before heading back to the car and lifting her as gently as I can, then bringing her back inside, and laying her down on what is hopefully a clean surface.

Her breaths remain even, despite the brief fluttering of her eyes, and as she curls in on herself, I take the moment to consider how much worse this could have been.

She shouldn't have been there—certainly shouldn't have seen half of what she did. But we don't treat women that way. Well, I don't, and there's no way I could stand there and let them hurt her, never mind watch it happen. Questions will be asked, answers will be needed, and whilst I killed one, the other had already bled out before I got there. I just didn't want that on her conscience.

Headlights flash around the room, and I pull the curtains closed, knowing I'm going to need some answers real fucking soon. After heading back down the stairs, I sneak out the back door and loiter in the darkness at the side of the building, watching the two people whispering quietly until their gazes catch mine, their steps quicken, and they follow me inside silently.

"What's going on? Where are you...?" Emmie asks, her questions trailing off as her fingers follow her gaze, inspecting every inch of my arms and shoulders, along with the blood staining my clothes, seeking out the wounds I asked her to help with.

She knows the risks we take. She's stitched the pair of us up more than once. It's not usual for me to ask for her help with someone else but... exceptional circumstances and all that.

"It's not me," I say. "She's upstairs."

"She?" her eyebrows practically hit her hairline before thunder cracks behind her eyes. "Show me."

With nothing more than a nod, I lead the way, my brother

silent as he follows the two of us, knowing just as well as I do whose house we're currently standing in and the shit storm that will likely follow.

Flicking on the floor lamp doesn't do much to illuminate the situation, but the dark patch expanding around her head is clear to everyone. Deferring to Emmie, I wait for her instructions, knowing she's the strength we need right now.

I can't fix this girl up—wouldn't even know where to start with it—but she can if only we can listen and do what's needed.

"Get me a chair, a bowl of clean, warm water, and whatever clean cloth you can find," Emmie demands, looking at Blaise before turning to me. "She shouldn't be asleep, and you damn well know it. Wake her up."

My stomach twists, already imagining the fight or flight that's going to kick in, no matter how gently I try to wake her. Hesitating at the side of her makeshift bed, I wait until my brother appears with a dining chair; his concerned gaze flickering over the girl before he returns to the task at hand.

Shaking off the emotion and the desire to run my fingers down her soft skin, I grip her shoulder and flip her over onto her back. Her eyes flicker briefly before flying open, her panic clear before the pain registers and she scuffles back, drawing herself against the wall and brandishing that little pocketknife she's held onto so dearly.

I should have taken it off her, put it somewhere safe where she wouldn't hurt anyone. Not that it's really going to be a problem. She's nothing more than a feral cat, her fur spiked out in every direction as she hisses at anything and everything that looks and sounds like a threat.

She doesn't say anything, just looks frantically from Emmie to me and back, her breaths heavy, and her confusion real.

"Come on, girl. If the amount of blood on that towel is anything to go by, we don't have a lot of time. Get your arse in this chair and let me stitch you up before you bleed out," Emmie says calmly.

Blaise appears in the doorway, slamming the light on with his forehead as he carries two measuring jugs into the room.

"Where am I putting these?" he asks.

Emmie looks around the room, moving the chair closer to a dresser before clearing the few things on there to one side and gesturing for him to put them down. Then she pins Ruby with a no-nonsense look—one that nobody has ever dared to argue with—before tapping the back of the seat twice, her expectation clear.

"Nobody here is going to hurt you," Emmie placates as gently as she can. "But if we don't get that cut sorted out soon, the hospital is going to be the only place that can."

Her mother isn't here yet, but none of us can know how long that will last. This needs to be done, and our cars need to be gone before she gets back. There will be fallout soon enough. But Ruby doesn't move. She barely takes a breath, stuck in her fight or flight instinct, with no idea what to do.

With a sigh, Emmie draws closer to her, not phased in the slightest by the terrified girl, poised and ready, brandishing a blade. I suppose, over the years, she's seen worse. Emmie grips Ruby's wrist, removing the knife from her hand and closing it back up safely and dropping it on the bed before *lifting her by her arm and taking her to the chair with not a single word, and Ruby lets her.*

For all the wildness behind her eyes, the fear that lurked there, something inside her knows we're not the threat her mind thinks we are. It's odd, really, considering the things we've done, and the man I'm being groomed into. Barely eighteen and already lethal, notorious. Not that she knows that. Not yet, anyway.

Blaise returns with cloths and hands them to Emmie before stepping back outside, clearly seeing the mistrust that plays on the young girl's features. And rightly so. Emmie asks her questions quietly, going through the motions as she measures and categorises the answers whilst doing her best to clean the area and prep for the stitches that will be needed, all while my feet are planted firmly near the doorway.

A tap on my shoulder jolts me out of my own head, where I was still picturing her limp body shaking in a man's arms tonight. Not the good kind of sated quivering you'd aim for at the end of the night, but the kind where you question if they're still even breathing.

I follow Blaise down the stairs, avoiding touching anything and everything as we go.

"What happened?"

Simple. Straightforward. That's my brother for you.

"Lance and Jameson came to do the drop. They were spouting some shit about not wanting to hand it over, about how we're profiting off their hard work, again…"

"Again," he repeats, rolling his eyes and crossing his arms over his chest.

"Anyway, I told them to take it up with Gregory, and

they paid up and fucked off."

"Except..." he says, gesturing to the stairs.

"Except Lance wasn't happy about it and kicked the fucking bin in his big, hard-man, temper tantrum. She was hiding behind it."

"Hence the head wound."

"Yep. If she's not sporting at least a couple of bruised ribs and a black eye in the morning, I'd be surprised."

"So, they started in on her, and you intervened. Couldn't have managed that a touch more diplomatically?" he asks, his jaw clenching.

Grabbing the cigarillos from my back pocket, I reach for my Zippo, only for Blaise to grab my hand and shake his head. He's right; I can't fucking light up in here.

He follows me outside, the two of us moving away from the barely broken door so the smoke and voices don't carry inside.

"You know I had to, right?"

He nods, taking a draw of the cigarillo he plucks from my lips before handing it back.

"They were gonna kill her."

"You're sure about that?"

"On my life," I tell him.

And it might be, depending on how this falls.

He already knows why I couldn't let them do that, even if the girl in question doesn't, but it's not going to make smoothing this over any easier.

Stamping the smoke out with my boot, I shove the butt in my pocket before we head back inside, hoping the worst is over.

"There you are," Emmie chides when our footfalls finally land at the top of the stairs. "Someone get this water changed, and one of you had better do something about that bedding. I'm not going to all this effort for her to end up with a fucking infection."

Ruby barely mumbles instructions, but it's enough for me to know where to get what we need and know that Emmie's given her the good drugs—the ones we almost have to be dying for her to bother with. I'm not sure whether that's a good sign, or not.

Blaise returns with clean water and then helps me with the sheets, pulling the dirty ones off to trade them with the only other threadbare set that was here. But they're clean, and the towel I lay on her pillow will help her overnight. Any more than that isn't our business. To be honest, this is more than we should be doing.

"Right, clean pyjamas and bed for you, girl," Emmie says as Ruby wobbles on the chair. "I'll leave you some tablets for tomorrow, but I can't do much more than that."

"It's fine, I can do it," Ruby slurs, trying to brush off the words and the drugs running through her system.

Her knees buckle as she attempts to stand, but I'm four steps closer within seconds, catching her before she undoes all of our hard work. Not that my hands don't meet Emmie's as we both reach for her.

"You good?" Emmie asks, not asking Ruby, but looking deep into my soul before choosing to let go and step back.

She knows me better than I know myself some days, that woman. She's seen me at my strongest, my weakest, and on the days where the world seemed so heavy, I just didn't know *how to carry it. She's seen it all, weathered it all, and she knows this girl is safe with me, even in the state she's in now. How many men in my profession could you say that about?*

"I've got this," I tell her.

Stepping back, she leaves with Blaise—nothing more than a head nod coming from him. There will be more questions asked, and more answers needed later, but for now, I listen for the sound of them leaving and the engine rumbling as he starts up and pulls away. I wait for far too long, with Ruby half-conscious in my arms, her face pressed against my chest.

"I just need a T-shirt," she mumbles. "Bottom drawer."

She lets me walk her over to the bed, wincing as her body curves to get down. Turning to go find what she needs, the drag of the zipper and the shuffling of fabric has me moving slower than ever.

This is not a girl I can care about or one I can see vulnerable. This is not someone I should be near at all. Equally, I couldn't leave her to die in the middle of a blood bath, either.

So, I slow my steps, find the biggest shirt I can manage in the half light, and I ask if she's decent before turning around. Chivalrous, I know. Her clothes and underwear lie in a heap at the side of the bed, her body tucked safely beneath the covers as she watches me but doesn't see. She won't remember any of this in the morning.

Maybe that's why Emmie gave her what she did, to numb the edges and protect me as much as she could. Maybe she's just as much as a sucker for a damsel in distress as I am.

Once I've handed over the shirt, I gather up her things

with the sheets and towels and drop them at the top of the stairs. I knock on the doorframe before coming back in for the water jugs, putting her things back on the dresser, then picking up the chair as I jostle the jugs in one hand.

She doesn't ask who I am—who any of us are. Doesn't ask why we helped her or what we want. She just watches me silently clear up and step back away. I put the chair back in the kitchen, rinse the jugs, and put them in what I think is the cupboard they came from. Then I grab the sheets and clothes, let myself out, throw them in the boot, and leave.

But I don't stay gone long enough.

I park the car somewhere safe and unobtrusive before making my way back to the house in the dark cover of gardens and alleyways, sneaking back in through the now-broken door.

The house is silent, broken and empty, much like the girl whose room I've just let myself back inside of. I move the tablets and water to the side of her 'bed' and find the darkest corner to sit in. The wood is cold, but I've been in worse places. The light reflects the tear tracks on her face—a vulnerability she waited until she was alone to release.

I can't leave, can't move.

I sit, I watch, I wait.

I count the breaths she takes, the way she moves and turns only to find it hurts, and she whimpers before curling back up to avoid the pain. I hear her mother come home and stumble up the stairs as the sun light begins to peek through the curtains.

She doesn't look in. She doesn't even check that her only

child, her only daughter, is home safe and sound. She has no idea of the darkness that lies in wait in her house while I rest and seethe, knowing I should leave, but I'm unable to make my body comply.

Get ready for the rest of Ruby and Dex's story, available soon on your retailer of choice:
Books2read.com/PerilousDesire
Goodreads.com/book/show/223905004-sweetest-sin

Perilous

DESIRE

H.L. PACKER

Secrets don't stay concealed for long in the criminal underbelly.

It's been going on for longer than it should, but Ruby Sheridan has a nighttime caller, and now, he's stalking her waking moments, too.

Dex Raymond has never kept something for himself before, but as he watches the approaching danger draw ever nearer to the object of his obsession, he can't walk away.

After all, Ruby doesn't even realise she's in the crosshairs.

There are some truths that can't be shared, and some lies that can't remain hidden, especially when the truth begs to break free, but will they make it out alive if it does? And what will be left of their relationship at the end?

Perilous Desire is a New Adult standalone story with mafia underworld ties and stalker themes. This story contains situations of a violent and sexual nature and is suitable for readers 18 years+.

Editor – Vicki at The Indie Hub

Cover Design& Formatting – LJDesigns

Playlist

Phix x Ryan Oakes – Underneath

Bad Omens – Death of Peace of Mind

Austin Snell – Excuse The Mess

Phix x Call Me Karizma – War

Lakeview ft Gideon – Money Where Your Mouth Is

Royale Lynn & Danny Worsnop – Death Wish

Bad Omens – Just Pretend

Austin Snell – Muddy Water Rockstar

New Medicine – Fire Up The Night

Warren Zeiders - Intoxicated

Author Note

Please note this story is set within the UK and is written in UK English where you need to be 18 to drink, 17 to drive, and where the age of consent is 16.

prologue
Ruby

It's been six weeks since *that night,* but I can still smell the cigar smoke in my room.

My logical brain knows it's a figment of my imagination, a safety blanket I'm conjuring to protect myself, but I can't help the warmth that sinks into my extremities thinking it might be real. That *he* might be real.

The skin on my scalp is still tender as I run the brush through my hair, tying the top half up in a bobble and leaving the rest to dangle over my shoulders, when something white peeking beneath the edge of the pillow catches my eye.

After peeling it back, I find a tiny polar bear keyring. It's definitely not something I've bought, and certainly not something my mother would bother to pick up. So, where did it come from? Looking around gives me no answers, the almost-barren room holding a secret I'm not privy to.

Who did this and why are questions I don't have time to ponder right now as Scarlett's driver blasts the horn, and she rings my phone.

I drop the tiny toy on the bed and snatch my bag from the chair, then head out, hoping the noise disturbs my mother enough for her to remember that I'm still here and alive, worth looking after. Just because the man she's chasing after decided that I need a better standard of education doesn't mean she's been turning up for me.

Thanking my new best friend, I climb into the car and look at the streets as we drive towards the shining beacon of my future: South Beach High. I never in a million years expected to be plucked from my public school and shipped off to a private one full of millionaire kids, but I've already learnt that not much is how you'd expect there.

Those millionaire kids, for a start.

They're the high-class type of bitch, the ones who will sooner troll your social media and cyberbully you until you want to kill yourself than throw a punch. I think I liked it better where I was before—at least I knew what to expect. And for a lot of them, the money they come from isn't something earned but given, and in worse cases, taken.

We pass through the dismal streets, moving from the cramped miserable place where I live through to suburban semis and towards the outstretched detached homes surrounded by expansive gardens and high fences, until eventually, we arrive at the big black gates of the school, and you can see the transition before your very eyes.

It may be only a stone's throw away from the sea, and it looks innocuous enough, but there are dangerous people inside the walls of this pretty building.

It's taken a few weeks, but I've finally got the lay of the land, no longer intimidated when the two of us climb out and make our way up the big stone steps before crossing the atrium and heading towards our lockers. Ours is an unlikely friendship, but when the girl forced to *be my buddy* dropped me like a hot stone in favour of one of the stars of the football team, Scarlett stepped up to the plate.

Her family has more money than sense, and nothing good is done by them, but who am I to judge? I'm just a girl who's been given an opportunity I'm determined to make the most of, best friend or no.

We make it to our form room with mere minutes to spare and slide into our set desks next to the partners already seated with a resolute sigh. Quarter of an hour later, we're almost ready to make our way to the first class of the day, until the teacher calls me back.

"Ruby, can I have a minute?"

Scarlett and I share a look.

"Miss Loughty will see you at your next class."

With nothing more than a narrowing of her eyes, Scarlett nods in my direction and leaves, closing the door quietly behind her.

"How are you finding South Beach, Ruby?" the teacher asks, gesturing to the chair closest to her desk and shuffling a couple of papers on the pristine surface.

"Yeah, fine."

"Good, good. That's good. Well, I'll make this quick." She folds one slender leg over the other. "An opportunity has been presented to a small number of girls to become part of a development team working with Timeless Inc. and the Big Sister programme. Your name has been suggested."

"Oh, that's… erm. What is that?"

"Let me introduce you to someone who has more information on this." Briskly, she heads to the door, opening it in time for someone who is definitely *not* a teacher to stride in. Even I can tell his expensive suit is not something available on teacher wages, not even the ones afforded here. "Mr Tasker will talk you through all the ins and outs, and I'll be back in five." She smiles and leaves us alone.

The stranger is blocking my exit, and every warning bell in my body goes haywire.

"Miss Sheridan, it's so nice to finally meet you." He doesn't offer a hand to me as he takes the previous teacher's seat, the smile on his face causing a chill to run through my veins.

This man is bad news, and whatever he is here for isn't going to be good.

Ice sluices through my veins as I consider the real reasons he could be here. I spent days after that night popping pain killers, wishing they'd just finished the job, only for no one to come. Following that, I spent weeks looking over my shoulder thinking that, any minute, this would be the moment my past caught up with me but, again, no one came.

What if he knows about the thing that happened all those weeks ago? What if I've not been as careful as I thought I had, and someone has put the pieces together? Maybe he was sent by whoever the guy was who saved me, or the people who came and helped him.

What if this is that moment?

That here, in the empty classroom, what I've seen is finally catching up to me?

"The Big Sister Programme links students from this school with counterparts at Pendleton Prep," he says, making himself comfortable. "The idea is to give you young ladies contacts for the future, and them the opportunity to garner some additional support and mentoring experience."

"Okay." But why have I been chosen? There's no way I'm going to need the kind of contacts these women have.

"*And* I'm hoping you'll be able help me out. There are a couple of people at Pendleton Prep I could really do with keeping tabs on, and I would be ever so grateful if you could keep in touch with my team and let me know what you find out about what's going on there."

"What, why?" I ask, confused.

This is nothing to do with what I thought, and whilst the panic that threatened to claw its way up my throat has subsided for now, a new concern stirs in the pit of my stomach.

If he's not here to see me because of what I've already seen and done, then why is he here to see me and not someone else? There are a small number of girls selected; that's what she said. So, why me?

"The reasons are unimportant."

Like hell they are.

"If the reasons aren't important, then how significant can the information I bring back be?"

His gaze darkens like a shutter coming down before my very eyes as he weighs his words carefully.

"Okay, let's try this another way. You care about your mother, don't you?" he asks as his gaze dissects my every movement. "Of course, you do. Well, I've got a proposition for you. You're going to join the Big Sister Programme, and you're going to feedback information to me. It's nothing awful, nothing arduous, just a few little details here and there, and in return, your mother will remain safe and sound. Whole. Complete. Sound like a plan?"

"My… my mother?"

"Rita Sheridan. A pretty red head with a terrible white powder problem. That's the one, isn't it?"

If I'd eaten any breakfast, I can guarantee you it wouldn't be staying put. I guess it's probably best I didn't as chills break out across my shoulders.

"There'll be a driver available to you as required. It's such a pleasure doing business with you." He stands, offering his hand out for me to take just as the teacher knocks and peeks her head around the doorway.

"Are we all good here, Josiah?" she asks, her smile wary as her gaze flicks between both of us. She knows just as well as I do that this man is dangerous and here with ill intent, but if the faculty isn't at liberty to refuse him, how can I?

"Just finishing up."

Josiah Tasker. That's a name I'm going to need to remember, even if I don't need to agree in order to do this.

"I'm sure the team will be excited to meet you after school," he says, smiling in my direction as though daring me to argue with him, his mask firmly back in place.

If the teacher picks up on the tension between us, she doesn't do anything about it, instead hovering in the doorway as the sounds of the rowdy class waiting outside drift into the room.

Josiah leaves without saying anything further, and I head to my next class, no wiser as to what the hell is going on here.

Who is this guy, and why does he want me to be the one in the middle like this?

***

Dex

Daniel leans against the car, his smoke curling up into the air as he puffs rings out, clearly bored and not paying attention to his surroundings. Josiah is a busy man, not someone you should argue with. I'd have expected more from the man tasked with keeping him safe. Not that I've ever bothered to look until now.

Josiah is the boss's second in command, and he's currently in the same building as Ruby.

I don't understand the edgy need to find out what's going on inside those walls, where he is, who he's speaking with. Does he know that she's here? Is that why he's come?

The man in question strides out the main doors, letting them slam behind him as he heads to the car, climbs in, and they leave, but I have no more answers than I did when he arrived, and no way to get them. So, for now, I step away, knowing she's safe inside those walls. Maybe there will be answers elsewhere, but I'm due back at the compound soon, and I need to get my head on straight before I walk back into the darkness.

The doors of the warehouse slam closed with a finality that no one is ever really prepared for, not that anyone on the other side is still alive tonight. That will probably be different tomorrow, and the night after that, and the night after that.

Letting the pain and suffering sink in far enough to allow my victims to see the error of their ways has become something of a hobby, and I'm getting good at it, but as the night draws in, I'm done. For some people that means it's time to go home, pour a beer, and shake off the depravity. For me, it means a pit stop first.

The streets are quiet as I make my way out of the industrial area and towards her house, parking a few streets away and grabbing the gift from the boot before letting myself in via the back door again. An old clock ticks away somewhere, the house dark as I move with practiced ease from one room to another, avoiding the step that squeaks and finally making it to her room unimpeded.

Once I silently push the door back, the lamp illuminates her sleeping form, her breaths coming slow and even as I slide into the room, drawing the door closed behind me. Ruby doesn't stir as I move around her inner sanctum and let the calm wash over me.

I don't know what it is about the air in this room, whether it's an incense she burns or a perfume she sprays, but the simple of action of drawing this air into my lungs calms my heartrate.

A booklet hangs from the edge of her mattress covered in nothing but hopes and dreams, and the logo catches my attention: Timeless Inc.

Josiah was there to drag her into the problems with Pendleton Prep. Fuck.

A chill creeps across my shoulders as I watch my darkness rub off onto her life.

I was supposed to be coming to say goodbye.

It's the same lie I've told myself night after night after I've snuck in here and watched her, waited, but as I place the new bed sheets on the floor and slide the booklet on top of them, I know there's no way I can leave her to face this alone.

Not now. Not ever.

one
Dex

Seven Months Later

His arm swings, fist closed as his darkened gaze flicks from one opponent to the other while deciding his next move, even as he sends one man flying. Sweeping another's feet from underneath him buys my brother more time to deal with the one trying, and failing, to sneak up on him. He side steps him with ease as he lets the man's momentum carry him forward into someone else.

They keep up the pace, though, one after another, after another, doing their best to get a hit in. One lands here and there, but they're nothing compared to the devastation Blaise dishes out until he eventually calls time. Four of them are doubled over, and one is collapsed on the floor while he looks over them, disappointment marring his pretty face.

Personally, I've missed this more than I care to admit.

It's more than just the movement and momentum for me. It's the complete and utter silence in my mind as I concentrate on taking out one after another, thinking about nothing except the problem in front of me.

Blaise barks out some scathing insult as he rubs a towel through his hair before draping it over his shoulders.

I push off the doorway and make my presence known. I'm sure he'll have been aware of me the entire time he ran the drill, but it seems nobody else realised their arse kicking was being observed. At least not until now.

"Better luck next time," I joke, tapping one of the guys on the shoulder.

He nods, wincing, as they all limp away.

I shake my head in fake disappointment. "If this is what we've got, I'm glad I'm out there on my own."

It's not true, though, and he knows it.

I've always been more comfortable with Blaise or Leo behind me, beside me, wherever. It's just who we are, who we've always been, but that shit's changing.

At the first given opportunity Leo's father packed him up and shipped him off as far away from Blaise and me as he could manage: Pendleton Prep. It wasn't like we couldn't have gone too, either. The money wouldn't have been a problem for him if he wanted Leo to have backup on site, but, no, we were left here.

Split. Separated. The three musketeers finally ripped apart.

It was only because he was holding our lives over Leo's head that Leo went in the first place. Now, it's complicated. There are other people he cares about, other people who matter.

I get it. It's cool.

Once his father managed to get Leo out and away from us, that's when they started doing their best to drag Blaise and I apart. It didn't work. Some bonds will never be broken, and once they realised so, they settled on sending us in different directions, hoping that would be enough.

I don't know why they bothered.

Together we're unstoppable, so why fuck around with that? That information is above my pay grade, I guess, but not Blaise's. Not anymore.

No, I'm the hired help. The ghost. The one they send out to 'fix' things.

Now I'm officially on babysitting duty while he's being trained up directly by Josiah to, when the time comes, become Leo's second in command. He knows more about what goes on inside these walls than I ever will, and I don't envy him for it.

Sure, I don't exactly leave my work at the door when I go home—I've been following my little charge for a lot longer than I'm supposed to have been—but it's certainly not the same as what Blaise is bringing home at the end of every day.

I've heard him pacing at night, the hushed whispers on the phone, and the early morning conversations with our mother. There's shit going on here I don't know and we can't talk about, and that's never been the case before now.

Maybe I'm delusional and they've managed to break the bond between brothers, because once upon a time there were no secrets between us, but I'd keep his secrets if I needed to. I'd keep his, Leo's, and Ruby's.

The rest of the world could burn, but I'd keep them.

"What are you doing here?" Blaise asks, ignoring my comment about his trainee's as I shuck my boots and the wayward thoughts of days gone by, toss my socks, and abandon my shirt, leaving them strewn across the gym floor as haphazardly as my mind.

If secrets and half-truths are what we have to work with now, so be it. He's still my big brother, and he's always had my back. I'll be here for him if and when he needs me, always and forever.

"Checking in." I roll my eyes at the ridiculousness of it all. Like a phone call wouldn't have done the job. "Have you got five minutes?"

I'm bored as fuck playing taxi driver *and* babysitter, keeping an eye on the girl I've tried to leave behind more than once. It's frustrating as fuck, and boring. So damn boring.

"Obviously not," he replies, looking around the empty room as I stalk towards him across the matts.

Long before it was the place we trained and honed our skills, you'd have found us kicking around the free weights and falling off the treadmills of this gym, trying to outrun each other, as well as Leo. Leo was always here.

It's never been one-on-one until recently.

Blaise sees my leg sweep coming long before I make contact, stretching out and warming up as we fall easily into old habits. We no longer scrap like little kids. Now we're significantly more intentional with those hits and neither of us hold back.

"It's a good job we don't leave weapons lying around down here," Josiah calls, catching my attention as Blaise's fist lands hard in my gut, knocking the air from my lungs before I crumple.

"Don't worry, boss. I've got the keys for the cupboard," Blaise replies, finally incensed.

At last, there's life in his eyes.

When I turned up, he was bored, lazy, going through the motions, and doing his best to train these guys. But they've got no drive or passion. And it's not that we enjoy knocking the fuck out of people. Well, not officially. It's just that it's so ingrained in us, it's one of very few things that reminds us we're alive. At least when it's done right. Not like whatever that was with the trainees.

Josiah throws a towel at me, still talking whilst I attempt to make my lungs work again, but I've missed every damn thing he's said.

"Well, it's good to know they're making progress, even if they're not quite there just yet. You're confident they'll get up to standard, though, right?" Josiah asks my brother, his too-put-together suit completely out of place in here.

"There's one I don't think will make it, but we'll see how he gets on over the next couple of days," Blaise replies confidently. "Weekends are always fun."

Fun.

They used to be in the days when Blaise and I went out to pick up money, remind people funds were due, and generally cause chaos. That was when we didn't have a *special job* in hand. Something darker and dirtier that couldn't be just handed off to anyone. Those were our jobs—the ones that needed keeping in house. Literally.

Now I'm on 'make sure Ruby doesn't do something

stupid like out herself to The Sect or the Five Families', watch, and that girl hasn't done anything fun or exciting in weeks. It's almost like she knows how much danger she's in and is being… careful.

So fucking weird.

"Aren't you supposed to be somewhere?" Josiah asks, looking me over before gesturing to his watch.

There was plenty of time when I came down here. Well, when I sneaked down here. Finishing up with the boss was supposed to be the end of it. I was supposed to be heading out to make sure Ruby got home from school without any issues. Instead I made my way to the gym, just for a minute. I couldn't pass up the opportunity to check in with Blaise and see what the hell was going on —training some very shitty recruits by the looks of it—and I couldn't leave without at least putting some of the fire back in him. What kind of brother could?

Nodding, I clean up as best I can and throw the towel in the basket before picking up my shirt and heading out, waving them off as I go with my boots in hand. I'm just the errand boy now who's not worth sparing a glance.

That's how it feels some days.

The other associates still give me a wide berth as I head upstairs with my lip bleeding and a whole bunch of bruising coming out that they can't see yet, but the security guys raise their chins or hold out a hand as I pass. Then I'm heading for my car and the job that awaits.

She's been more than a job for a long time. This little girl with a fire she keeps hidden deep, deep down is under my skin. I saw it the night that changed everything. I haven't seen it since, but it's in there, lying in wait.

Being moved onto her security team slightly changed things between us. If she remembered me from that night, or any of the nights I've sneaked in since, she's never made a show of it, but every now and again she looks at me like she knows something I'm not willing to admit. It's why I hate being on the day shift with her. When she's in the car with me, and her scent invades my space and clouds my thoughts, it makes me wish for things that can never happen.

No, the nighttime is safer. Then I can watch her from a distance, keep her safe, do the job I'm meant to be doing. When I'm on the day shift with her, I have to sneak in at night and bypass my own guys.

It's not the way it's supposed to be done, but what can I do? I'm not going to pass up the opportunity just because there's someone else keeping an eye out. Even I can admit that her proximity is about way more than protection these days.

We passed that a long time ago.

two
Ruby

A familiar, cloying floral perfume wafts around me, the scent getting right up my nose and turning my head before I even hear the voice I know goes with that smell. The person I used to call a friend.

"Tell me you're going to wear those silver heels tonight, Jasmine. They'll be perfect with that marine cocktail dress we looked at." Mariana chatters loudly as they pass our table, her heels clacking along the parquet floor.

"Obviously." Jasmine loops their arms together and flicks her hair over her shoulder, dismissing the rest of the world as they make their way across the silent library, with more than one head turning as they pass. Not that they notice.

They're impressive, the *it* girls of South Beach High. Or so I'm told.

Jasmine used to be nice, then her cute face and sweet nature got wrapped up with one of the football players, and suddenly she was besties with the bitches we used to hate, and too cool for the rest of us.

Well, fuck her. Who cares, right?

"Do you want to crash that stupid party at what's-his-name's place tonight?" Scarlett asks beside me, her clear-blue gaze peeking over the pile of books to catch my eye.

"Hmm, let me think. A party full of stuck-up arseholes who didn't invite me and would probably do their best to get me drunk and drown me in their pool. Yeah, I'm going to give that one a pass."

"*Try* being the optimal word there, my friend."

She high fives me over the books, then picks up her pen and goes back to whatever assignment she's halfway through.

You'd think that the last year at high school would be fun. It's not, and study leave seems like something we're never going to get to. It's this golden carrot the teachers are dangling ahead of us and pushing us towards, knowing it's always going to be out of reach.

They keep telling us that these exams will make or break our choice for sixth form, college, university, and the rest of our lives, and in the next breath they say we can re-do them if we need to. Talk about mixed messages.

Either way, my *benefactor* is only going to pay my way for so long, and I need to make sure I get as much out of the education he's willing to pay for as I can, because there's a good chance at the end of this school year I'll be on my own. Almost seventeen. Young and free. If only it was that simple.

"It's race night, and my brother has invited me to the trackt. You could tag along with me instead if you want to,"

Scarlet offers without bothering to look up.

It's not a pity offer just because she knows I didn't get an invitation to the football party even though she did. I may be a social pariah, but her family are practically royalty around here, and the only reason she's not one of those heel clacking, hair swinging, *it* girls is because she told them all to fuck off.

Her older brother is one of the kings of the sixth form, who's currently in his last year. If she stays on I have no doubt she'll show the girls of South Beach High just what a queen bee can do. Her family is wrapped up in a whole bunch of illegal shit. They're part of the Five Families.

Milligan, Wheeler, Osborne, Peregrine, and Loughty. Also known as Brent, Damien, Hugo, Everett, and Tanner: The Kings of South Beach High.

Nathaniel—Nate—Everett's younger brother, is in our year, and he swans around in his polo shirts and sweater vests like some Abercrombie advert, but his older brother is glued to the side of Scarlet's. I guess you can't have dumb without the dumber, and Hugo isn't usually too far behind. The terrible trio.

Nate is okay, I suppose, but I do everything I can to avoid the Kings of South Beach High, and turning up to their race night is not going to help me do that.

I've had an easy get out over the last seven months because of the Big Sister programme and my time with Timeless Inc. Let's just say it's been an interesting experience, and, whilst they might be a bunch of primped-up barbies and gym boys, some of them are okay, I guess.

Either way, it's made avoiding shit football parties

I don't get invited to and making excuses to my friend a distant memory. Until now.

Sure, the threats hanging over my mother's life are still hovering in the back of my mind, even if it's supposed to be going away. And, of course, I'm aware that more than one of those wonna-be barbies disappeared and never came back, but none of that is my problem.

I just need to keep my nose clean and wait it all out, that's all.

I did what I was supposed to, and it's all over now, as far as I know.

"I think I'm just going to go home and hibernate," I say, attempting to find an excuse I haven't used yet. "I'll probably stick a film on, make some popcorn, then hide until we have to come back here."

It's not a bad plan, even if that's not how my evening will likely go down because *he'll* be back. Watching. Waiting. The tension crackling, even as he sits across the road and watches my shadows move in the light of my bedroom.

Absentmindedly, I check my phone again, knowing in my heart that I won't have heard from the man charged to watch me and make sure I'm safe. The one who's been doing it a lot longer under the cover of darkness.

Dex Raymond.

He saved me once, what feels like a lifetime ago, and he never really went away. He just became a shadow I could never quite reach. But now he's here, in the daytime, couriering me from one place to another and making sure I get to the meetings with Ivy and the guys safely, then ensuring I'm tucked up in my bed at the end of the day.

It's amazing and horrendous. Yet another temptation dangling in front of my face.

"Abso-fucking-lutely not," Scarlett chastises, closing her book with a resounding slap, dragging me back into the conversation at hand. "You're coming to the race with me, and I'm not taking no for answer. We'll pick you up at ten."

"Ten? I'll be halfway to snoozeville by then."

I won't, but that's not the point.

"What's the problem? You can just sneak out. It's not like you haven't done it before."

My mum won't be home, and she wouldn't care even if she was. She'd smile, wave, and tell me to find someone pretty but stupid to take for a ride. Because that's the way to good things in life: sponging off someone else instead of making your own way.

I can't say much, I suppose. After all, it's someone else who pays for my tuition. *Her benefactor is also mine,* and the Big Sister programme has been funding everything else: my first ever bikini, an evening gown, winter boots...

Well, I've got to get something useful out of this too.

I've been doing my best to save what I can and to find a job, but nobody is interested in taking on a teenager. Not for anything legal, anyway.

If I wanted to pass around a few pills or connect a couple of people, there could be good money to be made in a place filled with bored teenagers who have more money than sense, but crossing the Five Families and putting my arse on the line for someone else's gain is not my idea of a good time, no matter how much money would exchange hands.

"I'm just trying to keep my nose clean and get through these exams," I reply, giving up halfway through the conclusion I'm attempting to write. "Who's *we*, anyway?"

Scarlett glances around carefully, her gaze flicking from table to table before she shuffles her chair closer to mine. "Do you remember that boy I was telling you about? Jeremy?"

"Yeah."

Someone set her up on a blind date, and she went. Idiot. She told me she trusted the person who set them up, even if she won't tell me who it was, but she still sent me the time and address, and that tells me exactly how safe she felt.

"Tanner invited me, and Jeremy's going to pick me up. We can get you in, too."

Sure, I'll jump in the car with a guy you've met all of erm... twice? Actually...

"So, you're planning on going to your brother's race with a boy you like? Someone they've not met before? And I say *they* because you know Everett and Hugo will be there to cheer the fucker on. Do you really think that's a good idea?"

"Fuck, no," she scoffs. "But we're doing it anyway. Are you in?"

A grin takes over my face. This is going to be a fucking disaster, and I can't wait.

"Well, I guess it looks like I might be going out after all."

three
Dex

The light goes off in her bedroom at nine thirty, the flickering of the television then showing through in its place. It's just another quiet, boring night at home for her. As much as I'd absolutely love to be out doing something, anything, it feels pretty good to know she's wrapped up safely watching some chick flick.

Although, I have no idea what she actually watches. Maybe she prefers murder documentaries or true crime thrillers. What if she's into all that CSI shit and is just working out how to make sure she gets away with whatever it is she's cooking up in her head?

No, she'll be watching that medical shit: *Scrubs*, *Greys*, *The Resident*. Maybe they're not any better, though, her working out how to kill me off and make it look like an accident. Let's go back to chick flicks and reality TV, even though I know for certain, one hundred percent, that is *not* what she's watching right now. Ruby isn't the kind of girl to be revelling in a romantic comedy or an emotional teen drama.

I can almost picture her wrapped up in a black blanket, surrounded by a bunch of shit you'd pull from a Tim Burton film. I know there's some of that in her room because I put it there, but that's not the point. Even before she found out about the darker side of South Beach, she wasn't the rainbows and unicorns type of girl, anyway. She's always been edgy, cool, herself.

I fucking love that nobody else gets it.

I shouldn't, but I do.

I left that morning, seven months ago, fully intending to never come back. I was supposed to leave the girl to her life while hoping and praying she never found herself in that same position again. Only I couldn't. What if someone saw her there, saw us there, saw me leave?

I told myself it was just whilst she healed up, to make sure she was good until she could protect herself. In the end she was fine, physically, but then she started at South Beach High, and Josiah came to see her. I knew she was being wrapped up in something dangerous and she had no idea about it. So, at the end of each night, I'd find myself back outside her house, watching the shadows moving around and waiting until all was still, because being across the road wasn't enough. I had to go inside.

I needed to see the life she lived. I needed to live it myself, to breathe it, and once I had, I couldn't not do something about it. I started with small things at first: replacing a broken lamp, straightening up the cupboard door that hung off its hinges. Two minutes, no big deal, right? Then she came home to the banister repaired and the hallway lino replaced, next the sofa, the bedding, the towels.

I didn't know who she thought was doing it back then and who *is still* doing it now. Maybe she thinks her mother is finally coming through for her, taking care of the place they live, like she's supposed to. I don't know, and I haven't asked. It's my form of payment, a penance of sorts, for the watching, for the way I've memorised her breaths as she sleeps, the way her smile lights up a room, and the feel of her thick hair through my fingers.

A V8 crawls along the road, the sporty car and rumble of the engine completely out of place in this run-down street, intriguing me further when it pulls up outside her house.

Leaving the TV on as background noise in case her mum comes home isn't an option, not that it's needed, as the TV flicks off and the house goes dark, only for Ruby to appear at the front door just seconds later.

She doesn't see me hiding in plain sight from the house across the street. Her gaze darts left and right as she checks the coast is clear before Scarlett fucking Loughty climbs out of the passenger seat, high fives Ruby, then drops the seat for her to climb into the back.

My, my little mouse. Where are you planning on scurrying off to?

With her, tonight? That doesn't take a genius to work out.

I raised my concerns about this *friendship* a long time ago with my brother Blaise, and then more recently with the boss, but neither of them understand my issue. B told me to leave her the fuck alone, and the boss shrugged it off like he couldn't care less, but he's got Marcus and me sitting out here watching her for some reason.

Not that I haven't been doing it on my own time for way longer than is reasonable.

I watch her petite frame fold itself into the back of the car, the denim she wears hugging curves I wish I knew more intimately. Her signature spiked belt glints in the dim glow of the street lamps, and I know her favourite pocket knife will be shoved down the inside of her boot. The outline would be way too obvious in her practically sprayed-on trousers, but I know she never leaves the house without it.

I watch them leave, giving them a head start and making a note of the registration before locking up and heading for the car, knowing exactly where I'll find them.

The night is still young, and with only one set of races this month, they've all been set for the same place. It will go on for hours, race after race, the party raging as winners, losers, petrol heads, and those turning up for the atmosphere tumble in to a night of overindulgence.

Don't get me wrong, I like a fast car as much as the next guy, but I've never felt the need to turn it into a dick-measuring contest.

I make my way to the abandoned airfield, knowing that's where tonight's 'event' is being held. Too many boys with their toys, too many girls looking for a stiff drink and a quick fuck. Not somewhere Ruby really *wants* to be, I'm sure.

The carpark is heaving as I slide along the rows, looking for somewhere unobtrusive to hide this thing. It's not that me being here is an issue as such, but as a general rule, we leave the Five Families to it and collect our cut when it's due, which doesn't always goes seamlessly, but there's no need to get any more involved than that.

Until something like this happens.

I reverse into a spot and check the clip before shoving the gun down the back of my jeans and covering it with my shirt. Hopefully nobody looks too closely, and I don't need to use it.

I've never realised how well insulated this car is until I open the door, the noise hitting me like a baseball bat as the bass reverberates through my feet. Maybe being hidden behind the hanger isn't the best idea? Looking up, I make my way around, trying to work out where the girls would start their night out.

It's loud and busy—neither of which Ruby particularly likes, but maybe she makes exceptions for her friend. She's made them before for other people. I even saw one of those Pendleton Prep girls hug her once. That was a moment I didn't expect, and neither did she if the look on her face had been anything to go by.

As I stand on the edge of the carpark, quickly grabbing a beer from what can only be considered a bar in the entrance to the hanger, I know she won't be in there. Not sober, anyway. So, I bypass said bar, then the dance floor, and meander through the gathered crowds to follow the sound of engines. Exhausts pop and bang, and music plays from over-tuned sound systems, hoping to draw people closer to ogle their lit-up engines and overpriced boy toys.

I know Ruby's not afraid of a little thrill, but this amount of ego is not her thing, so why the hell is she here? It doesn't make any sense to me.

Before her friend arrived at her place, she'd honestly looked like she was settling in for the night—a nice quiet one to make it through to the end of the school year. That's what I know she's been doing, staying out the way of the Five Families and to make it to the point where she can get away.

And now, she's here, in their domain, with their little sister, kicking up dirt and causing chaos.

So much for keeping your nose clean, girl. Now, where the hell are you?

four
Ruby

I think Scarlett is as keen as I am to get out of this tin box. The cloud of overpowering aftershave Jeremy has on is thick enough to taste when he eventually stops the car, and she flings the door open. Instead of waiting for him to come round and offer her his hand, she just climbs out. Not that he moves anywhere other than to yank a hipflask from the glove box and offer it to me expectantly.

"Really?" I eye him with trepidation. "No, thanks." There is no way in hell I'm going to let myself get drunk in a place like this, and even less chance of me accepting some unknown concoction from a complete stranger.

I can honestly say the thought of getting back in the car with him repulses me, and not just because the boy has no idea how much aftershave to wear, but because he drives like a fucking idiot and is now drinking.

Although, the car fumes as I climb from the back aren't much better. What on earth was I thinking?

"Come on, Scar. You'll have some, right?" Jeremy asks,

shoving the hip flask into her hand.

"Scar," I mouth, looking at her, but all she does is roll her eyes and throw back a shot of whatever is in there. If her brother finds her here with this tool, drunk, neither of them will make it home in one piece.

Not my circus, not my monkeys.

It's totally my problem if I get stuck here, though.

"So, what do we do now we're here? Racing?" I ask.

"Yes!" Scarlett replies excitedly.

"Err, my baby's not going up there," Jeremy counters, stroking his hand down the paintwork.

"So… no racing, then?"

"I'll stick it out here for a bit," he replies before opening the bonnet and flicking some button that makes the whole engine bay light up. "Show her off a bit, you know? Why don't you girls go find someone worth showing off to, huh?"

Turning away, I cringe as Scarlett wraps her arm through mine and waves over her shoulder, throwing way too much sway in to her hips, almost knocking us both over.

"Where did you find this guy again?"

"Oh, uh. He's a friend of a friend," she hedges.

"Please tell me he's not linked to your brother."

"Tanner? God, no." She bursts out a laugh, shaking her head. "You think I'd look twice at any of his idiot friends? You must be out of your damn mind."

"Maybe I am," I grumble as we meander through row after row of cars, the music pumping at odds with each other. "Who introduced you, then?"

"Promise me you won't laugh?" she whispers, leaning close.

"Absolutely not."

She smiles, though, knowing I was never going to agree to that before throwing out, "Nate."

"Nate? As in Nathaniel Peregrine? The younger brother of your brother's best friend. Let me get this straight. You won't look at *Tanner's* friends, but his bestie's younger brother's friends... that's all good. Really? Jesus." Shaking my head, I attempt to wrap my mind around this. "Actually, I can't imagine Nate having any real friends."

"Hey, he's a good guy."

"Are we talking about the same person?" I look around. "About this tall..." I hold my hand up above me. "Dark hair, soulless eyes?" A body half the year drools over on the regular at the swim meets. "More ego than I have ever seen in real life. In fact, he's nearly as bad as that guy from Vampire what's-it Diaries."

"You're terrible." She laughs, dragging my hand down and threading it back through her arm as the "track" finally comes into view. "And just so you know, Damon Salvatore is an absolute sweetie, he's just misunderstood."

"Because defending red-flag fictional characters shows me just how great your discerning ability is. Look, I'm just saying the guy is a tool. Jeremy, not Nate. At the very least he needs airing out for the next few hours, because that aftershave is just... wow."

Scarlett just shakes her head with a satisfied smile as we move towards the starting line. There are no cars currently lined up, but who knows how long that will last.

"Look at that! Ask and you shall receive."

"I think the phrase you're looking for is 'speak of the

devil'. Nobody has been asking for Nathaniel Peregrine," I counter.

"You're wrong there. Haven't you heard the gossip?" she asks, lining her hands up in a way that could only be describing the size of his cock.

"Oh, God."

"Heard that before," Nate says, catching the end of our conversation, but luckily missing Scarlett's hand gestures as she quickly shoves them into her pockets; a smirk covering her face. "You might want to shuffle off, though. Tanner will have a fucking fit if he finds you here."

"Hey, I was invited," Scarlett argues, flicking her dark hair over her shoulder. "And not just by you."

"Where's Jer, anyway?" he asks, distracted by the clipboard in his hand.

"Captain Asshat is sitting pretty with his lovely, lit-up dick extension."

Nate splutters out a laugh, his dark gaze meeting mine. "I can't imagine anyone has ever called him Captain Asshat before, but maybe they should. You need me to get rid of him?" He asks the question to Scarlett, but holds my gaze, the conversation turning real dark, real quick, and part of me wonders what would happen if I were to say yes.

But I've seen firsthand what that looks like, and my stomach turns with nothing more than the memory of that wet slapping sound echoing in my ears. There's so much about that night that's still not clear, but there's no one to ask, no one to clarify, and I'm not sure I'd want them to if they could.

"Don't be silly," Scarlett says, bringing me back into

the here and now with a jolt as she brushes off his wayward comment. "I thought there were supposed to be races going on? Not just a whole bunch of petrol heads loitering about."

"You usually get a better view at the finish line," Nate comments, waving a pen in Scarlett's direction. "But the next set will be up in five, and Brent's racing in a bit, so you might want to scoot."

"You think I'm scared of Brent Milligan?" Scarlett scoffs.

Whilst Nate and Scarlett's brothers are almost joined at the hip with Hugo Osborne, there are two other guys who make up the Five Families, and the two sides don't get on. Brent Milligan and Damien Wheeler are two boys with more belligerent charm than I've ever seen in real life, and I have absolutely no desire to get in their way. Especially not with freedom within reach.

I honestly thought with the number of cars loitering in the immediate vicinity that it couldn't get any louder, but it turns out I was wrong. An engine roars behind us, making me jump just seconds before it slides around us, and despite it probably being a foot away, it feels like it's nothing more than inches as I yank Scarlett back into me, panic rushing through my veins.

Nate barely moves, though, and as the car comes to an idling halt in front of us, I realise why. Scarlett's brother Tanner hangs out of the window, waving obnoxiously and whistling loudly.

"Baby sis! Fancy seeing you here," Tanner calls, his blond hair blowing in the breeze.

"Fuck you!" Scarlett shouts, laughing as she leaves me

loitering with Nate to go and berate her brother.

I'm quietly confident there aren't many people in this world who can clip one of the heirs to the Five Families around the back of the head in public and get away with it, but he does nothing more than chuckle at her attempts, dragging her up against the car door in a bear hug that pulls her off her feet.

"I thought he had a motorbike?"

"He does. That beast is Ev's," Nate replies appreciatively.

"Careful, Nate. I think you've got a little drool there," I comment, gesturing to his plump bottom lip, watching as it curves up into something similar to a smile. It's not quite a smirk, but it's not really a smile either.

"Don't worry, princess, I'll get my pick soon enough."

"Princess? So cliché. You couldn't come up with anything better? Surely, if anyone is the princess here, it's Scarlett."

"*Technically*, Damien's sister Annabel is the oldest of the siblings." Nate taps his fingernails against the cut of his cheekbones as he steps in to my personal space, drowning out the rest of the world.

An awareness prickles against the back of my neck, and without a doubt I know *he's* here.

Well, it's about time.

I was beginning to wonder if he didn't care anymore.

"But the chances of me ever calling Annabel Wheeler *princess* and living to tell the tale are slim to none," Nate says conspiratorially, his breath fanning against my neck.

"Might be the same outcome if you were to say that to Scarlett, too," I reply, doing my best to supress the shudder of anticipation that threatens to cascade over my shoulders down to my fingertips. He may misconstrue it to mean I'm interested in him instead of the man I know is watching us.

"I guess that means it falls to you."

Nate's fingers skirt across my collarbone before slipping inside the back of my jacket to tug my collar up, warding me against the cold. Then he steps back, the ghost of his touch still humming beneath my skin. Or is it the knowledge that my stalker is here somewhere, watching and waiting.

Did he see? Does anger vibrate beneath his skin, or is he used to seeing me around other people, other guys? Maybe it doesn't bother him in the slightest. Maybe I'm just some girl he has to watch now. Another part of the job.

"Come on," Nate says, his hand sliding to the bottom of my back as he guides me towards the truck, the engine still idling but the cab door open as his brother leans over from the passenger seat, his arm hanging across the steering wheel.

"I can't believe you let him drive this baby, but I don't get a look in," Nate complains loudly, reaching out to shake Tanner's hand and raising his chin to his brother.

"There's this odd thing called the law, little bro," Everett replies with a chuckle. "You ladies want to come for a drive? Leave the kids to their toys."

"There's no way I'm getting in there," Scarlett replies, wrinkling her nose up like there's a foul smell emanating from the back of the truck. "Things to do, people to see. You know how it is."

"People to see. Now, that sounds like something we could get behind," Tanner says, jumping out of the truck and throwing his arm over her shoulder. Never in my life have I been more grateful to be an only child. "So, little sis. How did you get here? Who drove…"

He steers her away from the truck, Everett climbing out before saying something quietly to Nate and turning to me. "Shall we?"

Just because I've been hiding from them all this time doesn't mean I'm going to swoon at their every thought and be led around like a puppy.

"Your fake as fuck gentleman schtick isn't going to work on me, Everett."

Ignoring his outstretched hand, I stride past him to follow Tanner and Scarlett instead. I'm interested to see where this is going to go. I know Jeremy said to bring someone back worth talking to, but two of the co-organisers of the event were probably not what he had in mind.

And as much as Nate introduced them, or his friend did, I'm not sure Jeremy really knows who and what the Five Families are involved in. He certainly didn't seem like he had the backbone to be illegal as fuck, even if he did have the balls to turn up here with Scarlett.

I have no idea the conversation Scarlett and Tanner are having as they weave us through the cars without so much as a backwards glance.

"Is he always this sociable?" I grumble, wishing it was just Scarlett, me, and a bottle of something strong chilling out in my back garden.

"Yep," Everett answers, surprising me. "You should see it when he and Hugo get started. They're a nightmare."

His presence hangs ominously beside me, the dark

shadow to Tanner's light and welcoming self. But his darkness sits well against mine, the two of us waiting as Scarlett and her brother head closer and closer to the boy he's about to chew up and spit out, all while my secret observer is here to see it.

I can't even tell you how I know *he's* here, and not one of the other guys. It's a sixth sense. A tingle at the back of my neck. An awareness that vibrates through my fingers. Something unspoken but understood, and my body responds to it like it knows, even when he doesn't acknowledge it.

They sting, those moments when I'm in his presence and he acts like he has no idea of the connection that burns between us. I get it. He's just supposed to be the man driving me from here to there, the one on the clock, but it's not like that deep down.

He's been hiding in the shadows since *that night*, watching, waiting, changing things. I've acted like I didn't notice. I played along, pretending the gifts left on my bed were from my mother. That she finally decided to spend some of that money she earns making sure our house is liveable. But they weren't, and she isn't. It's him. It's always been him.

Luckily, Everett doesn't attempt conversation, and he doesn't stop to engage with every single person we meet on the way, either. The two of us simply weave our way along behind our respective best friends in silence.

Jeremy is leaning over the bonnet when we eventually find him, grinning and pointing something out to the blonde, whose tits are practically hanging out of her top. *Pervert.*

Tanner bangs twice on the propped-up bonnet, scaring

the ever-loving shit out of Jeremy, and I can't deny the smile that pulls at the corners of my mouth. Scarlett is a fucking catch, and he's here drooling over some track bunny. Idiot.

"Well, well, well. What have we got here, little sis?" Tanner asks, dropping a tatted arm over Scarlett's shoulder and pulling her against his side.

With a disgusted tut, she shoves his arm off and skips towards Jeremy, completely oblivious to the girl, until she gets closer. Then suddenly, Tanner, Everett and I are nothing but background noise.

"Who the hell is this?" Scarlett hisses, eyes narrowed at the offending blonde.

"Nadine was just asking about the intake system," Jeremy replies with a wink, clearly impressed with his own bullshit.

Until Everett takes three strides closer, peeking around the side of the group and pointing out exactly were that would be, and it certainly isn't anywhere near where Jeremy was. The bullshitting, sleazy fucker.

"You're…" Jeremy says, eyes wide as he really looks at the two men in front of him. "And you… you're Tanner Loughty." He visibly swallows, paling in front of our eyes. If he could drop Scarlett and run away to hide in a corner, he would, and it only makes my smile wider. "Shit."

The blonde girl shrugs and makes her escape whilst everyone looks at Jeremy in confusion.

"You know my last name. Who else did you think my brother was?" Scarlett asks, doing her best to rein in her temper. "We're coming to watch him race… duh."

Jeremy's mouth opens and closes like a fish out of

water, all the pieces falling into place.

He didn't know who she was, but he sure as shit knows who *they* are, as well as the heap of trouble he's found himself in.

"You came to watch your brother. That's so sweet," Everett comments, his tone saccharine sweet as he turns that wicked glare on to Jeremy. "And you brought us a toy to play with."

"No," Scarlett raises a finger like she's about to scold a toddler.

"Someone who was flirting with another girl the second your back was turned," Tanner adds.

"It wasn't like that," Jeremy attempts. "I wasn't—"

"Sure looked like it to me," Everett says, cutting Jeremy off as he rests his hip against the side of the car and crosses his arms over his chest. "You sent poor little Loughty out here to find her big bad brothers whilst you entertained your next fuck. Classy."

While pressing my lips together to suppress the smile dying to break free, I take a step back. If this is going to go from bad to worse, I don't want to be in the direct line of fire.

Jeremy drops Scarlett and takes a step towards her brother with his hands outstretched, an apology, an explanation, something on the tip of his tongue.

"Let's go," Everett decides, coming up behind Jeremy, grabbing him by the back of the shirt, and dragging him away.

"What?" Jeremy screeches, his feet barely touching the ground.

"You brought Scarlett here—strike one. You've been drinking—strike two. Then you're flirting with some other bitch—strike three," Everett rattles off. "That's three strikes and you're out, my friend."

"*And* you don't even know who the fuck she is," Tanner adds, following.

"Jesus," Scarlett says on an exhale, throwing her hands in the air. "You coming?"

"I'll leave that one with you and grab a drink. Call me when you've picked the bits of your once-upon-a-time boyfriend up off the ground, yeah?"

"Thanks for the vote of confidence." Her laugh tinkles out as she skips away, more at home with this chaos than the quiet of the library from a few hours ago.

Shaking my head, I make my way back towards the hanger in search of something in a sealed bottle. Surely this place isn't completely full of dickwads, even if there's one hanging around here who's definitely more dangerous than your average, over-zealous racer boy.

five

Dex

One pissed off looking Everett Peregrine stalks straight towards me, with some kid hanging off the end of his arm pleading his case while Tanner Loughty follows. Scarlett isn't far behind them. I turn as they near, just another racer talking cars for all they know, my gaze tracking back to Ruby without a second thought.

Hopefully, they're too distracted with whatever *that is* to notice the semi-familiar face in the crowd. There are probably lots of people here who they half know anyway, but my interest isn't in them, it's in Ruby, and she isn't following them. Instead, she's heading in the opposite direction, alone.

So much for a nice, quiet night at home.

When I said I would be up for a little excitement, throwing myself into the middle of a Five Families race night was not exactly what I had in mind. The fucking fumes get right up my nose.

While keeping one eye on where she walks, I pluck my

vibrating phone from my pocket and see Blaise is calling.

"Hey, bro," I answer. "What's up?"

"You're not where you're supposed to be."

"I'm exactly where I'm supposed to be, but *she's* not where you expected her to be," I correct, ignoring the fact that he's checking up on me.

"Great." His sarcasm isn't missed as I track Ruby's movements, hanging back.

He doesn't usually call for a catch up—we do that that at home—so, why the hell is he interrupting me?

"What do you need?" I ask while watching Ruby stop to speak with someone by the starting line.

"Nothing. This is just a heads up."

Fucking great.

Somebody has clocked me and called it in.

"Thanks for that," I say, weaving through the cars far enough away from Ruby so it's not obvious to anyone watching, because I can be damn sure someone is.

"I'll see you later, then?"

"Sure thing," I reply before ending the call and pocketing the infernal thing that's keeping me at such a distance.

I watch Ruby smile, and *he* laughs, his hand coming deceptively close to the small of her back, and my molars grind.

Doesn't he realise she's mine? Doesn't she know that I'm here?

Nathaniel Peregrine.

Youngest son of Keaton and Odette Peregrine, brother to the one and only Everett Peregrine, heirs to the *entertainment* side of the Five Families' businesses. They run escorts, high class and expensive. They're hookers in another disguise, and by all accounts Everett already has quite an eye for it, but Nathaniel's is, unfortunately for him, on Ruby tonight.

That can't happen.

It's bad enough that Ruby is traipsing around with Scarlett Loughty, because she's flying far too close to the sun for my liking. Not that anyone else seems to care about her tempting fate with the Five Families. That's what I'm here for, as well as the rest of the team.

Crossing the open space to follow her as she heads to the hanger is trickier than following her through the throngs of people, because nonchalant behaviour is not my go to, but I tag along behind a group of wannabe racers and hope nobody else is paying much attention.

With Everett and Tanner off dealing with Scarlett's little boyfriend issue, there's only Hugo likely to be loitering around, unless Brent and Damien are here. With this being a last-minute jaunt I didn't have time to check the race logs.

I hate being unprepared.

Taking a swig of my drink, I follow the racers towards the hanger, holding back as Ruby plucks a bottle of beer from an open cooler. I chuckle when her cute nose wrinkles before she shoves it back in, looking around for something else. I can almost imagine her distaste.

I push ahead, mere steps away from her now as I pass and move deeper into the hanger, then delve back into the shadows, just another nameless faceless person at the meet with the music pumping through my feet.

The draw to brush my fingers along her back as I pass is

almost too hard to hold back, but that would give the game away, and the way her head turns to seek me out is enough of a thrill. She knows I'm here, knows I'm near, but this game of cat and mouse is getting more dangerous.

I'm supposed to be watching and keeping her safe. Those were the orders from the boss. But what he doesn't know is that I've been doing this a lot longer than I should have been. That even after the threat from the Five Families passed, I stayed. I couldn't help myself.

She's off limits. Too young. Too naive. Too innocent. Too perfect.

Nothing my bloodied hands should be near.

But when she looks up at me with those deep brown eyes, lust warring with a desire she doesn't understand, it's getting harder and harder to refuse.

It was one thing when it was just me in the shadows because I could keep my distance, but now that I'm on official babysitting duty and I'm with her in public, it's a nightmare. Pick up. Drop off. Watch and wait. Hand her care over to Marcus and hope he doesn't make a mistake.

It's when we're enclosed in the car, her fragrance wrapping around me, her eyes beseeching for something she knows I can't give her... those are the moments weakening my resolve. They're slowly but surely chipping away at the distance I keep placing between us.

But she has no idea what's on the line, what's at stake, and why would she?

She checks the seal on a bottle of water handed to her, when someone familiar enters from a side door, striding past with his cousin at his side.

I wasn't expecting Damien Wheeler to be making a show tonight, but then I haven't exactly had time to do any recon. I just need to keep her away from him, as well as Nathaniel, and get her back to Scarlett in one piece. Except the guy who brought the two of them here might be dismembered imminently, which means watching her get in the back of a car with Tanner, Everett, or Hugo.

Before I've had time to work out what the best thing to do is, Ruby is making her way towards the speaker cases and the side door Damien just came through, far too close to whatever deal is going down. Because there's no way he's come to race night in what's pretty much enemy territory without an agenda. Not even to watch his bestie wipe the floor with the rest of them.

Fuck.

It's like a car crash you can't help but watch when there's nothing you can do to intervene. I'm on the wrong side of the hanger and too far away to effectively redirect her, short of making my presence known, and that, here, would be a mistake.

There's no dispute between my employer and the Five Families as such. There's an understanding that they can go about their business unimpeded, providing a percentage of their earnings come our way. So, whilst me being here isn't problematic, it's certainly not ideal, and if they knew that *she* is the reason I'm here, they'd finally look further into who she is and why she might need my protection.

That would open a whole other can of worms.

I draw closer, praying she doesn't stop and look behind the speaker cases, that she just walks straight to the doorway and out into the safety and anonymity of the night. Even as I wish that were the case, I know it won't be.

I watch Ruby get to the cases then dip behind them and out of my sight as I push on through the crowd. I shouldn't have strayed and dared to go past her, deeper into the hanger. I should have known she'd want to be out of this noisy, people-filled space as quickly as possible, and stayed nearby, but the temptation to confirm my presence was too strong.

So strong that I've left her open and alone with Damien and his dodgy dealings in the vicinity. My personal feelings should have never entered into this space. I'm working. On the clock. In charge of keeping her safe and protected. If Marcus had done this, I'd have his balls in a fucking jar.

As I turn the corner round the speakers, I'm silently praying the door is open and she's nowhere to be seen, but Ruby stands there, pressed against the side of the case, her ear cocked to listen to whatever is going on.

Completely out in the open.

If this was one of their team and not me, she'd be fucking dead, throat slit and dumped in the back of a truck, left in a river somewhere or dropped over the side of a boat twenty miles out at sea, never to be seen again. I'd have been doing a seriously shitty job to let someone else get that close to her, but even so, the threat lingering in the air pulls me down the tiny, makeshift corridor.

And she doesn't stir.

She's so engrossed in eavesdropping that she's completely oblivious to the danger that lurks directly behind her.

I quickly close the distance between us, slide a hand over her mouth and one around her waist before I pick her up and push through the side door, praying it doesn't slam behind us. Once we're out of the door and rushing into the night, I make for my car, with Ruby kicking and screaming in my arms—only realising the noise could have alerted someone to our presence as an afterthought.

If anyone sees us this plan is totally fucked, but what other option do I have?

After dropping her at the side of the car, I press her against the back door with my hips while fishing out the keys from my pocket as I keep the hand over her mouth, making sure she can't reach for that knife stashed in her boot.

I'm surprised there isn't another one somewhere on her body that she's managed to unsheathe and plunge into my skin yet… but I guess there's time. Finally finding the keys, I unlock the car, throw her in the back, climb in behind her, and lock the doors quickly. It would be just my luck for her to climb out the other side as I got in, escaping without so much as a confrontation, but I've barely got the door closed when she lets out a cry for help. The sound echoes around the small space as she crowds against the opposite door.

"You don't want to do that, baby girl."

She continues trying the door handle and banging on the window as she calls out, too fuelled with fear and adrenaline to realise I'm the one who saved her, not the one who wants to hurt her.

"Hey, Ruby. You're safe. It's me."

She's still lost in her instincts, until she whips round, her frantic gaze finally connecting with mine, and suddenly all that energy is heading in my direction, her tiny fists raining down on my face, chest—anywhere she can connect.

I'm just glad the knife has remained tucked away. That could have been problematic.

As the seconds pass, her anger turns inward, her upset taking over as the slaps to my face and body slow until she's clinging to my shirt and climbing into my lap, panting as tears track down her cheeks.

"I thought…"

That she'd been caught watching something she had no business watching. That the Five Families had got hold of her.

"I know."

"But it's you…"

Someone safe… er. Someone not looking to hurt her.

"Yeah."

"Fuck." She hiccups.

That about sums it up.

"What did you see, Ruby?" I ask, knowing if I'm going to get this information from her, it needs to be now whilst it's fresh.

Once the adrenaline wears off, what she saw will change. Her brain will morph it into something more palatable, something it can handle. But I need to know what she's witnessed and what they might come after her for.

"I don't know."

"*Who* did you see?"

"Damien. Damien was there with two guys." She shakes in my arms.

I want nothing more than to wrap her up in my embrace and feed her chocolate, to let this go and look after her like she needs me to, but I can't. I can't keep her safe if I don't know how much danger she's in.

And it isn't just me anymore. The boss will want to know, too.

I wrack my brain, attempting to remember what each family looks after, what she might have seen. More recently, Blaise and I have been the men *collecting* from those not likely to hand over the cash—the ones who are going to need to pay in blood and bone, and that has never been the Five Families.

"What were they doing?"

"Dealing," she admits.

Drugs. Of course. It's the 'Wheeler' powerhouse.

"And they didn't see you?"

"I thought…"

"You thought they had because I got you out of there. You thought I was them."

She nods, sniffling.

"But now you know it was me, did they see you?"

How much blood will need to be spilled to make this right, and whose will it be?

"No, I don't think so," she admits quietly.

The relief that courses through my veins is unwarranted. Just because she hasn't been spotted by Damien and the guys with him doesn't mean his cousin didn't see her. It doesn't mean they weren't on their way when I got her out of there, or that they didn't hear the door and know someone else was with them.

There's a good chance she's not safe yet.

"I'm taking you home."

"What about Scarlett?" she asks, pulling back.

"She's a big girl. She can make her own way home."

"That's not what I meant." She sniffles before wiping her face, her eyes dark in this light. "What am I supposed to say to my friend when I just disappear halfway through the night?"

"Seriously?" That's what she's worrying about right now? No more than two minutes ago, she was sobbing into my chest thinking she'd been taken by fucking drug dealers, and now she's contemplating the lies she'll have to tell her friend about leaving early. "Tell her you found a friend, and he took you home."

"Friend?" she throws the word out into the space between us with disgust, rearing back like I just slapped her.

She's not a friend. She's a job. Just a job.

She has to be.

"What? You'd rather tell her you found a hookup and ditched her?"

It's cold, and we both know it, but the taste of her fear on my tongue and the feel of her tears on my skin is a euphoria I can't get used to. I'm not the good guy in her story. I never will be.

Pursing her lips, she nods twice, finally seeing the line drawn in the sand.

"I'll tell her some arsewipe pissed me off, and I walked home." She reaches for the door and yanks on the handle but gets nowhere. "It wouldn't be far from the truth."

"Nobody is believing you walked back, baby girl."

The term of endearment slips out unintentionally, and I get to watch firsthand as it slices through her chest.

I should unlock the door, let her out, and give us both some space before we say things we can't take back, or do things that could fuck up my life and hers irreparably, permanently, but I've never been smart like that.

"I don't think anyone saw you, so you should be able to go find your friend, and I'll keep an eye on the situation."

Logically, wait and see is the best option right now.

If I take her away, then we'll have no idea if the Wheelers saw her, or me, and then we're on the back foot. If we wait, they'll either approach her whilst I'm here and waiting for it, or they'll come for me. Either way, this ends here and now, and I don't have to spend the next week looking over my shoulder or explain to the boss that she got in harm's way.

At least this way it'll be me that goes down for it.

"Are you going to unlock the door, then?" she asks despondently, refusing to turn and look at me. Her fingers grip the handle, and her back is towards me, refusing to acknowledge me or the pain my words have caused. The dismissal.

"Ruby," I try.

I hate this... this... distance, but it's a necessary evil. At least that's what I tell myself.

"Don't," she clips, cutting me off. "Don't *Ruby* me now." Her irritated glare pins me over her shoulder.

We've tiptoed around the tension coiling my limbs for a long time. It's the same one that doesn't want to press the release button.

Sure, she's younger than me by a couple of years. She's younger than anyone in their right mind should look at this way, but it's not like that. The air is charged with something, but it's not lust. It's not *only* lust.

I have no doubt that if I'd sincerely offered her that hookup, she'd have said yes. I'm not just being a cocky fuck, but it's more than sexual attraction. She's the first person I've ever wanted to protect outside of B and Leo, but they're family. She's the flame I'm drawn to, the light at the end of the tunnel. She's the broken, beaten, little girl who still attempted to get up on her own. The one who has been handed very little in this life but makes the most of every second, regardless.

She got dropped into a preppy high school by the boss, despite not having enough money to feed herself properly. She got handed an education she's absolutely destroying, with a whole bunch of bitches who do nothing but tear her down, and she still managed to find a friend amongst it.

That friend might only be there to keep an eye on her after what she witnessed, but I don't know that for certain, and I'm not going to ruin it for her. She's strong, so strong, and she deserves the world handed to her on a silver platter wrapped in gold ribbon. She deserves everything, and I can't give it to her. Wouldn't even know where to start.

So, as the seconds stretch on, her irritation ebbing and waning, instead of pulling her into my body and pressing my lips against hers, I unlock the doors, and breathe in the cool, crisp air as she climbs out, disappointment sinking like a stone in my stomach.

If letting her go is the right thing to do, then why does

it feel so bad?

six
Ruby

I stand and straighten my shirt, tucking it back into my jeans as frustration swirls in the pit of my stomach.

I don't know why I expected anything different from him.

Chauffeur. Shadow. Protection. Ghost.

Those are the labels he likes and holds onto.

He doesn't realise that every time he pushes me away it hurts more and cuts deeper. He's driving a knife into my chest every time he treats me like something he wants, someone he wants to keep, only to turn around on the next breath and push those walls back up.

But I see the cracks, and they match the knife wounds in my chest.

He's not going to let anyone hurt me but him. So, I shake it off, breathe the cold night air into my lungs, square my shoulders, and head back towards the front of the hanger.

I have no idea where Scarlett went, or where Everett and Tanner would have taken Jeremy to kick his arse, but

I know where Nathaniel is, and that's got to be as good a place as any to start. So, rushing my steps, I make my way through the cars and back to the starting line.

Before I get too far, I hear the car door behind me close, and see the lights flash as they lock, lighting up the vehicles around us, but I don't turn and acknowledge the shadow that follows me. I can't.

I know the Five Families are into some illegal shit, so why the hell did I stop?

Stupidity. That's the only thing I can come up with.

My curiosity was piqued when I got behind the cases. The thud-thud-thud of the base was finally relenting, and I just wanted to enjoy the peace and quiet for a moment—just a second of time without having to put on a face for all the people around me—and then I heard the voices.

I should have walked away. *Haven't I said that before?*

I should have just kept moving. *I've definitely said that before.*

Instead, I stopped and listened, peeked around the corner.

I'd barely been there a moment, and I'm still not one hundred percent sure what I saw, but they were undeniably talking about drugs, and that was money I saw Damien shove into his pocket. It doesn't take a genius to put two and two together.

Then I was flying through the air, with a hand over my mouth and no way to get free. The panic that rushed through my blood was terrifying, intoxicating. Maybe it's because, in the end, it was Dex and not my impending death.

A shiver threatens to ripple through me at what could

have happened. Perhaps I'm not an adrenaline junky after all. All those might-have-beens and what-ifs are still rattling around my mind as I make my way back to the noise and the clatter, with the engines revving as people gather around the starting line.

The cars rush off, whatever noisy race they're in finally getting started, and, as the people begin to disperse, I make my way back towards the truck still abandoned at the side. Nate is chatting with some guys at least five years his senior, his clipboard in hand. He smiles when he sees me walking their way and steps away from the nearby crowd.

I've never paid much attention to Nate Peregrine, he's always been on my do-not-touch list, but the happiness on his face as I approach looks good on him.

He'd be a much better choice that Dex. He's my age, cute, if you like that kind of thing, but he's also wrapped up with the Five Families. Nathaniel Peregrine is nothing more than another dangerous man I should stay away from. Man, boy, whatever. Though there's nothing boyish about the knowing smirk on his face as we meet at the side of his brother's car.

"Found that drink you were looking for?"

"Yeah."

His gaze drops to my empty hands, and I realise I must have dropped the bottle of water I'd found at some point. I can only hope and pray that it's spilling all over Dex's leather seats right now. The fucker. It would be pay back for him scaring the shit out of me.

"Oh…"

"Hang on. I bet Everett will have something in here," he

offers, pulling open the boot.

"You know I don't drink, right?"

"Water… he has bottled water in here," Nate says, shuffling through a gym bag. "Might have electrolytes in or whatever, but other than being in with his sweaty gear, it should be fine."

"Such a gentleman."

"Hey, you're more than welcome to run that gauntlet again."

Yeah, there's no way I'm heading back in there, and he knows it. After accepting the offered bottle, I crack the top, feeling the bristle of the man watching from a distance. I never checked the seal.

"He just leaves this thing open?" I ask, gesturing to the truck.

"Nobody here is going to do anything to this beauty." Nate chuckles before turning to the list in his hand.

"That safe, is it?"

He raises an eyebrow in my direction as if to say, *what do you think*? I guess he's right. Tanner usually runs these races, and nobody in their right mind is going to mess with his bestie's ride.

"Where are they, anyway? I thought they'd be here by now."

Not that I don't want to stand and chat shit with him. Well, I don't really, but if I have any chance of getting the hell of out here, then I need Scarlett. And where Tanner went, Scarlett followed. *How long does it take to teach the sleazy mess a lesson?*

"You tell me." Nate looks up from the clipboard. "There

are less than ten minutes until Ev is supposed to be on that starting line, and the two of them went off with you and Scarlet, but you're the only one who came back. What's up with that?"

"Captain Asshat was perving on some blonde when we got there. Tanner and Everett weren't happy with that, or the fact he'd been drinking whilst supposedly driving Scarlett, so they took him off for some kind of *chat.* I didn't go with them."

He shakes his head, rolling his eyes.

"I'm assuming *Jeremy* didn't realise who Scarlett is in relation to your family, and hers."

"Really?" Nate asks, sarcasm dripping from the single word.

With a shrug, I take a drink and look over the growing crowd as the first car pulls up.

I know absolutely nothing about cars. Tin thing. Four wheels. Goes, so long as it's not broken. It's the kind of thing I'm not likely to have for a long, long time, anyway, so why bother?

"Back in two," Nate says, stepping away to check in with the driver.

I'm sure he's not supposed to be the one doing this, but the driver doesn't seem to give a shit as he high-fives Nate, then revs the engine. Luckily for them both, Tanner comes jogging through the cars, waving to the driver, who hands Nate some money.

Ah, yes, more legalities.

"Can I talk you two in to joining us for this one?" Everett asks, appearing at the side of the truck as he pulls the door open, one foot on the step. "We can drop you home afterwards."

"We?"

"They found Hugo en-route," Scarlett explains with a roll of her eyes and a swig of her pop bottle.

As if on cue, Hugo sticks his head through the cab, a joint in one hand and a lazy grin on his face.

"Come on, Scarlett. Bring your friend, and we'll make sure you get home safely."

"I'd rather get in an unmarked taxi," she quips.

I shouldn't be jumping into a car with the two of them, but at least I know I'd be out of the clutches of Damien Wheeler. Better the devil you know and all that. Not that anything has happened since Dex whisked me out of the building, and if I'd been seen, it would have, wouldn't it?

I can't imagine if they had any inclination they'd been seen they would just be shrugging it off. They'd have followed us, found us, done something.

Carefully, I look around, knowing that Dex is going to be somewhere here if only I can find him. The smell of cigars wafts on the breeze, and I know he's nearby.

"Fine. Tanner it is, then," Everett declares, drawing my gaze back to the task at hand as he jumps in, revs up, and reverses to the start line.

"And what *exactly* is Tanner?" the man in question asks, avoiding Everett as he moves the huge truck with a practiced ease I'm sure I'll never find.

"What happened to our ride?" I ask, interrupting Scarlett's no doubt irritated response. I don't exactly want the answer, but at this point, I think I need the confirmation that Jeremy isn't going to be the one taking us home.

"Who?" Tanner asks, confused as he looks between the two of us.

"Jeremy."

"Still no clue…"

"The no-longer-a-boyfriend you and Everett disappeared off with."

"Oh. Yeah, he's not driving you anywhere," Tanner replies dismissively, stepping away to meet the next driver at the starting line.

"Tanner is gonna be stuck here until the end, so Ev might be your best bet," Nate suggests, bumping his shoulder against mine as he passes. "I'd offer but… no car."

Remind me again why on earth we came here?

That's right. Because Scarlett was bringing her new boyfriend, and shit was going to hit the fan. Well, I guess it did, just not in the way I expected.

"God, I hate that fucking guy," Tanner grumbles, marking another name off his list when he comes back, quicker than before.

"Don't worry. Ev and Hugo will wipe the floor with him," Nate comments, looking on proudly.

"That V8 is a beast," Tanner says, way too much appreciation in his tone for the anguish on his face as he looks over some blacked-out, shiny BMW. "It'll be close, but I'm not sure Ev is going to manage it."

"He'll manage it," Nate counters.

"I have no idea what on earth you're going on about, but I'm done with this noisy, smelly mess. Let's go find something fun to do," Scarlett says, attempting to wrap her arm through mine.

"That's Brent Milligan, and you're not going anywhere other than straight home," Tanner argues, stepping in her way as he waves some girl towards the cars ready and waiting at the starting line.

She winks and blows him a kiss before sashaying past us, and I practically have to hold Scarlett back from ripping the girl's extensions out.

"And this is exactly why I don't invite you here normally. How's anyone supposed to get lucky with their little sister threatening every hot bit of arse within a two-mile radius?"

Get lucky...

"You're an absolute pig," Scarlett hisses, and I'm suddenly reminded how grateful I am that I'm an only child.

It might have been nice to have someone else around, but I can't imagine how much worse these last few years would have been if I had siblings to take care of, too. Mine isn't exactly 'Mother of the Year', but at least she's here, and if I had brothers or sisters then I'd have to deal with this sort of shit. Hard pass.

Besides Tanner, Scarlett has two younger brothers, too. Their house is complete chaos on any given day. It must be.

It falls silent as the engines roar, the girl doing her thing and starting the race. Where Nate, and even Tanner, have barely paid the races a moment's notice, this one has them both rapt, watching their best friend and brother pit themselves against their enemy.

Brent pulls away first, but Everett is almost nothing behind him, and the two of them head off down the race track, with the other cars following at a distance. There's nothing major at stake here, just money and status, but you can almost feel the tension as the four of us watch them all disappear down the road.

"Are you good here?" Nate asks, looking at Tanner.

"Sure."

"I'm just gonna go find Jer, check he's in one piece."

"Just about." Tanner shrugs.

I don't want to know. I *absolutely* do not want to know.

"You up for an ice cream on Monday, princess?" Nate asks, turning away. "I'll come find you after school."

"Me?" I ask, confused.

"Yes."

"Yeah, that's a no," I reply, taken aback.

Why the hell would he want to spend time with me? I've been nothing but rude to him tonight and on every other interaction we've had over the years. I have never, ever, not once, suggested I could be one of those hair-flipping, googly-eye-looking, mob wife wannabes. If anything, I want to be as far away from these families as I can get, especially after the incident not even an hour ago. The one I got rejected after...

On second thought, maybe I should give this a chance. Not that he seems to give a shit what I think as he continues the conversation regardless.

"All I heard was yeah," he says, striding away. "See ya on Monday, princess."

"What?" I screech. "Absolutely not. Don't bother. I'm not going anywhere with you. And that is *not* my name."

He doesn't turn around, look, or acknowledge me, just

waves over his shoulder and continues marching in the opposite direction.

"What the hell?" I ask, looking at a confused Tanner Loughty and his amused sister.

"Well, at least one of us got something out of this evening," she comments.

"Yeah, you. I'm pretty sure you brought Captain Asshat here for your brother to scare away. Job done," I reply, reeling from the bomb Nate just dropped.

Tanner barks out a laugh, pointing a finger in my direction. "You get to name all her boyfriends from here out. One of the boys will be here in two to take you both home, and I don't want to hear another word about it."

"Ugh," Scarlett growls. "Do I even get to have a drink before we go?"

"No," Tanner and I reply in unison.

"I like you, princess." Tanner smirks, his eyebrow piercing glinting in the streetlights before he goes back to his clipboard. "But you're both getting home safely tonight. Alone. And sober."

Sounds fucking perfect to me, but Scarlett is less than impressed when her cousin pulls up.

"That's not my name," I grit out.

"Hey, if Nate gets to call you it, then I do, too."

"Princess. I like it." Scarlett grins, accepting her brother's outstretched fist as she bumps hers against it, opening the door and gesturing for us to get in.

"*He* doesn't get to do shit, and neither do you. Either of you."

Scarlett climbs into the back of the car with less

argument than I expected, clearly knowing she's not going to win this one. I follow, the door closing behind me with finality.

I shouldn't look out the window, hoping to see Dex loitering in the darkness, hoping to see his lights idling somewhere nearby, but I do. He was so near, so close. I can still smell the aftershave from his shirt, remember the way his arms wrapped around me protectively as he let my emotions cloud both our judgements in the back of his car.

Just for a second, I thought he'd been about to kiss me. I could almost hear when his restraint snapped and feel the press of his lips against mine, but it was all in my head. I'm nothing more than a *friend* to him. A job.

"See you soon, princess," Tanner calls through the driver's window, tapping on the roof as we peel away.

Like a bucket of cold water poured over me, I'm suddenly reminded of what happened before that and how dangerous this place and these people are. She may be my best friend, my only friend, but Scarlett Loughty has people looking after her with the kind of money, power, and influence I could only dream of.

seven

Dex

My phone rings as I watch her climb into the back of blacked-out car.

I answer it without looking, reciting the license plate in my head until I can write it down.

"Call in for a night cap, won't you?" Josiah asks, even though it's not a question. *The boss wants to see you.*

"I'll be there in thirty."

"Marcus is home. Make it twenty." *Marcus is already sitting and waiting outside Ruby's house. Come here.*

The line goes dead, and I watch Ruby drive away, the taillights of whoever is driving her home disappearing down the track in the opposite direction to where I need to be. I guess it's good that Marcus is already there waiting for her, because there's no way I'd have made it to her place and then to the boss in thirty minutes, never mind twenty.

While scrubbing my hand through the length of my hair, I take a swig of my beer, knowing I'm going to need it before throwing the mostly-full bottle into the closest bin and making my way back to the car.

Twice in one day isn't good news, and there's no need to guess what he wants to ask me about. Damien is standing in the side entrance's doorway as I pass the hanger, his shoulder against the frame and a smoke in his hand. His gaze narrows as he watches me pass, but I don't have time to consider it too much. I need to get the hell out of here and get back to the house. Josiah hates being kept waiting, the boss even more so.

Once in the car, I start it up and pull out to head straight to the boss's house, wishing I was following Ruby back to the quiet safety of her home instead.

Security wave me into the compound, and my spot is empty when I pull up. Josiah is standing waiting in the doorway once I get there, *which is not a good sign.* Neither is his silence as we head straight to the office.

The boss is quiet when I arrive, and he gestures to the seat opposite as Josiah stands at the door behind me. *Definitely not good.*

Vincent Windsor sits silently behind his desk, his shirt loose across his shoulders, the top buttons undone, and his jacket long discarded. It is almost midnight, after all. Luckily, he seems to be sober but pissed off, his jaw clenching as he weighs his words, allowing enough time for the fear to sink in to lesser men.

"Tell me, Dex, why the hell I've had Theadore Loughty on the phone asking questions about our involvement at the race night?" he asks.

"No involvement, sir. Ruby went out with her friend, and I followed."

The least amount of explanation I have to give here, the better. He doesn't want the details unless they're pertinent.

"So, nothing happened?"

Now, that's a trickier question to answer.

And if I'm here, and he's heard from the Five Families, then he probably already knows, and my stomach turns realising this could get messy.

"With the race? No. The boy who picked Ruby and Scarlett up offended Everett Peregrine and Tanner Loughty, but they took care of him. I haven't had any involvement with the race tonight."

"But you were seen. That's not very incognito, is it?"

"I'm supposed to keep an eye on her and keep her safe. I do that as quietly as possible, but sometimes that isn't achievable."

Like when she's watching a drug deal go down. But why the hell would Theodore Loughty be calling up to complain about that? Damien Wheeler is an arsehole, but he's not friends with the Loughtys. What did I miss?

"And this wasn't called in because…?"

Because I don't ring in every change of plan she has, every time she steps out of the house and goes shopping or to meet a friend. I just get on with the fucking job.

"She was already on the move before I had chance, and I was conscious about locating her in the overcrowded event where there are more ears listening than you think there are."

He nods, humming and hawing about my explanation. If he thinks someone else could have done a better job, he's fucking wrong.

"And there weren't any other issues this evening? She went, she saw, she left."

Oh, if only it was that simple.

I knew I wouldn't get out of here without having to explain it, but my stomach still churns at the thought of it sounding like failure on my part.

"She went, she saw something, I got her out safely, then she left."

"She saw what?" he asks, his gaze piercing as his head snaps my way and his forearms land heavily against the desk. "What did she see, Dex?"

"Damien Wheeler was dealing, and she may have got an eyeful of it. I got her out of there as quickly as I could, and nobody saw her."

"You're sure?"

As sure as she was that they had her and were going to hurt her. As sure as I am that she wanted me to kiss her as she lay cradled in my arms. I'm as sure as I can be about her safety, now and always.

"She was around for a little while afterwards, with Tanner Loughty and the rest of his group. Front, centre, and visible. If Damien or anyone from their side had seen her there, they would have confronted him, her, and anyone else they thought was involved."

"They would, would they?" Vincent scoffs out an unimpressed laugh, the sound crawling underneath my skin. "Tell me, why do you think I put you on this job?"

To keep me away from Leo and Blaise.

"Because I'm the ghost."

"The ghost." He nods, humming. "Not the 'wandering

around in plain sight' guy?"

My teeth ache from clenching my jaw so tightly, but I manage to hold back from answering him.

"Not the 'banging through doors and making a racket' guy, no?"

"No, sir."

"If you can't do this job, then I'd better get a few calls made. Perhaps I can see if she could be lined up for Pendleton Prep in September. I suppose she'd be younger than the rest of the cohort, but if money can buy her in, then why should that matter?"

Ice slides down my spine, but I can't let it show. He's not sending her away; I won't let him.

"That won't be necessary."

"No? Because if she's watching drug deals go down in the middle of a fucking Five Families event, I have to consider how effective you're being right now." His voice gets louder as the words roll from his tongue, spittle flying from his lips as he leans over the desk towards me, his irritation barely restrained.

"I have made my concerns regarding this friendship clear," I comment.

It's about as close to *I told you so* as I can get without having his fist or boot in my face, and I'm not surprised at the silence that stretches out between us. Blaise and I have been afforded a whole lot of leniencies over the years—the perks of our bond with Leo, I suppose—but Leo isn't here to back me up, and neither is Blaise.

Now I'm standing here, alone, facing the wrath of the man who can make or break me with zero fucks left to give.

I did my best, and if they'd listened to me about Scarlett Loughty in the first place, then we wouldn't be here.

"You report every fucking thing in. Every move. Every conversation. Every. Thing."

"Yes, sir."

"Marcus will do the next twelve hours. You can take over from him at lunchtime tomorrow," Josiah says from behind me.

At least I'm going to live until tomorrow. That's something.

"She's going out with Nathaniel Peregrine on Monday afternoon," I admit, swallowing thickly.

"But they didn't see her, no?" Vincent steeples his hands on the desk, dragging a breath in through his nose and closing his eyes momentarily. "You report every single thing in. Every question he asks. Every place he holds her. I want to know exactly what they talk about, his hopes and dreams for the future, I don't give a shit. If they suspect her of anything at all, I want to be the first to know about it mere seconds after you do. Do you understand me?"

Gritting my teeth, I nod, waiting to be dismissed.

I'd rather be anywhere than watching her out with some other guy, and of all people, Nathaniel Peregrine. Talk about walking out of the frying pan and jumping straight into the fire. For both of us.

"You can go," he says, standing and offering his hand out to me. "But if I get another call from the Five Families before you, you're done."

He doesn't mean *taken off her security detail,* and it's not an idle threat. I'll be shoved into dirty work so deep, I'll never be found again.

Clasping his hand, I nod. Message received.

Turning, I head for the door, surprised when I meet Josiah's right hook, the bone glancing across my cheekbone, splitting the skin, and making me stumble to the side.

"You weren't close enough, and you were seen. You're supposed to be better than this," he hisses, running his tongue along his top teeth before stepping back. "I expect better."

It swells almost immediately, but retaliating isn't in the cards. With a nod, I take the hit and walk out, striding down the corridors and out of the front door, not even bothering to look in the mirror before setting off and heading home. Or, at least, that's where they think I'm going.

If I'm going to have to sit my arse nearby and watch her with another man in nothing more than two days, then I sure as shit need to get to her now.

After leaving the compound, I make my way across town towards Ruby's house, where I park three streets over and make my way to the back door in the darkness.

Marcus will be watching the front, looking for movement in the rooms and on the street, but I'm the ghost, and despite that nickname proving ineffective in the middle of enemy camp, this place is as familiar to me as my own home now.

Once I've flicked open the lock, I let myself into the kitchen, noting the empty glass by the sink and the sound of a television humming somewhere nearby. It's Friday night, and there's no party at the compound, it makes sense that her mother is home.

Unfortunately, I have no idea when she came home or if Ruby had to deal with any fall out from going out with her friends tonight. Fucking boss. I guess the report Marcus leaves for me will have the details. Even so, it's frustrating.

I slink past the partially-closed living room door and note the flickering light. Carefully, I wait a moment to see if her mother noticed the dark shadow passing. When she doesn't move, I make my way up the stairs and slide towards Ruby's room unannounced.

I suppose, for normal people, they'd get in from a night out, grab a drink, and get comfortable on the sofa with some easy watching for a while to come down from the excitement of their evening. Not Ruby.

I can't think of a single occasion when she's been in that room. She spends time in the kitchen diner, and in her bedroom, and that's it. If she's watching TV, it's in her room or on her laptop, but never downstairs.

I've often wondered why, but we don't exactly sit and chat. Maybe one day I'll get to ask her.

Until then, I slide through the doorway of her bedroom and soon find myself watching for the steady cadence of her breathing before taking up my spot in the corner.

She moved the dresser here once, and it must have taken her ages because it's heavy as fuck. Unfortunately, I only got to imagine the horror on her face when she woke up the next morning to find it back where it was before, but the thought still makes me chuckle.

"I know you're here," she comments quietly, not bothering to turn over.

When I don't reply, just rest my elbows over my knees,

feet planted on the floor as my back rests against the wall, she turns, her wary gaze meeting mine.

If our lives were normal I'd be asking how her evening went, if she had a good time, or what she thought about her first visit to the tracks. But they're not, and I'm not even supposed to be here. I'm just a ghost in the dark, but she can see me. She's always seen me.

Maybe that's some of the reason why I kept coming back here long after I should have stopped. Not because she's a weak, distressed, little thing who I need to protect—I think she debunked that theory a long time ago—but because I see the strength beneath her armour, and she sees the weakness beneath mine.

No one has ever taken the time to look for those before.

What I want to do is crawl across the floor and curl her into my body, feel the beat of her heartbeat against my chest and the rush of air as it passes her lips. To be intimately aware of the life that courses through her veins at this very moment.

Right now, she's walking a tightrope, and she has no idea how precarious it is.

She sighs when I do nothing more than cock my head but makes no comment about the state of my face. It must be obvious even in this dim lighting. Instead, I wait until her eyes eventually close and sleep pulls her under. Only then do I move by slipping onto the floor bed and pulling her into my embrace.

I may not be willing to give her this false sense of security whilst she's awake, but I can sure as shit lie to myself for a little while longer. The hours pass, and I know

I need to leave, even as her body seeks out mine when I pull myself away. Eventually, after pressing a gentle kiss to her forehead, I make my way out of her room, down the stairs, and across the gardens, back home to where Blaise waits for me with more questions.

eight

Ruby

The corridor is busier than I'd like it to be while everyone gets their things from their lockers, me included.

"You'd better be quick with filling me in on the rest of your weekend, because lover boy is going to be here any minute," Scarlett rushes out, looking around as she rests her shoulder against the locker beside mine.

"Not this again," I grumble, opening my locker and fishing out the books I need for the last classes of the day.

The two-minute run down I gave her at break was clearly not enough, but with her having netball practice over lunch, we haven't had time to catch up properly. I don't have anything to tell her about my weekend, though. There's nothing she doesn't already know.

I spent Saturday running over the thoughts of what happened on Friday night and scaring the shit out of myself that Damien Wheeler and Brent Milligan were going to come storming through my front door at any given minute.

Thankfully, they didn't. Dex or whoever was on

babysitting duty would have been there anyway, but still, I spent two days hiding and freaking myself out about the Five Families. The last thing I want to be doing is heading out for a nice stroll with one of them.

A shiver ripples over my skin thinking about being trapped with them, but Scarlett interprets it differently.

"Excited, are we?" she winks, stepping back. "Here he comes."

She's practically vibrating with excitement, and I have zero idea why. I have never, not once suggested that I could be interested in anything with him—with anyone. I'm quite happy hiding in my corner and getting on with my life.

I just need to get through these exams and get out to a college somewhere far away from these pretentious arseholes.

"Meet you out front at half three, princess?" Nate asks, propping his shoulder against the locker Scarlett has just moved away from.

I can hear it starting already. *"Princess?"* being echoed down the halls, the whispers, the looks. So much for keeping myself to myself.

"Yeah, thanks. I'm gonna pass," I reply, closing my locker in his face and giving him my back. That pretty, dark-eyed face that so many of the girls here flock towards. Not me. Never me.

The boys of South Beach have always been off-limits, those linked with the Five families especially. I'm not supposed to be here. I only got a place here because my mother's benefactor paid for it and continues to do so. Once his benevolence runs out, I'll be thrown back into the public school with the rest of the masses.

Not that I fit in there, either.

The small number of friends I had there haven't so much as text since hearing I was moving to South Beach High. Some friends they were. If only they knew the strings that came with the move, my mother's life hanging over my head being at the top of that list.

And whilst that pressure seems to have eased off, it's no easier navigating these privileged bitches than it is the ones back there. If anything, I could have done with a little bit of the day-to-day normalcy that comes with laughing about the shitty hand you've been dealt with people who get it.

As much as I love Scarlett taking me under her wing, she has no idea the life I've lived, the things I've seen, and she's never going to understand. In the same way that I have no idea what goes on behind closed doors at her house, either. I won't ever be able to fully comprehend that.

"I heard yeah again. I love that you're so in to this," Nate adds sarcastically, pressing in against my back. "See you then, princess." His words are whispered over my shoulder, his aftershave banding around me before he walks away without another word.

And I let him.

I don't argue with him again, don't knock him back in front of all these people. I just ignore the words tumbling from his lips, the pet name I hate, and I let him go.

Pushing back against him isn't going to get me anywhere other than further into the limelight. The girl who publicly turned down Nathaniel Peregrine isn't one who's going to be left alone, especially when she's as unworthy as I am in the eyes of ninety-nine percent of the school.

It's easier to lean into it. He'll be bored in ten minutes flat, anyway.

After sliding her arm through mine, Scarlett turns us away from the hushed words of the other girls by our lockers, throwing them a death glare for good measure as we walk towards English.

"If you really don't want to do this, just say the word and I'll go complain to big brother," she whispers.

"No, it's fine," I reply, my defeat evident. "Can you imagine the field day this lot would have if I let my best friend go crying to her brother to get me out of a date with the hottest piece of arse in here."

"Hottest?" she asks, a smirk kicking up one side of her mouth.

"You know what I mean." I shove my shoulder into hers playfully.

I can admit he's good looking, even if he's not for me. Swallowing thickly, I can't help but think about the man I'd like to go grab an ice cream with, the one who would never even consider something so… expected.

Dex would never be seen walking hand in hand down the promenade, laughing and joking with an ice cream. I can't even imagine what a date with him would look like. There's no point thinking too hard on it, either, because it's never going to happen.

So, until Dex pulls his head out of his arse and sees what's right in front of him, I'm going to enjoy this ride. It's time to see what all the girls are drooling over and find out if Nate's personality is as toxic as the dips in his abs.

I'm the talk of our last two classes, and when more than one unimpressed and confused look is sent my way, it's clear the gossip girls are on form. Well, if they're going to talk, and Dex is going to watch, then we may as well give them a show, hadn't we?

With more confidence than I intended, I stride out of the last class, shove my books in my bag, slam the locker door, and make my way to the school entrance to find Nate already leaning against the stone railing of the stairs.

"Shall we?" he asks, stepping away from the couple of guys loitering.

Scarlett practically shoves me at him, and I glower at her, managing to get my footing before doing something as girly as landing against his chest or waiting for him to scoop me up. Surprisingly, my stomach does some kind of stupid flip when he drapes his arm over my shoulder as familiarly as Tanner did with Scarlett on Friday night, and all the girls around us collectively gasp.

I guess that means it's official. Everyone knows, and I'm not even mad about it.

"Call me!" Scarlett shouts after us, and I can't help the chuckle that attempts to break free.

"Not the kind of attention you're used to?" Nate asks quietly, the heat from his body pressing against mine as confusing as it is welcoming.

"Definitely not."

"We can either grab a ride with Ev, or we can walk if you'd rather?" he asks, turning down the street.

"Erm, can we walk?"

"Course. Two secs, though." He stops at Everett's huge

truck and throws his bag and blazer into the back before telling him he'll grab a ride later, then slamming the door with a chuckle. "Apparently, I'll never get any without a big arse truck to fuck in the back of."

"Good to know," I comment with a grimace.

"Let me carry that for you," he offers, gesturing to my bag.

"Oh, no, I'm fine. It's not that heavy."

He shrugs, and the two of us walk in awkward silence.

"Did you have a good weekend?" I ask, plucking my first thought out of the air.

"Uh, yeah. I stuck it out at the track until the end and got a ride back with Tanner, so that was cool."

"Are you usually so involved? I thought they were kind of his thing." Not that I know much about it, only the little bits Scarlett has mentioned in passing.

"They are, but Tanner was supposed to be racing, so he asked me to cover for a bit and get a feel for it."

"Cool. Oh, was your friend okay when you found him?"

"Jeremy? Yeah. He's not really my friend, just, like, a friend of a friend or whatever. But he asked me to introduce him to Scarlett after swimming one day, and he seemed okay so…" He shrugs, popping the button on his shirt and shoving the tie into his pocket. "Guess I was wrong."

"Totally." The silence stretches out again as we walk towards the beach front.

"Here, let me take that," Nate offers again, noticing when I adjust the strap on my bag for the fourth time. "Please."

Relenting, I hand it over with a roll of my eyes, noting

the sleek, black car that passes us for the second time.

"So, you swim?" I ask, attempting to fill more silence.

We spend the next ten minutes talking about everything and nothing, filling the time with talk of our hobbies as we near the beach front. The cackling surprise of the girls at school eventually turns to nothing more than a distant memory, and I begin to wonder why I was so against this in the first place. Sure, he's the younger brother of one of the SBH kings, heir for the Five Families, but with my bag thrown over his shoulder, and a smile on his face, he's nothing more than a normal guy. Gone are the dark shadows that hovered around him on Friday night, the perceived threat from what he stands for. Now he's just a boy taking out a girl for an ice cream. There's nothing untoward about that, is there?

"I actually have an ulterior motive for this," he admits, holding the door as we step back out of the ice cream shop, the weak spring sun shining down on us once more. "Your favourite ice cream flavour says a lot about a person, you know?"

"I didn't realise this was a test," I admit, pushing down the nerves that spring from nowhere. "Go on, then. What does strawberry shortcake say about me?" Something good, hopefully.

We meander across the road. At the right time of day in summer, you can take half a dozen steps down to the sand and walk along the beach, but not today. The soggy sand stretches out along the wall, the sea receding inch by inch as it crawls back out.

"Well, some people would say you're too sweet and you

wear your heart on your sleeve, but others would say your sweetness is nothing more than a deception to get what you want."

Bristling at the suggestion, I wonder, once again, if this is a ploy to get information out of me. A way for him to find out what, if anything, I saw on Friday night. There may not be any love lost between Damien Wheeler and Everett Peregrine, but how far will enemies go to keep their secrets hidden?

"So, I'm either too sweet for my own good or I'm manipulative. I don't think you're winning any bonus points here. Tell me, what does that cookie dough swirl say about you, then? That your head's bigger than it should be and you can't make a decision?"

"Well, not quite. From what I remember, it means I'm diplomatic and can see both sides of an argument, or that I get overwhelmed attempting to do everything at the same time. Also, that it's fucking tasty!"

I wasn't that far off, then.

"I think I'll stick with my sweet treat, thanks." I dismiss his opinion without much thought, looking out at the road, wondering where that black car has gone and how far away Dex is right now.

What would he have picked? Something dark and mysterious, I'm sure. Triple chocolate or caramel twist. Nothing light and breezy. No, there wouldn't be any cappuccino for him. Rum and raisin? No way. With a chuckle, I try to picture him with sprinkles on top of a vanilla cone, and the unimpressed look on his face is one I can imagine all too well.

"What's tickled your fancy?" Nate asks, nudging his shoulder against mine as we move to the side, letting a guy pushing a pram pass us.

"Uh, just thinking about a friend and what their ice cream choice might suggest."

"Scarlett? Yeah, I think she'd be a mystic potion kinda girl, don't you? Caramel and honeycomb wrapped up in that not-quite-vanilla ice cream seems her kind of thing."

Not who I was thinking about, but a definite get-out-of-jail-free card if I've ever needed one, because that could have been an awkward explanation.

"I'm sorry to break this to you, but hers is raspberry ripple."

"Really? You think you know a girl." He shakes his head, amusement curling the corner of his lips.

I know Scarlett is close with her brothers, and that Tanner's friends look out for her, but I've never really understood the extended family dynamic of their situation. To be fair, I haven't asked, either. I've been too busy trying to keep my nose out of it when maybe I shouldn't have been.

Maybe Scarlett is more than just the girl who took me under her wing when my supposed friend-turned-*it* girl dumped me quicker than the empty ice cream tub in my hand. Maybe she's a friend who will last, even when we break out of the confines of this high school hell and move on to whatever freedom comes next.

"I was going to ask if you know each other well, but I think you just answered that question." I smile, looking at him as his fingers brush innocently against mine.

"We get thrown together at family events a lot." He

shrugs, turning his dark gaze on the tumultuous waves that lap at the shoreline. "She's good people."

I know.

"You seem like good people too," he admits.

"Thanks," I reply, finding a bin for my now-empty ice cream tub.

He slides his fingers through mine, confidently taking my hand as we continue our walk, and, once again, I let him.

I know Dex is somewhere nearby, watching and waiting, but he's made it abundantly clear time and time again that there's nothing between us, no matter how much I wish there was. So, I enjoy the feel of Nate's warm hand wrapped around mine, even if it's just for the moment.

"Did you have a good time on Friday night?" he asks.

The question is innocent enough, but disappointment sinks into the pit of my stomach as I wonder exactly where this offer came from. Was this really just a spur of the moment thought, or was this orchestrated because of what they think I saw? Is this nothing more than a convenient excuse to butter me up with ice cream and ask questions about my friend, only to finally get around to what he's after—details of what happened and what I saw.

"Well, the night started off with being choked to death by a cloud of aftershave, followed up by a display of utter manliness by Tanner and Everett, polished off with the thing we were actually there to see: racing. Except we were at the starting line and not the finish, so I have no idea who won."

I do my best to sum up the night whilst skipping over the parts he probably most wants to hear about. The coolness of the speaker case against my cheek as I peered around that corner, watching Damien Wheeler and his lackeys trading cash for little bags of pills and potions. God, I don't want to know what was in them. I really don't.

"Not Everett, sadly," he admits. "It was close though, so I'm told."

"That counts for something, right?"

"Sure. He'll get it next time. That M5 competition Brent runs is a serious piece of machinery, and he doesn't fuck around."

"I know less than nothing about cars," I admit, not willing to touch on the fuck around and find out policies of Brent and Damien, or the rest of the Five Families' heirs. "They're nothing more than tin boxes with four wheels as far as I'm concerned."

"Yeah, I didn't have you down as a petrol head. If you were, you'd have been all over a trip in Ev's Raptor."

"That's one extra-large tin box." I shrug.

He chuckles at my lack of knowledge, shaking his head.

"You know, there are tonnes of girls who would die for the opportunity to get in that car with him, or with him and Hugo, or Tanner, but you just turned it down like you'd rather walk with me."

His surprise isn't lost on me. Despite how he looks and who he is, he's just as insecure as the rest of us. He honestly thinks anyone would pass up time with him for his brother or their friends, but I suppose maybe they have. The gaggle of girls that flit around the kings of SBH are legendary, and more than one of them has already attempted to stake their claim. Not that it ever does them any good.

The notoriety Scarlett and Nate live in is slightly

different, but no less significant. Whilst Scarlett chose to ignore the limelight and hide in the darkness with me, Nate revels in it, so to hear his vulnerability is surprising, especially for someone he barely knows.

"You know that there are tonnes of girls who would die for the opportunity to walk with you," I say back to him, and whilst it's not supposed to come out flirtatious, somehow it does.

We both heard the whispered words of confusion as he told me to meet him, and saw the confused looks we got walking down those stairs at school, didn't we? It's not because I'm the star of the show and he's some nobody I found in the library.

His phone rings before we have the opportunity to take the conversation any further, and after a quick conversation with someone, he draws back, the walls going back up as he clenches his jaw, nodding despite whoever is on the other end not being able to see him.

"I'm sorry about this, but I'm gonna need to call it here and head off. There's a car coming for me, but we can drop you home first," he says, offering no further explanation as he ends the call.

The disappointment that sours my stomach is confusing, because it's been nice hanging out with him. I've spent half our time together thinking about what Dex would do or say, pondering on whether or not he's here, watching, or if it's someone else, but it's still been kinda fun.

I'm not one of those hundreds of girls lining up for their chance with Nate. Maybe that's why I'm here and they're not. Perhaps everything doesn't have to be cloak and dagger.

"It's okay. Thanks for the ice cream."

The words hang in the air between us as we stand at the side of the road, our fingers intertwined as I watch a myriad of thoughts flicker behind his eyes. After shoving his phone in his pocket, he reaches up to trace the column of my neck, cradling my jaw as we lean closer together.

This is it, the minute his lips brush against mine and I realise what an absolute mistake this is, but I can't make myself stop or even care. I've already forgotten whatever it was I'd seen, ignored how dangerous he could be, and thought nothing more about the man watching my every move.

Right now, Nate and I are just that boy and girl walking beside the sand after eating ice cream like nothing else matters, like life will wait for us. I swallow, my tongue feeling six sizes too big as Nate's skin rubs gently against mine, his thumb rubbing behind my ear causing heat to pool and goosebumps to break out. It's a something and nothing gesture that's still too tender for the moment, full of promises I don't really have any intention of letting him go through with, but when he leans in and whispers in my ear, I'm done for.

"Let's do this again, princess." His thumb drags down my bottom lip before he steps back, taking his heat and promises with him as a car pulls up beside us.

Shaking off the anticipation with a shiver, I reach for my bag. "I can walk back from here, but thank you."

"You sure? We can take you wherever you want to go…"

Anywhere but inside my own skin right now. "No, I'm

fine. You go do what you need to do. I'll see you at school."

Stepping back, I watch him climb in, and the car drive away until the taillights disappear, and it isn't long before Dex pulls up—the sleek, black car a shadow I can't seem to shake. I haven't wanted to until now.

But that's nothing more than the desperate complaint of a woman who knows that the man she wants doesn't want her back.

nine

Dex

I don't hear the door closing or the clip of her seatbelt in the back. The only thing I can hear is the blood rushing through my veins.

He touched her.

He was going to kiss her.

But she's mine.

Mine.

The word echoes through my consciousness with a vengeance that surprises even me.

I pull out from the kerb and drive away. Away from the spot he sullied with his gentle touches, with a look that promised so much more than a moment of rapture. A future. One laid with blood and danger.

Not that I could offer her anything different. I couldn't ever offer her anything at all.

But that doesn't stop the voice in the back of my mind that chants, *Mine. Mine. Mine.*

That girl is mine. Not his.

Calling it in, saying the words aloud, was the hardest

thing I've ever done—taking the life that saved hers all those months ago was nothing but child's play in comparison— but the knife to the heart was the way she looked at him. She wanted it.

If he'd pressed in and put his lips on hers, she'd have let him. She'd have kissed him back. And as much as I said she's nothing more than a job, we both know that's not the truth. We're half way back to her house before I snap and pull into the first layby I find.

"What the hell?" The words are barely out of her mouth before I'm climbing out, slamming the door, and practically ripping hers from the hinges so I can pull her out, too.

"You think he can touch you, breathe your air? You think he's worth that, huh?"

I'm practically feral as I press her against the passenger door, my hips holding her in place as I slam my forearms down against the cold metal of the car either side of her head. I need it, the pain, to remind me what a bad idea this is.

"Is this what you wanted? Jealousy? Possession? You want me to be so unhinged that I take everything I know I don't deserve from you."

"Yes," she replies breathlessly, not in the slightest bit frightened by my reaction, but there's more light in her wide gaze in this moment than there was with *him,* and that's the only justification I can give myself as I slam my lips down on hers.

She tastes like sunny days and sugar as I plunge my tongue between her lips, licking and tasting every inch she'll give me access to. Claiming. Owning. Devouring. She steals the breath from my lungs, allowing me everything, taking as much as I do.

My hands sink into the thick of her hair, the tips of my fingers raking against her scalp as I drag her closer, if that's even possible. Her fingers twist in the front of my shirt, bracing herself before she's lifting herself and wrapping her legs around my thighs. Pulling my hips back, I drop one hand and drag her up, pressing her core against my thickening length.

Fuck, I want this girl. I've wanted her for longer than I dare to admit, and she wants me, too. Her kiss is as desperate as mine, her nails digging into my chest as I grip her backside and squeeze, the rumble at the back of my throat unintentional as I feel the slide of the skirt.

I could drag my dick out and plunge it into her heat, feel her slickness surround me, claim her here and now, but I can't. I won't. Not at the side of the road in a jealous rage, even though I want to more than I've wanted to do anything in my life.

"You wanted it, didn't you?" I rasp, pulling on the lobe of her ear with my teeth. "*Him.* You wanted his lips on you."

"Yes," she admits, unashamedly.

"What else did you want, baby girl? Do you want to be his princess?" My teeth dig into the corded muscle of her neck, pressing hard enough for her to cry out before I soothe the burn with my tongue. "Well, you can't. You're *mine.*"

My fingers loosen in her hair, sliding down to grip the perfect handful of her tit and squeezing, her nipple already taut behind the delicate fabric of her shirt. She may have wanted him in that moment, but this attraction that's been sizzling between us is all consuming.

"Prove it," she throws out, her chest bouncing.

We've tiptoed around this for far too long. Her wanting me, yet me pushing her away... in the daylight hours, anyway. She doesn't know the gentle way she puts me back together in the darkness with nothing more than breathing, but now I've crossed a line and done something I always said I wouldn't, and she wants to know I mean it.

Locking my gaze with hers, my fingers blaze a trail around her tight bud. A moan slips free from her lips before I press lower, hitching beneath her skirt. We may be nothing more than twenty feet away from the road, and I might not be willing to stuff her full of my cock right now, but there's more than one way to claim her.

After pushing the soaked fabric of her underwear to the side, I bide my time, sliding my fingers up and down her, learning every place that makes her twitch and tremble in my arms before gliding a wet digit up and around her clit while claiming her lips again. I swallow down her moans and whimpers, lapping them up like the starved man I've become, desperate to keep every second of this pleasure for my own. She gasps in a breath as I push one finger into her, working her open inch by inch, until one becomes two, and the heel of my hand presses against her clit, her body rocking and grinding as she chases oblivion.

"That's it; you're so wet. I can feel you. You're so close."

She whimpers, her head tipping back against the car, and as much as I'd like to wrap my hand around her throat and watch her ride my hand until she comes apart at the seams, holding her up by nothing more than the finger in her pussy doesn't seem like the safest solution.

Instead, I curl myself over her, squeezing the globe of her perfect arse through the skirt as I nip along the column of her neck.

"Come for me, baby girl. Show me just how much you want me," I purr in her ear, swallowing her cries as her orgasm crashes through her.

If there was ever any hint that she wasn't absolutely perfect, that was erased the second she gave in to my suggestion and tumbled off the precipice as ecstasy wraps around her. Unfortunately, with reality comes everything else, and the knowledge of what I've just done and who I've just done it to pours over me like a bucket of ice-cold water.

Blinded by a jealous rage, I took things too far, and I can't take it back.

She must notice the shift because she clips out, "Don't you fucking dare," even as I pull myself from her body, righting her skirt.

I don't feel bad for it even if I should. Instead, I take the time to suck the soaked digits into my mouth, getting my first taste of her on my tongue, then kissing her hard. I shouldn't have kissed her or got her off, but I don't regret it. I only hope she doesn't, either.

"Let's get you home," I say, knowing there's only so long before they're going to want an update. I'm surprised my phone hasn't gone off already.

"No," she replies huskily. "I want more."

You and me both.

"Time to get home, baby girl." I place her feet back on

the ground, open the door, and wait for her to get in before adjusting the obvious hard on I'm left with as I climb back into the driver's seat.

The journey back to her house is quiet and awkward as we both fall into our own thoughts. I wish I knew what was running through her mind, but I'm too chicken shit to ask, and before I manage to pluck up the courage, she's grabbing her bag and stepping out of the car, walking away without a backwards glance.

I watch her go in, lock the door behind herself, and go up to her room. I can imagine the stilted conversation with her mum as she loiters in the hallway. "Yeah, my day's been fine. No, nothing exciting happened." Liar.

Not that I can say anything different.

"The bird is in the nest," I repeat, checking in with Josiah, as promised.

"Anything to be concerned about?"

"No."

Whilst there's a good chance that Nathaniel was taking her out to find out what she saw on Friday night, he left on the back of a phone call. So, either something else came up that was more important, or he doesn't believe she saw anything. It could be a combination of both.

I'm not willing to admit there's even a small chance that he asked her out because he likes her. She's gorgeous, sarcastic, funny, and she's mine.

"Marcus will be there at midnight. If she moves, I want to hear about it."

"Yes, sir," I reply, but the phone goes dead in my hand.

Without wasting a second, I lock the car up and make

my way up the path to the house opposite Ruby's. If anyone on the street has noticed their new 'neighbours', or the way we to-and-fro in time with Ruby, they wouldn't dream of commenting about it.

Vincent Windsor is a force to be reckoned with, and only someone with nothing to lose or a death wish would cross him. Not even someone in this neighbourhood would be desperate enough to wave a red flag in his direction.

So, I make myself comfortable in the chair at the window, the one-way tint making our observations much less noticeable, and I wait for movement in her bedroom. It's a Monday night, what could go wrong?

I'm sure I said that about Friday and look where that ended up. I failed to keep her safe and had to rescue her from herself before she ended up in the clutches of the Wheelers. I've got the black eye to prove how badly I fucked up, and Blaise had nothing good to add when I got home.

Even though I was dragging my arse in through the door at some god-awful hour of the morning, he was up and getting ready to go for a run. He cleaned up my face without the lecture I was expecting, threw a packet of painkillers at me, and left. Not what I was envisaging, but a reprieve I took all the same.

Ruby pulls the blind halfway down, loads her laptop up at the desk, and flicks on the lamp, but she doesn't look out or dare to peer across the road, knowing I'll be sitting here watching and waiting but unwilling to acknowledge it.

I grab the sandwich I left here earlier on, keeping one eye on where she works as I unwrap and eat. She disappears downstairs, reappearing two minutes later with a cup of noodles that she raises in my direction before sitting down and getting back on with her work.

With a chuckle, I watch her work from my vantage point, the lights behind me coming on automatically at some point until the night draws in and she's illuminated by nothing more than the glow of her computer.

I can feel her weariness from across the road, and all too soon she's shutting it down, changing, and turning out the light before crawling into bed alone with her thoughts about what's happened today, no doubt.

As much as I'd love to go curl up and comfort her, I'm on the clock, and Marcus will be here in less than hour. If he turns up and I'm not in this fucking chair, my arse will be deep in the shit. Deeper than it already is.

So, I wait until he arrives, pull my car around the corner, and head back in the darkness. She's asleep when I get there, but her entire body relaxes when I pull her back against my chest, and whilst she may not know I'm here, her body does.

I give myself an hour before sneaking back out and heading home, leaving her to her dreams while hoping they're of me, not him.

"You're late," Blaise clips out, his voice rising from the darkness of the kitchen as I slip in the door.

"Had something to do."

"Or someone."

"Don't know what you mean, brother." I dismiss his words with a shrug, not taking his bait. He doesn't know shit about shit.

"He's looking into it, you know? Pendleton Prep."

He throws it out there like the gauntlet we both know

it to be.

It's where the boss sent Leo to initiate into The Sect, and whilst he wouldn't be able to guarantee her a spot in the secret society, she'd make useful cannon fodder for their sick games. Either way, she'd be gone and lost to me.

"What do you want me to do?" I ask, exasperated.

I've been keeping her safe for months, doing my best to keep her off the radar of the Five Families, but literally the second I'm two steps behind her, she's walking into the fire with them. Now, because she's on their radar, the boss wants to send her away. If they didn't know she was important before, they would once they found that out. I don't know what contacts they've got in there, if any, but just getting wind of the suggestion could be enough to pique the interest of the Five Families. Hopefully not.

"I don't know what you can do," he replies, pushing a beer across the dining table towards me. "I know she's more to you than she should be, and I know losing her will break you. What I don't know is how to redirect the balls that are already in motion."

"That's why you're up at half past one in the morning, drinking beer on a school night, waiting for me to come home."

"Pretty much." He shrugs. "You're my brother. How could I leave you to the wolves?"

That's where we're at, isn't it?

Stuck between keeping her off the radar of the Five Families, even while she goes out for *ice cream* with one of them and sits in the library with another three nights a week, keeping her out of the secret society that's already stolen our other brother—the one not bonded by blood.

ten

Ruby

"I think the cliff notes version you gave me at lunch must have been missing a few points," Scarlett says, pointing her pen in my direction. "You, my friend, are very distracted."

"Huh?"

"Case in point. Distracted."

She slides a highlighter between the pages of her open book, places her pen down, and gives me her unwavering attention. "Spill."

"There's nothing to say," I bluff, attempting to remember what I told her at lunchtime. "We walked to the beach, had ice cream, walked along the boardwalk, and then he had to go. Simples."

"Then, what is all this about?" she asks, waving her hand across my entire self.

I can't tell her it's because Nate almost kissed me and I wanted him to, or that the man I've been dreaming about for months finally caved and gave me the best orgasm of my entire life in a jealous rage.

Sure, I've kissed guys before, had the odd one attempt to slide their hand inside my pants or up my shirt, but absolutely nothing in this world could have prepared me for the onslaught of emotion that crashed over me as Dex absorbed my moans and stole my breath.

I sat at my desk for hours after I got home, horny and confused. I wanted to storm across the road and ask him to finish what he started, because I know there's more. I want to feel him move inside me, fill me, complete me, but I can't do that.

I don't even know what came over me when I threw the phrase "Prove it" out there. It was a whole bunch of confidence that I seriously don't have.

"Is he really that good?" she asks. "I've seen the devastation when Nate's turned girls down before, but this starstruck look on you is weird."

"Starstruck?" I pull the pen from the corner of my mouth. "I have not been blinded by Nathaniel Peregrine's magic dick of charm."

"Magic dick. You and your nicknames." She chuckles.

"God, don't let him hear us say that. Can you imagine? He'd never let anyone live that one down."

"Least of all you."

"True."

"So, if it's not his unmentionables that have you all tangled up, what's going on?"

"I'm just thinking about the future, that's all. Do you know I put in for the art college?"

"*Yeah.*" She gestures with her hand for me to get to the

good stuff.

"Well, I got a conditional offer from them. If I manage to get the grades I'm supposed to, I get a place in September."

It's what I want, so I should be excited, but there's this weird swarm of terrified butterflies that erupt in my stomach every time I think of leaving the safe confines of these halls.

I may not have chosen South Beach High, but this is where my mother's... what is he? The guy she's been fucking for the last ten years. The man who pays her bills and makes sure there's a roof over our head, just. He's the one paying my tuition at this school, who held her life over my head in order to get me to spy on someone who became a friend.

Anyway, him. He may be paying the bill for me to come here, but it came just after the incident that brought Dex to my door, and I've always felt some safety in the knowledge that whoever and whatever I saw that night, it can't hurt me in here.

It's probably all in my head, and the danger is likely much closer than I think, but it's hard to tear the incidents apart in my mind. *That* happened, and I came here, where the worst things to happen are the bitchy girls. It could be so much worse.

So, leaving here fills me with a sense of dread I don't know how to compartmentalise, but I don't have the funds to stay here without money from my mother's... *him*, and I don't know how I would even ask for that or what it would cost me.

To be honest, I was surprised to still be here after the Big Sister programme ended and I was of no further use to him. I was half expecting to show up one day and be turned away at the doors, but for some reason, the tuition is paid up until the end of the year, and I get to finish my exams here.

I can't say I'm sad about it. Just confused.

"O.M.G, that's awesome," Scarlett says, raising her hand in a high five. "I haven't heard anything back from them yet, but I think Daddy is hiding the post."

I'm not the only one with hopes and dreams, and whilst mine are dependent on money and safety, hers aren't.

"Why would he do that?" I ask, confused.

My mother doesn't care enough to even realise I've been applying to college, never mind have an opinion on it enough to hide the responses I get, but at least she's here. That's one more than the sperm donor who ran off the second she said, "Surprise, I'm pregnant." What a dickhead.

"Because he wants me to stay on here where my cousin is. Aka: where he can keep an eye on me." She rolls her eyes. "Tanner will be starting at South Beach Uni in September, all being well, so that means I'm free and clear of him breathing down my neck. If I could get out to the college with you, I would, but that's just not going to happen."

"Why is your education dependent on someone being here to keep an eye on you?"

"I'm a risk, you know. A liability. A commodity that might be useful to someone, somewhere, someday," she replies, mimicking her father.

"You're a person."

A person who has every right to live her life free of her parents' condescension.

"I know, but not everyone sees it that way." She sighs,

looking down at the books in front of her. "I keep thinking, if I just stay for a-levels and do something basic, I could still go on and do what I want to at Uni. It will just take me a bit longer, that's all."

"And is that what you want?"

"Err, no. I want to be out there in the big world with you. Going to parties and meeting boys. I want to be free."

Maybe our hopes and dreams aren't too dissimilar. We're both looking for a way out of our lives, and whilst those lives look vastly different, that's what melds us together. One of the things.

"Well, I've been applying for funding, so we'll have to see what happens."

Because it's not just about what I want, but what I can afford. And it doesn't take into consideration the shadow that's been following me for the last seven months.

If I left, would he follow? Or is this entire connection only in my head?

It's not. It can't be.

I can still feel the vibration of the word *mine* through my chest as he rumbled it in my ear yesterday. That kind of possession isn't normal, I'm sure, and the switch that flipped in us both should be a warning in and of itself, but we've been ignoring the feelings swarming around us for months.

Every time I climb into the car with him, I feel the tension pulling at the air around us. It's thick and dense, and it's been the elephant in the room for too long. I'm only sorry it took someone else showing an interest in me to force his hand, but even that didn't last.

I thought maybe he'd have come over once I settled in for the night, to sit in the corner and keep watch, but he didn't. As always, I woke up cold and alone, with nothing but the scent of his cigars swirling around the room.

"If I ever get a letter I'll let you know," Scarlett says, pulling me back into the conversation at hand. "Until then, what's going on with you and Nate?"

"He thinks your favourite ice cream is mystic potion," I reply, remembering the confusion on his face as I dashed his confidence to shreds. "I'm not sure I can give someone with those kinds of smarts the time of day."

"You like him," she comments with a small smile. "He deserves someone like you."

"Sarcastic?"

"Someone who will call him on his shit, but who cares with her whole heart."

I do, but not for him, and it makes the knot in my stomach pull even tighter. "Yeah, maybe."

He was so... normal. For a little bit, anyway. I could see it, the two of us grabbing a drink in a bar or playing pool with friends, but it would never be like that between us because our lives aren't like that. It's a pipe dream at best.

"And you do, too, you know. You deserve someone who will give you the world."

"Wow, this got heavy," I comment, attempting to break the spell we've fallen under with an awkward laugh. "I just hope one day you'll find someone who will remember your favourite chocolate."

"Ugh, can you imagine ending up with someone who repeatedly buys the wrong thing?" she asks.

"For your birthday."

"And Christmas."

"Anniversaries," I add with a click of my fingers and a smile, our homework long forgotten. "That would be horrendous."

"Totally," she agrees. "Well, I suppose I should finish this. These Biology notes aren't going to remember themselves."

"Right," I agree, but it's clear neither of us are particularly in the mood to finish the work in front of us, both too inside our own heads now.

She flicks her pen distractedly, and as I peer around the quiet library, my mind wanders. Where is he now? What is he doing? Is it Dex waiting out in the carpark for me, or is it one of the other guys?

I refuse to let my thoughts stray to the confusion that is Nathaniel Peregrine and Dex Raymond, and I won't touch what might come after these exams. Exams I'm going to fail if I don't get my arse in gear and get this work finished.

After a while, I manage to shove down my wayward thoughts and turn the page to make a start. If either of us are going to make our own futures, we're going to need to do as well as we possibly can in these exams.

The teachers can wax lyrical about how there are other routes to the careers we'd like to have, and money can certainly buy you those options, but I think we're both aware that if we want to make our own way in life, then it needs to start here.

I turn off thoughts of the future, and of boys I should like but don't, and the one I shouldn't but do, and concentrate on getting to the end of the work laid out. Forty minutes later, I'm tired, hungry, my concentration is shot.

"I think I'm gonna call it a day here."

"I've just got ten more minutes, I think."

"I can hang on for you if you'd like?" I offer, closing my books.

"Nah, you get yourself home. It'll be getting dark out there. Everett will be finishing at the pool any minute now, so if I text Tanner I can get a lift with them. He's probably tucked up in a corner smoking with Hugo and waiting for him, anyway."

"You sure?"

"Of course. Swimming never finishes early." She rolls her eyes and grabs her phone, her fingers flying across the keys at breakneck speed. "See. Done."

"Fine. Well, text me when you get home, okay?" After shoving the last of my books into the backpack, I squeeze her shoulder and leave, more than ready to shake the last hour off.

The walk home would have probably been cathartic, but as the harsh wind whips around me, I'm secretly grateful to know there's someone out here waiting for me. It just depends on whether it's Dex or not...

We were both quiet in the car on the way back to my house yesterday afternoon, and even as the disappointment that he wasn't there this morning soured my stomach, I knew it was for the best.

It is, isn't it?

He's been drawing that line and pushing me away for so long, I'm not sure either of us know how to break through that barrier now even if we wanted to.

I can picture walking hand in hand down the road with Nate as he makes jokes and I laugh, throwing sarcastic jibes back his way, but that's not his life. Not most of it, anyway. What I can't do is envision any future where Dex and I do the same.

Am I just chasing a feeling with no substance? A connection with no future? Is this just lust?

I'm distracted as I pass the slipway to the art department, lost in a cloud of confusion as a shadow steps out, wrapping one long arm around my torso, attempting to lift me up.

Instinctively, I scream, but the sound is lost to the gloved hand that covers my mouth, a pair of bright blue eyes looking at me from underneath a black balaclava as a second guy steps forward.

"Like taking candy from a baby," whoever it is says, a wicked glint in their eyes that I don't want to see come to fruition.

I don't fucking think so.

Throwing my head back, I catch the guy behind me off guard as the back of my head smashes into his face, and his arm loosens, one leaving me completely to get hold of whatever soft tissue I just hit.

But taking a step forward doesn't get me anywhere as the guy in front of me twists to wrap me in his embrace and clamps his arm down over my mouth with an oomph.

"Fucking hell, bro. She just hit me," the one behind me splutters as I wriggle in the other guy's arms, desperate not to become another statistic—a student who left school and never made it home.

I'd just be some poor girl that was given an opportunity at a better life who squandered it by disappearing one day. It would be my fault, obviously, and nobody would even question it. So, I move, and I do my best to shove my shoulders into the solid one behind me, but he doesn't budge, doesn't move.

I'm met with nothing but a steadfast solid wall.

eleven

Dex

It's the smell of weed that hits me first, the voices following mellower than expected as Tanner Loughty and Hugo Osborne come into view. *Just what I had in mind.*

"Enjoy your night at the races, did you? Heard you disappeared around the same time as Scarlett, and here you are waiting outside her school. Not cool, man," Hugo comments with a disapproving shake of his head.

Because of course they think I'm following their little sister around. Hugo hasn't got any siblings of his own, and Everett only has Nathaniel. Nothing to worry about there. So, their biggest concern is the girl that mine has been wrapped up in.

"Do we have a problem? Because this is starting to get weird," Tanner adds.

Yeah, I bet it is from where they're standing. They think they're protecting Scarlett from me, and I'm doing my best to protect Ruby from them. Ironic, really.

"We don't have a problem, and I'm not here for Scarlett.

Just picking up a friend."

There we go with that word again. Friend. I can practically picture the look of disgust on Ruby's face almost as clearly as if it were in front of me right now. The unimpressed curl of her lip, the down turn of her gaze.

"They let you guys have friends? I've heard it all now." Tanner laughs, the sound echoing across the almost-empty carpark.

"What are you two doing loitering around here after hours, anyway? Looking for some young girls to pick up and pawn off?"

It's a low blow, but that's where I'm at right now.

The Peregrines deal with the Five Families escorts, and none of them are underage or there because they have no other choice. They're high class, highly vetted, kept safe and clean. Treasured. There's nothing basic or desperate about their operation.

Nor the guns that the Osbornes peddle, or the races that the Loughtys coordinate. I don't think they're supposed to participate in the night's entertainment, but what Daddy Loughty doesn't know won't hurt him, I'm sure.

"Love me a high school girl, sure." Hugo rolls his eyes, the green orbs lightened from the smoke pumping through his system. "Or not."

"Everett's got swimming practice," Tanner explains.

"And the three of you are joined at the hip," I add, putting all the pieces into place.

Where one goes there's usually another one not far away, or, on this occasion, two. Loitering around after school, smoking a little, killing time until their friend is ready to go home. Oh, if only we were all able to be so lackadaisical about life.

They may only be a couple of years younger than me, but it feels like an entire generation when they're like this. Soft. Easy. Two words that have never been used to describe me or the life I've lived.

At eighteen I was cold, closed off, a stone-cold killer. I don't doubt that they've been inducted into life with their families, but I have a feeling the real dirty work is done by someone else.

It's in the warmth of their conversation and the playful way they are with each other. Neither being things I've had the pleasure of for a long time.

"Not quite, but we'd better get—"

Whatever excuse he was going to give to leave me here is lost as a scream reaches us. A feminine scream. From the direction of the library.

Significantly more sober than he was two minutes ago, Tanner straightens, shouting, "Scarlett!" at the top of his lungs and running. Hugo and I are nothing more than a step behind him as I push up off the car and follow.

Once we round the corner, we find Scarlett hanging on the back of some guy while Ruby is being held by another as she does her best to break free, the pair of them nothing more than a handful of steps from the safety of the library before all this chaos commenced.

Tanner goes to reach for Scarlett as I race past the two of them, only interested in the one holding Ruby, dragging her closer and closer to the alleyway they must have slipped out of. That leads to the art department and the overflow carpark, and from there they have direct access to the main road and the opposite direction from where I'm parked.

I get to her just as she slams her boot down on the top of his foot, loosening his hold enough for me to swing and not hit her, smashing my fist into the side of his face. Bones crunch with a squelch that's lost amongst the rest of the commotion.

To hit me back he has to let her go properly, but Ruby's already manoeuvring herself to get away, and his hand falls from her mouth as she sinks her teeth into the flesh, acting on pure instinct.

The scream this time isn't from Ruby or Scarlett, but from the big, hard man that thought he could take my girl without any retribution. Grabbing the top of Ruby's arm, I drag her out of his hold, pulling her into my body as I catch him with an uppercut that knocks him backwards until he's hitting the floor with a loud thud.

Hugo has the other one pinned to the wall while Tanner talks to his sister, but I don't bother waiting to find out who either of these idiots are, instead hauling Ruby into my arms and getting her the hell out of here.

They don't need to know who she is and whether or not I was here for her in the first place. If I'm lucky, they might just think I'm happy to be the white knight in this situation. It's not often that gets to happen. Although it is becoming more of an occurrence with Ruby.

"Are you okay"? I ask quietly as we near the car.

"Yes," she replies, sniffling. "No. Just get me out of here."

My pleasure.

But where the hell can I take her that's going to be safe while we find out who the fuck that was and what they wanted? There's only one place I can think of, but there's something else I need first.

Placing her safely in the car first, I then slam the door and lock it before heading back to where I just found her. The guy is still passed out on the floor as I stride past Tanner and Hugo, then yank him up and throw him over my shoulder.

I may not get answers from him, but it'll be fun finding out.

"What the fuck?" Everett asks, coming around the corner and almost walking into me.

"Hey, we can take it from here," Tanner calls.

"Sure thing," I reply, not stopping or handing the idiot back over.

I'm sure they have their ways and means of getting information out of people, but none of them will be as fun for me as taking the payment out of his skin. They don't stop me before I get to the car and dump the guy in the boot before climbing into the front seat, locking the doors, and getting the hell out of here.

Everett is on his way towards the car as I slide out of the space, call my brother, and hit the accelerator.

"B, we've got a problem."

He's on full alert the second the words fall out of my mouth, asking, "What do you need?"

"Someone attempted to take Ruby. Scarlett, Tanner, and Hugo were there, and I've got cargo, but I need a safe space for Ruby."

"Bring them to the house."

"Not happening. I'll take her home and bring him to the warehouse. It's closer."

"Boss isn't going to like it."

"She's safe, and I'm going to get him answers one way or another. He doesn't need to know where she is."

The bloodlust in my voice isn't missed on him, or Ruby if the look in her eyes is anything to go by when I check the rear-view mirror. Luckily for both of us, the Five Families' boys aren't anywhere to be seen, but I have no doubt they'll be calling this in any second, and my car is going to be enemy number one.

"I'll meet you there," he says, ending the call.

I don't know whether he means home or the warehouse. Either way I need to get her to safety before I take care of the gift currently waking up in the boot.

"He can't get in here, right?" Ruby asks, looking at the centre seat with concern.

"No."

That push through was welded shut a long time ago. This isn't my first rodeo.

"You're sure?"

"Positive."

She relaxes into the seat until he kicks the back of it.

"Climb through here," I offer. "Just keep your head down."

The last thing we need right now is someone clocking this car with a girl in the front. All hell will fucking break loose.

"I thought you said we were going home," she says, not recognising any of the streets we pass.

"We are. I just didn't say it was your home."

Sure, there are so called 'safe houses' I could take her to, but none of them have the kind of facilities I'd like for our guest in the boot, and there wouldn't be anybody there to keep an eye on her. I couldn't see any bleeding, but that doesn't mean she isn't hurt.

At least this way I have someone to keep an eye on her and make sure she's okay. When her brain catches up with what the hell just happened, her adrenaline is going to crash, then she's going to feel like shit, hurt or not.

So, she rests back in the seat, sliding as far down as she can, and I turn the radio up, drowning out the banging and clattering coming from the boot as I make my way through the winding streets to take her home.

I can still feel the rage bubbling beneath my skin at seeing someone with their hands on her, someone in black, someone who really should have known better. Whoever this fucking idiot is must know the mistake he just made, and if he doesn't then I'll have fun finding out what the hell he does know.

Eventually, we pull down the small cul-de-sac and slide into my space outside the corner plot. If Ruby is surprised by where we are, she doesn't show it, instead looking around with interest.

"Wait here," I say, climbing out.

After heading through the side door, I grab one of my hoodies from the pile of washing in the utility, quickly explaining the bare minimum of the details to my mother before going back out to the car.

"Stick this on before you get out, and make sure the

hood's up."

All the neighbours know who Blaise and I work for, and none of them are stupid enough to share information about who comes and goes from this address without thinking twice about it, but just in case, I'd rather she wasn't instantly recognisable.

Someone wanted her, for what I'm not sure, but I'm not taking any risks with her or my mother's lives.

Sitting on my sofa is not somewhere I ever expected to see Ruby Sheridan, sinking into the corner of the fabric and wrapped beneath a pink, fluffy blanket with a steaming cup of tea in her hands. It's unnerving, but I don't have time to dissect it too far. Instead, I thank my mother and head back out to the car, more than ready for some fucking answers.

My mother didn't do much more than raise one concerned eyebrow and put on the kettle before dragging a mug from the cupboard and asking what Ruby wanted to drink. She knows I wouldn't bring anyone here if I didn't have to or if it wasn't an emergency, and I certainly wouldn't be leaving them there with her unguarded.

Blaise and I had earned enough to move out and buy somewhere nicer, better, and safer a very long time ago, but Mum wouldn't have any of it.

"I picked this place to raise my sons, how could I leave it?" was her argument.

How could either of us argue with that?

In the end, we stayed and made a few adjustments here and there. Like the state-of-the-art security system she doesn't know the full details about that's linked to the compound. Just because *that* drunken old man wasn't going to turn back up to hurt her doesn't mean there aren't people out there looking for a way to get to the two of us.

I don't doubt that *he* was connected somewhere. You don't get those kinds of tats, that kind of reputation, and that amount of angry without having learnt a thing or two. So, we fortified the place and let her keep her dream of raising us there.

We might be adults now, with more money than makes sense for the average three up, three down we live in, but that doesn't mean we aren't in the exact place we want to be.

There aren't many people in my life worth protecting, but my mother has always been at the top of that list, and it's the reason Blaise and I went to Vincent in the first place all those years ago. Two preteen boys can't do much to stand up against a very angry drunk man who thinks he's owed something, and when Blaise stepped up to try, it was almost the end of him.

I've never felt fear like it, watching the blood come out of my brother's mouth as he coughed, dark red dribbling down the side of his face as it came out of his ear, and hearing my mother's cries when she couldn't do anything to get to him, to us. Held back by the big hard man who felt the need to take his frustrations out on nothing more than a boy as his boot connected again and again. I still have nightmares and hear the sounds. It's what fuels me in those dark moments when I need to do things other men would only baulk at.

If someone that deranged can walk the streets unimpeded, then what horrendous things do those that we sort out do? Much worse, I imagine.

I turned up at Leo's door covered in blood and crying, and when his father was done, there wasn't anything left of *that* man. He took care of it personally; he told us so. It's a debt we swore we'd repay.

I'm sure we have, time and time again, but we're here now, and this isn't a life you can walk away from. I can't imagine the kind of job interview where my *skills* would be needed, and I'm not sure I'd want it even if it existed.

Blaise is standing outside the warehouse when I pull up, the engine nothing more than background noise as the shutter rolls up and I see his car parked to the side, leaving the perfect space to slide mine into.

"He's not happy!" Blaise shouts over the noise of the metal rolling down, waiting until it's clicked firmly into place to look for anything like an answer from me.

"Me neither."

With a shake of his head, he cracks his knuckles, ready to dive in with whatever I need. "What happened?" he asks, watching me slide a pack of smokes out of my pocket and light up.

It's a habit I keep telling myself I'll quit and then don't, but I need a minute to gather my thoughts, to channel the anger still sitting just beneath the surface into something productive. When I open that boot, he's going to come out kicking and screaming.

Sadly for him, there's nowhere to go and nothing to help him. There's no-one here to save him. The only thing waiting for him here is pain, if I'm feeling benevolent and decide to let him live, but I guess that depends on the answers he gives us.

"Open it," I say, gesturing to the boot.

I guess it's time we both find out exactly what happened.

twelve
Ruby

It's so… normal.

Thick, cream-coloured curtains hang across the bay windows. The TV plays some daytime television gameshow I've never heard of as I hold the steaming mug of tea in my hands and snuggle deeper into the comfortable sofa.

Maybe it's the steady rush of adrenaline that tore through me when I heard that man kicking and banging in the back of the car, but I can't help feeling safe. Much safer than I should to say that I've just been taken by the man meant to look after me and bundled into a car—one he told someone not to share the location of.

I trust Dex, don't I?

He wouldn't do anything to hurt me, would he?

"Is he coming back?" I ask, looking towards the door Dex walked out of half an hour ago only for the lock to engage automatically.

Despite how average it looks, I'm sure it's not normal for locks to engage like that, or for the wall lights to click on automatically as they do just now, making me jump. I'm sure there is much more to this house than the quiet suburban home it appears to be. Otherwise, why would he leave me here? How could he know I'd be safe tucked up in this blanket with this woman. She doesn't look like she could protect herself, never mind anyone else. If someone were to break in here, it would be me doing the saving. Of that, I'm sure.

"They always come back eventually," she replies, dipping a biscuit into her cup while she perches on the edge of the sofa, the soft knit of her jumper more expensive than you'd expect from this neighbourhood.

We fall into silence, the TV playing as we drink, and she eats, offering me a biscuit intermittently. She doesn't ask me any questions, doesn't want to know who I am or why I'm here, or what I've done for Dex to drop me here in the middle of the afternoon.

Eventually, she takes the empty mug from my hand, and I pluck up the courage to ask, "Who are you?"

It's the first of twenty-four trillion questions running through my head, and I'm impressed it's the only one that tumbles free.

"Me?" She smiles, a warmth I'm not used to in her gaze. "I'm Emmeline Raymond, Dex's mother."

Mother.

Swallowing my panic, I plaster a smile on my face.

When he said he was taking me home, I thought he meant mine, and then we came here, but I never thought any further into the destination itself than that. What I have been pondering is if he'd take me to a girlfriend or a wife, and if that's the reason he's been putting walls up between us.

I guess not.

He's brought me home to his mother.

She rinses the cups, washing them out and setting them on the draining board before asking me if I'm hungry. She throws it out there easily, like I'm just someone Dex has brought home from school—I suppose work, in his case. As if I'm just a colleague who has popped in and is waiting for him to get here, not some girl he's been watching for way too long, that he just yanked from the arms of someone who was trying to kidnap me.

"Erm, a little?" I offer.

My own mother isn't the kind to be sitting in the kitchen when I get back from school, ready and waiting to make me something to eat or to check in on the progress of my coursework and revision. So, why is she?

"You like eggs? Scrambled, fried, soft boiled with soldiers, maybe?"

"Erm, scrambled would be great, thank you."

It's weird, awkward, and I don't know what I'm supposed to do or how I'm supposed to behave. Am I guest or a prisoner? Is this for my safety or hers?

Without any answers I take a breath, pushing back the craziest afternoon of my life and get up. "Can I help you?"

She smiles, lines crinkling around her eyes as she nods and gestures to the bread bin on the side while she pulls a carton of eggs and a mixing bowl from a cupboard. Together, we make food, neither of us paying attention to the television in the background anymore, instead taking our plates and sitting at the weathered-wood dining table.

"Do I know you from somewhere? You look surprisingly familiar," I comment, wracking my brain. It's been driving me crazy the whole time we've been cooking, which, fair enough, has only been the last ten minutes or so, but her perfume is triggering some kind of memory or something in the back of my brain, and I can't for the life of me place it.

"We've met once."

"We have?"

"I came to your house one night at the end of the summer and helped my boys with something," she admits.

Me?

She helped them with me?

Suddenly, my appetite is gone, lost to memories of the things I saw that night. To the stitches I have no recollection of getting, and the ache that permeated every breath for months on end. She was there and she was the one who helped.

"Oh."

It's a ridiculous thing to say.

The words coming out of my lips should be *thank you*, or *how can I repay you*, or *that was a moment*—one I mostly don't remember. Well, the details of what happened *after* are hazy. The event itself is ingrained in my mind's eye in technicolour detail.

"Indeed," she agrees. "If Dex was worried enough about you to bring me there then and to offer you respite here now, I don't need to worry about you, do I?"

Her gaze hardens, and she's no longer the placid woman I've spent the last hour with. After all, a parent so easy going and laid back would be out of place with the person I know

Dex to be: cold and cut off.

That had to come from somewhere—nowhere good—and it looks like it's the same place she is mentally now. Gone is the woman answering the gameshow questions with a smile and a shake of her head, replaced with someone looking out for her son's wellbeing.

I'm not sure what would constitute a problem as far as she's concerned. After all, someone just attempted to kidnap *me*. Maybe they followed Dex's car and are coming here right now to try again? Or maybe I'm overthinking it.

I'm assuming he brought me here because he knew I'd be safe, because he thought his mother would be able to sort me out when my jumble of thoughts finally tumbled over. Because, right now, I'm doing my best to not think about how close that was and how easy it was for someone to know where I was and how to get hold of me.

What would have happened if Scarlett hadn't followed me out with my book in her hand and seen what had been going on? There would have been nobody to help me, nobody to scream on my behalf and alert the masses. It would have just been me and the two people who wanted to take me away.

"You don't need to worry about me. I'm not going to be a problem, Mrs Raymond."

"Good." She nods before going back to her food.

I do my best to do the same, but I can't help all the thoughts tumbling around in my head, not least of all who else lives here.

"Earlier on, you said *they*. They always come back eventually. Who did you mean?" I ask.

Maybe he has a girlfriend or a wife. Maybe that's who *they* are. Dex and his partner. Even just thinking the word has my stomach turning, but if there are more surprises coming my way, I need to know them now and give myself time to prepare before I'm faced with them.

"Dex and Blaise, of course."

"Blaise?"

What the hell kind of a name is Blaise? She must be a leggy blonde with tits shoved up to her eyeballs with a name like that, surely.

"Oh, child. Do you have any idea who the man is that just dropped you off?"

"Well…" I thought I did.

"Blaise is my eldest—Dex's big brother. Not that there's a lot in it."

"Your… His… Oh."

She chuckles, shaking her head and standing as she takes her plate to the sink.

He may know me better than I know myself, but it's pretty clear I don't know anything about the man who's been shadowing my every move. Although, if there ever was an opportunity to change that, this is it.

The big, scary man who knocked someone out and whisked me up into his arms, bringing me to his home to keep me safe has a whole other life, and finally, I get to peek into it.

"Can you tell me about them?"

"Well, that depends. Do you have someone waiting for you, because your phone's been going mental for the last ten minutes?"

"Shit."

She raises one eyebrow as I cross the room to drag it from the backpack that lies haphazardly on the floor by the blanket that slid off the sofa.

Swiping my PIN in, I note the twelve missed calls and five text messages waiting for me. Scarlett is doing her best to find out where I am and if I'm okay if the voicemails she left are anything to go by.

"They can't know where you are," she says pointedly. "If I need to confiscate that thing then I will, but I'm willing to give you the benefit of the doubt… for now."

"Why?"

"Why am I trusting you? Or why can't they know?" she clarifies, pouring herself a glass of wine. "I think both of those things are pretty self-explanatory, don't you?"

Because Dex hid me here to keep me safe, and because she trusts him. That's what it boils down to. And even though Scarlett is my best friend and the one who jumped in to save me and bring the cavalry to the rescue, I can't let her know where I am. I can't put Dex in danger, or his family.

I nod my understanding and read through the messages again before replying to say I'm safe and I'm okay, wondering again if that really is the truth or just something I'm telling myself.

Two people attempted to kidnap me, and they meant it.

This isn't like the other night at the tracks with Scarlett, when Dex picked me up and ran off with me. These people wanted to take me, and I have no idea why or what for. I'm only glad that Scarlett was there, and that Dex came to the rescue.

If he thinks I'm safe here, and she wants me to keep the location to myself, then I can do that for now. There's nothing to say I can't fill Scarlett in later if I need to, because what if Dex turns out to *not* be the good guy here?

After all, he's been watching me for months—lots of months. He turns up in the middle of the night, sometimes covered in blood and, whilst he hasn't hurt me, that isn't normal, right?

"Friend?" she asks, gesturing to my phone as we make ourselves comfortable on the sofa again.

"Yeah. She was there… before we came here." I swallow the lump that rises in my throat. "I've let her know I'm okay, but I haven't said where I am, just that I'm with a friend."

There's that word again. The lie we keep telling ourselves and others.

If Scarlett was worried enough, she could go to my house, but I don't think she will. She knows just as well as I do that my mother wouldn't care. She'd just shrug it off as silly teenage bullshit and wait for me to come back at some point.

She might ask me what happened when I got home, or she might have snorted enough to have forgotten all about me and the drama that comes with a daughter of my age. Either way, she won't be rushing to get a search party together to find me. She certainly wouldn't be whisking the man away who hurt me and be doing… whatever it is that Dex is doing right now. The less time I spend lingering on that the better. Just because he turns up in the middle of the night covered in other people's blood doesn't mean I have no idea how or why it got there.

"Good. Now that you know who I am, who on earth are you?" she asks.

So, he's not just my secret. I'm his, too.

"I'm Ruby Sheridan, and your son saved my life that night."

It's not something I like to think about. In fact, I do my best to avoid leaning too hard into the memory, but if she wants to know who I am, then she ought to have the truth.

"I'd like to think I had something to do with it, too," she adds with a smile.

"Yeah," I agree, but there wouldn't have been anything left to stitch back together if he hadn't got me out of there in the first place.

Sadly, it wasn't the last time he had to step in and save my arse.

"I think he did it again today, too," I add quietly.

"Ah, he's always had a soft spot for a damsel in distress, that one." She nods knowingly. "Blaise, not so much."

It's something I thought about a lot at the time. What if it had been someone else there? Someone who wasn't *Dex*. And what if they'd left or weren't able to take on two men? Especially ones so twitchy and unbalanced.

The odds were not in my favour to make it out of that scenario in one piece with anyone else, and even after it was all done, after the two men who hurt me were dead, Dex picked me up, took me home, and took care of me.

Now I realise that not only did *he* take care of me, but he asked his family to as well, and it soothes something jagged in my chest as I wrap my fingers into the softness of his clothes and the comfort of his sofa.

"Is Blaise quiet, too?" I ask.

"More so, but what is it that you really want to know?"

"Tell me everything."

He knows everything about me. I think it's time to even the score a little bit.

thirteen

Dex

His rasping breaths echo around the room, but finally, we have answers.

"He's five minutes out," Blaise says, throwing me a hand towel from his back seat.

All the clean-up shit I usually keep in the boot is in ribbons or strewn along the floor of the warehouse from when this idiot jumped out, hoping and praying a bottle of sanitiser was going to give him enough of a head start to get away from us.

Unluckily for him, he's inside a locked building he doesn't have the codes for. The plan was always to let him out and wait for whatever adrenaline was rushing through his system to do its thing, but I could have done without the mess.

"What are we doing here?" he asks, leaning back against the car.

Gesturing to our barely conscious *colleague* doesn't seem to appease him.

"Who are you trying to protect her from?"

Again, I thought that was pretty obvious.

She's been getting under the feet of the Five Families for a long time, they just haven't realised it. Or they hadn't until recently. But it's more than just the looming threat of the Five Families. She doesn't know what we know and doesn't see the danger around every corner.

"Everyone," I reply.

Picking through the mess on the floor with the toe of my boot, I pluck the still-useful things out of the pile, opening one of the bags and sliding the wipes and empty bottles into it. Just because we have good news doesn't mean the boss wants to see all this shit.

"Are you sure she wouldn't just be safer at Pendleton?"

"Absolutely not."

I heard what they did to Jacob, one of Leo's partners. I saw the marks on his skin, heard the cries down the phone, and I did what I could to help keep him going in there. Ruby wouldn't make it through that, and there's no way she could win the kind of games The Sect play.

Secret societies stay secret for a reason, and it's not because they let anyone and everyone walk in, take a look around, and then walk out. Once you're in there, you're not coming out. Then she'd be lost to me forever, and I won't have it.

I'm tucking the last of the mess into the back of the car when the shutters open, followed by two cars cramming into the increasingly small space.

It's showtime.

The boss climbs from the back of the first car with his

bodyguard and driver, Josiah from the second, along with two others, and it looks like our presentation has garnered more attention than I expected.

"So, what do we have?" Vincent asks, shaking my swollen hands while looking at Blaise.

Gesturing to the man currently slumped over the chair, we all go together.

"Wakey, wakey," I say, slapping the side of his face twice. What's left of it, anyway.

It must hurt like a fucker, because he wakes up with a start and thrashes about.

"I'm going to need you to recite that last little titbit, if you don't mind."

"Huh? What?"

His confusion is an issue as he looks from me to the boss, then to Blaise and back again, hoping for someone to be the saviour and get him out of here, no doubt. Sorry, man, you're shit out of luck.

"What were you doing outside the library this afternoon?" I ask, cracking my knuckles.

If we need to start back at the beginning, so be it.

"Library? What library? Wait... oh, fuck." His eyes widen as his body finally acknowledges everything I've put it through over the last God knows how long.

He's not going to make it out of here alive. Releasing him from his miserable existence is the most he should be allowed.

"The girl..." he says as he coughs, spitting blood onto the floor.

"What about her?" Blaise asks, disinterest laced through

his tone.

"We were told to get the girl and take her to the safe house."

"Why?" I ask again, hoping we get a different answer to before.

"I don't know, I'm just the lackey. They don't tell me shit."

"Who?"

This is the key.

The seconds tick over while he deliberates repeating the words he confessed to us earlier. I'll hurt him until he repeats them, we both know it. It's not that the answers aren't good enough to be passed on via Blaise or me, but hearing them from the horse's mouth in this instance is important.

"Mr Osborne," he rasps.

Pursing his lips, the boss nods twice, and I slide the knife from my leg strap and finish him off. We've got what we need.

"So, the Five Families have Ruby in their sights," Josiah confirms, rubbing his fingers along the stubble on his jaw before shoving them in back inside his jacket.

After wiping the blood off the knife, I strap it back in place as our *guest* gurgles and dies, the life draining from him in nothing more than seconds. It's probably a relief after everything he's been through, but this sounded like a simple job, likely for good money. Why wouldn't you take it?

With a nod from the boss, two of the guys come to unstrap our guest and get rid of him, only, instead of going to him, they grip me. Attempting to grab an arm each, they have no idea who they're fucking with when I throw one across the room, but the other one snags me, and with assistance from a third, they manage to force my arms wide with an elbow between my shoulder blades.

The confusion that swarms through me isn't missed, but as I look up, one of the other guys holds a gun to Blaise's forehead, and any fight that was ready to burst forth simmers beneath my skin. I'll peel his fucking fingers from his body with my bare hands if he hurts my brother, and I'll take great pleasure in doing it as slowly as I can *after* I've spent hours stripping slabs of flesh from his body.

If my confusion is evident, then the madness that now sits behind my eyes can't be missed, and neither is the rage behind Blaise's.

"Where is she?" Josiah asks.

Because of course, this isn't just about who attempted to kidnap Ruby, but where she is now, and if they're seriously considering sending her to Pendleton Prep and away from me, there's no way I can tell them.

"Safe."

That elbow peels from my shoulders and bangs into the back of my head before going back to its original position, leaving my ears ringing.

"You didn't honestly think that getting me an answer on who ordered this was going to mean you'd get away with hiding that girl from me, did you?" the boss asks, leaning back against the bonnet of his car.

Well, kind of, yeah.

Someone tried to hurt her, but I saved her, found out who wanted to hurt her, and gave them retribution. What the hell kind of thanks is this supposed to be?

"I'm not paying for her tuition at that school because it's fun, and I'm not paying to have people watch her out of the goodness of my heart. She's an asset. *My* asset. And I want to know where she is."

The guy I threw across the room limps over, clutching his side before reaching back and hitting me hard in the chest. With my arms outstretched, there's nothing I can do to stop it or shield myself. I take the hits as they come, one after another with a relentless force I should have expected.

It's payback, and it was earned.

By the time he's taken retribution, my lungs are screaming, at least one rib is broken, and my knuckles aren't the only things swollen and bleeding. There's nothing Blaise can do but watch and wait, praying and hoping I give in and tell them exactly what they're looking for.

But this isn't a secret I'll be spilling, and he knows it.

"Keep going. If you kill me, you'll never know." I throw the words out there, hoping for sense.

All I get is the click of a safety coming off, and you could hear a pin drop in the silence of the room, nothing but the fire burning in my lungs keeping me grounded.

"And if you kill him, finding Ruby won't be your biggest problem," I seethe.

If they think they've seen me wild and worrisome, they're wrong.

Dragging the deepest burning breath in that I can, I press my chest backwards, digging in towards the pain between my shoulders before I haul whoever is holding my arms forwards; my right shoulder dislocating. After the longest half second of my life, the pain between my shoulders abates, the guy losing his footing as I drag the two of them forwards and use their own momentum to smash them together.

The one in front of me hesitates, and that's his ultimate downfall. With enough space to do it, I duck, bringing my fist up square and hard across his jaw. If he didn't have a concussion before, he does now.

I'm bloody, beaten, breathing heavy and spitting blood, but there are three unconscious bodies at my feet. The man holding a gun to my brother's head meets my gaze, swallowing thickly as I take a step towards him.

The boss and Josiah are in the room somewhere, but all I can see is the red of that threat. The one I'm going to eliminate.

"They knew I was watching her—had Tanner and Hugo keep me occupied whilst they slipped around the building to get to Ruby. They weren't expecting Scarlett Loughty to come out and get involved, but she did, alerting us all to what was going on and diving straight in to keep her friend safe."

Wiping blood from my forehead, I take another step towards him, the fury barely repressed in Blaise's gaze.

"*I* saved Ruby. *I* got her out of there. *I* took the perpetrator and got you answers so that you could make sure she continues to be safe."

"I'll keep her safe, son," the boss says, his voice calm and placating. "I kept both you and Blaise safe all those years ago. Let me do the same for Ruby."

"You can't kill one of the leaders of the Five Families."

We both know it.

He has no way of stemming this problem, and no way to know whether they're only circumstantially interested in her, or whether they know the truth. And that's the biggest problem. There's no way to know how much shit she's in.

The only other option is to hide her, and I won't be separated from her any more than I would Blaise. Knowing that Leo was a bloodline member of The Sect, that he'd been through initiation with Blaise and me, was different.

He's strong, mentally and physically, and he was walking into it with his eyes wide open as a man. Despite what we all might think, secret societies are a man's domain. Nothing good can come for Ruby by being there.

I won't let them take her away.

"That is my problem, not yours," the boss clips out, slowly losing hold of his calm persona. He strides towards Blaise and takes the gun before turning and aiming it at me.

Blaise takes the opportunity to turn the tables on the man who dared to threaten him, getting him in a head lock quicker than he can blink as someone wakes up behind me, the moaning clearly pained.

Instinctively, I reach down for my knife, needing to get this shoulder popped back in before the nerve damage takes too long to rectify, done waiting around for someone else to hurt me.

The shot echoes around the warehouse, and it takes a second to register the pain that radiates through my leg. My gaze goes to Blaise's, my teeth gritting against the shock as he pulls his knife from the man he was holding, letting him slide to the floor, much like I do, but he's quicker.

Shoving an arm underneath mine, Blaise hauls me up,

my pained moan joining the rest. And when nobody else moves and nothing else is said, I take this for the opportunity it is.

"She's safe, and I'll keep her that way, so long as this ends here."

I won't hurt her—couldn't even if I tried—but he doesn't know that.

Blaise props me against the side of his car, bracing my bad shoulder on the cold metal before shoving it back in place. That's one less thing broken, but it hurts like a motherfucker.

Another shot rings out, and I pause, waiting for the pain or the darkness, but when neither come, I look to my brother, frantically checking him over, only it isn't him, either. Josiah finishes off the other two men piled on the floor, and realisation sinks in.

There can be no witnesses to the deal he's about to broker, the concession the boss would never offer to someone as lowly as me.

Vincent and Josiah share a look, an entire conversation without words. It's something Blaise and I can do. Leo, too. When you've worked alongside someone long enough, you learn every thought, look, and tell that runs through their minds, but I think we're all on the same page that this is a make-or-break moment.

There's nobody here to hurt us if I won't tell him. Nothing I want enough to bribe me with. He's already threatened Blaise, and how did that end? Leo's safely tucked up within the confines of The Sect now, preparing to take over from his father.

Whilst hurting Blaise or me wasn't a great idea on his part, bones heal and bruises fade. A death is not something he can cover up, and Leo isn't going to take to that very kindly, and he's our ace in the hole.

"Can I get your word that she's safe?" Josiah asks, looking up from the death surrounding his feet.

"She's safe."

"I'll be in touch."

With a nod, Blaise lowers me into the front seat of his car. "I'll be back for that later," he says, gesturing to mine before climbing in and waiting for someone to punch in the code to release us. He doesn't comment about me making a mess of his interior, just pulls up two minutes away, slides his belt off, and wraps it around my thigh before dropping a pack of wipes in my lap. "That was fucking stupid."

"Tell me about it," I reply. "They only brought four men and thought it would be enough. Fucking idiots."

"Who exactly are you protecting her from by keeping this information to yourself?"

"Him."

"You think he doesn't want her to be safe? That's why he's had you, Marcus, and the rest of the team on her for the last few months?"

"The picture is changing. She's at risk from the Five Families, sure, but he doesn't have *her* best interests at heart either. You heard him. She's a commodity, an asset. She's nothing but a pawn in the games he plays, and if I give her to him now, there is nothing to say she won't be handed over to The Sect."

"And? Maybe they'd keep her safe." He practically

shouts his logic at me, hoping it will penetrate. "What the fuck are you going to do now? You can barely keep yourself safe."

Pain twists in my chest like a knife plunged too deep as I cough out a breath, and a small part of me knows he's right. Maybe The Sect can keep her safe. Maybe the Five Families only want to know who she is and what she wants from them… aka: nothing.

Or maybe the Five Families want to keep her close and find out what she knows, and The Sect want to break her and induct her into their nameless, faceless ranks. Either way, they can't have her. Neither of them can. She's mine.

fourteen

Ruby

"He was totally covered head to toe in mud," Emmeline says, waiting until I've caught my breath before continuing as tears of laughter stream down my face. "And that wasn't the end of it. I'd barely got him in the tub before Blaise followed. Yet another set of muddy footprints across the damn floor." She bursts into laughter, too, the two of us creasing up at the mental picture she's drawn. "I never did find their shoes after that either, the cheeky little shits."

Our laughter is cut off the moment the side door bangs open and a tall, dark-haired man whose irritated gaze looks way too much like Dex's to be anyone other than his brother strides in, yanks out a chair, and yells, "Get the kit!"

He walks back out, and Emmeline sobers immediately, throwing the blanket back and rushing off up the stairs.

"Was that blood?" I ask, but there's no one here to answer as I sit in the corner of the room, alone and confused. I don't have to wait long to find out, because seconds later, he's back, and there's a bleeding Dex hanging from his arm.

He drops him into the dining chair as I rush over, trying to work out what looks like the worst of it. Blood seeps down his leg, turning the dark denim a dangerous colour, but there's blood dripping down his forehead, too, covering his face and hands. It's everywhere.

"Ruby, get me the scissors from the kitchen," Emmeline says, snapping me out of the stupor as I find myself standing there watching him unhelpfully.

"Shit, yeah."

Moving to the kitchen, I open and close just about every drawer while Blaise rattles a list of war wounds off that's way too long to be real. Eventually, I find the scissors in a pot on the work surface, and I rush back to take in the angry set of Emmeline's jaw.

"That one guy did all this?" I ask, looking him over. The guy was comatose when Dex threw him in the boot. Not so much when he got him out, though. And if this is what he did to Dex, what the hell would he have done to me? How much worse would I be looking right now if it weren't for Scarlett and Dex.

And here he is, like this, because of me.

Emotion creeps up, lodging a thick lump in my throat as my eyes well and tears threaten to tumble for an entirely different reason than they were a few minutes ago.

"It was a bit more complicated than that," Dex offers before bursting into a coughing fit. "Fuck, that hurts."

"What doesn't?"

"Probably a shorter list," Emmeline clips out, handing Dex a syringe from her pack before grabbing the scissors.

"Ruby, get me the bottle of vodka out of that freezer, will you?"

Dragging my gaze away from where she slices through the jeans to where she's pointing is harder than I imagine, but at least he's here, breathing, and as dry witted as ever. This isn't the moment to clam up and become useless.

When I needed help, they were there, all of them.

Shoving that emotion down, I go to the kitchen and get whatever she needs. Vodka, warm water, clean cloths from the bathroom cabinet. Blaise throws sanitiser on the tools Emmeline needs like they've done this many, many times before while I stand there attempting to be as helpful as I can be.

After all, this is my fault.

"Do you need me to call Catherine?" Blaise asks, watching his mother inspect Dex's leg, concern etched on both their faces as she cleans God knows what out of it. "If not, I'll set the security system."

"No, I think I can get this. It's only just in the bone, so that's good news."

"That's good news?"

"At least it's something firm to yank it out of. Harder to minimise the damage with soft tissue if it's lodged in there firmly," she explains, dragging a breath in through her nose.

"Are you sure?" Blaise asks, clearly not convinced. "I can call her if you think—"

"I'm good. Drink some more of that, and get that security system on," she says to them both. "I've given you some painkillers, but nothing that will kick in quick enough, and this is gonna hurt. Blaise, hold his leg."

Gritting his teeth, Dex grips the arm of the chair, and Blaise places his hands where his mother points to. I can do nothing but grit my teeth and press crescents into the palm of my hands as I watch Dex take a big swig of vodka just before Emmeline picks up the wicked-looking pair of tweezers and digs it into the hole in his leg.

I can feel the groan that rumbles from him in my very soul, even as it twists into a roar as she needles the wound, attempting to get hold of the tiny piece of metal that someone tore through his body.

It goes on for the longest seconds of my life, even though it's probably nothing more than a minute. Dex bucks and twists, writhing in agony, but Blaise holds his leg steady so that when their mother eventually yanks the metal things out, she's wearing the most triumphant smile.

"Got it."

After releasing his brother, Blaise moves to a black bag on the side, and there's something vaguely familiar about it... until he pulls out a blow torch and a knife.

"What the fuck is that for?" I ask, horrified.

Dex has just been beaten half to death and shot. What on earth could they have in mind now?

"Got to stop the bleeding," Emmeline explains, inspecting the hole.

"You can't just stitch it up and call it a day?"

"Too much risk of compartment syndrome and infection if I seal it up. I'd rather not have to slice his entire leg open or amputate it if we can help it."

"You're not cutting me up," Dex groans, looking paler than I've ever seen him.

The blow torch bursts to life, the menacing sound something I'm not likely to ever forget.

"What can I do?" I ask.

"Just sit," Emmeline says while Blaise concentrates on heating up the knife.

Pulling out one of the chairs beside Dex, I slide his swollen and bloody hand into mine, wrapping those digits up like I could keep them safe in my lap. *If only.* The least I can do is stay here and give him any comfort I can whilst they finish up putting him back together.

Taking the opportunity, I tune out and watch Dex's older brother. The one that I didn't know existed until a few hours ago. He's got the same dark hair and irritated countenance as Dex, a dark stubble lining his jaw, and stormy blue eyes several shades darker than his brothers normally are.

They work together like a flawless team, with Blaise changing out the water as Emmeline cleans and preps the area ready for whatever comes next.

Fixing up the now-empty bullet hole in Dex's leg.

Bullet hole.

I wouldn't have survived that.

Don't they usually put people under anaesthesia for this kind of thing? And don't you normally go to a hospital?

I'm reasonably sure that digging bullets and burning wounds is not a normal dining table activity. Although I wasn't refusing the assistance when it was my table we were sitting at, and I wouldn't have been going to a hospital, either.

"This is gonna be worse. Are you ready?" Emmeline asks, looking from Dex to me and back again, waiting on confirmation before taking the red burning knife from Blaise.

She's not wrong.

The yell that bursts from Dex is hard to listen to, and thankfully short lived, because he passes out. Not that I think that's any better. Emmeline finishes with the knife, and Blaise rushes to the sink with it, plunging it into cold water before returning with a bottle of smelling salts.

Dex wakes up with a start, and my heart stutters. He's gone through so much and is still going through so much instead of me. It should have been me.

Nobody would go to these kinds of lengths with a girl who doesn't know anything. It'd have been over and done within an hour. I'd have been dead, but Dex would have been safe. I wouldn't be missed, anyway. Everyone's lives would continue on without pause if I weren't here. It would have been fine. Instead, he stepped in and saved me, and this is the thanks he gets.

"Let me check that shoulder," Emmeline says as Blaise disappears with the rest of the instruments. "And your ribs."

Sadly, the picture only gets worse when the three of us manage to get his shirt off, with Dex groaning as his mother presses along the bruising on his chest. She manipulates his shoulder before checking over the cut on the back of his head and adding a couple of butterfly bandages to the list of wounds.

"Well, I think you'll make it through the night," she declares.

Blaise must see all the colour drain from my face as my stomach threatens to revolt. He could have died because of me.

"She's joking," Blaise says, the first words he's uttered intentionally in my direction. "Mostly."

"Mostly?" It's supposed to come out strong and sarcastic, but the word squeaks out sounding way too mousey for the moment.

"Try some weight on it; see you how get on," Emmeline instructs, holding her hands out as if she can help Dex up.

He's a good six or more inches taller than she is, and at least half as broad again. If Dex was actually incapacitated, the only person who stands a chance of moving him is Blaise, and he doesn't seem inclined to do so.

Instead, I release Dex's hand, and he grips his mothers in one and the edge of the table in the other, pulling himself up to standing before testing his weight on his bad leg. Wincing, he shuffles the weight back off it, testing it again with a step.

"It could have done with an X-ray, but I think you're good," his mother says, watching the tentative steps he takes along the edge of the table as I step back out of their way.

"Yeah, I think we're good," Dex says, stopping when Blaise interrupts his movement to hand him a glass of water and a couple of tablets.

"It's just paracetamol. I'm assuming you've already given him the good drugs?" Blaise asks, looking at his mother for guidance.

"Yeah, give it another ten or fifteen, and he'll be out like a light," she replies.

"I'm still here you know?" Dex comments, amusement mixed with irritation laced through his tone while I wait awkwardly at the side of the table.

"You need a hand getting cleaned up?" Blaise asks.

"Just some water and a washcloth would be great. I'll manage with a little bit of help. Do you have some of that arnica shit, though?"

With a nod, Blaise disappears up the stairs, an unimpressed turn to his lips.

"I'll just—" I say, gesturing to the sofa, but I don't know what I was going to say. Get out of the way? Wait over here? Make myself invisible and wish this day never happened?

"I don't think so. Get your arse up these stairs," Dex grumbles, gripping the handrail and hauling himself up.

"Erm…" I'm not really sure what the protocol is here as I look from where Dex is struggling to his mother, and back.

"Go and give him a hand. You're old enough, almost an adult, and nobody says no to that boy," she replies, fondness radiating from her.

I can't imagine how hard this must have been for her, hurting him like that only to make it better in the long run. I'm not sure it's something that I could do for my child. Not that I have one or am going to have one. I'd have to have a boyfriend first…

"Ruby," Dex growls, the sound echoing down the enclosed staircase, and I hurry my steps to catch up with him.

Water is running somewhere when we make it to the top of the stairs, but Dex shoves open the door in front of us and limps through, dropping heavily to the bed as sweat slicks across his shoulders.

"I'm gonna need a hand with these if you don't mind"?

"Yeah, sure." I nod as he unhooks the belt at his waist, the only thing holding up the tatters of his jeans.

This is most definitely not how I've planned on getting his clothes off him recently, and I certainly won't be doing any of the things I'd have liked to do had this moment ever arisen between us, but he took all this pain for me. The least I can do is help him to get comfortable.

He stands, waiting for me to shove the material over his hips and down his thighs before dropping back to the bed. The cut edge falls uselessly when I pull the leather from it and carefully manoeuvre it over his good leg.

And that's where I wait, on my knees between his legs, with his trousers in my hand, the proof of his devotion surrounding us. It's in the blood soaked into the fabric in my hands and the bruises that mar his skin. It's in every wince and ragged breath, and if I ever thought there was something deniable between us, I was wrong.

His usually-clear-blue eyes are dark as they gaze down at me now, and despite the swelling, the blood, and the ridiculous amount of pain he must be in, he still manages to make me feel like I'm his entire world.

"No soap, just water, and try to keep that wound dry," his brother says, banging his fist on the door and throwing a tube of cream on the bed beside us, making us both jump. "Think you can manage that?"

"Sure thing. Thanks, bro."

Blaise places the bowl of water and a handful of towels on the floor beside the bed, not daring to look my way before he disappears again. The thudding of his steps on the stairs is the only signal that he's not still with us, disappearing otherwise silently as Dex attempts to stand.

"Uh, yeah, you can knock that shit right off. Sit your arse down," I clip, abandoning the discarded pants and moving towards the water.

"You may as well bin those," he says with a sad smile, dropping back down to the bed.

I have no idea where or how to, but… sure.

Making sure he stays seated, I grab the pants and drop them by door, determined to do everything I can to make this easier for him. It's the least I can do, after all.

fifteen

Dex

When I called her up here, I just needed to know she was safe and in one piece, that nothing had happened in the time Blaise and I had been out getting answers.

Logically, I knew she was okay, tucked up in the confines of this house, but when your mind is overwhelmed by pain, it seems to short circuit a little bit that way.

Now, though, she hovers at the side of the bed, looking warily at the cloths Blaise left there, clearly not knowing what to do or where to start. The least I can give her is an out.

"I can do this myself, it's fine. I'm probably just going to sleep, anyway."

It's not like I need to be ship-shape and sparkly clean or anything.

"I think we'd better get the blood off you first," she comments, dropping onto the side of the bed and taking my hand into her lap, apparently not bothered about the blood anymore.

She soaks a cloth, ringing it out before wiping along the back of my hand, taking extra care around the split knuckles and swelling. That's how we spend the next ten, fifteen, forty minutes or more. I don't know how long it takes, and I don't care.

She works from my hands to my shoulders, picking carefully around the tape on my head as the painkillers finally kick in, and the edges of agony soften. It's like sinking into a blanket, warm and inviting, and as much as this is not how I wanted Ruby to see me half dressed for the first time, right now, I really don't care.

She works along my chest, rubbing the cream Blaise left into the aching muscles and cracked bones. It won't fix anything, but it'll help it all heal faster, and somewhere in the back of my mind I can register that this isn't over. That I need to heal as quickly as I can if I want to keep her.

I've never kept anything for myself before—anyone.

There have been girls, women. The compound is swarming with them most weekends when Vincent throws his parties and does his best to keep the top line associates on side and on board, and with a reputation like mine, it's not hard. They all want the chance to tame the bad boy, to fix the broken parts of me and placate the beast that rages under my skin. But it's not like that with Ruby. She's different. She's an itch I can't scratch. A problem that hovers in my periphery when she's not near. A question I can't answer.

As I sat there watching her that first night, when she was broken and beaten but not out, I wondered what she would do in the morning. Would she call the police? *That would sign her death warrant.* Would she curl up in a ball and cry, wishing for it all to be over? *No, not my girl.*

As far as I can tell, she got up and dressed and went to school. She put on a brave face and got on with this shit, and I've never seen anything so beautiful in my life. The strength it must have taken to get her hair up over that wound, covering it up as best she could, would have been intense.

People must have noticed the way she wasn't her usual self, or maybe they didn't. It was her first day at South Beach High, and they didn't know her at all. She was frightened, in pain, and alone, except for me watching in the shadows.

Which was where I stayed, for the most part.

Making sure that the Five Families didn't suspect her and that she healed up well gave me the opportunity to see her become *herself* again, and it was amazing.

I'll never forget the way her face lit up the first time I left a soft toy on her bed. Watching from the other side of the street wasn't ideal, but I at least got to see it, and that's more than I got when I fixed the kitchen or replaced the lino in the hallway.

No, that would have been a sight to see.

Instead, I had to make do with the amusement and confusion in her mother's voice when I overheard her talking about it at the compound. I only wish it hadn't been needed in the first place. What kind of person lives like that out of choice?

Ruby changes the water more than once, the cloth running red quicker than I think either of us expect, and when she's done, she tiptoes back into the room.

"I'll just leave you to sleep," she whispers, pushing the hair back off my face.

I wish she'd press her lips against mine and crawl into my skin, keeping me safe and warm and finally letting my mind rest. Instead, I pull her down, more than willing to blame the drugs in the morning as I awkwardly turn to my side and press her back against my chest.

"Just stay here with me."

She doesn't respond, but she doesn't move either, staying tucked up in my embrace as slumber finally drags me under.

When I eventually wake, she's gone, and my brother is sitting in a chair with his feet propped up on my bed.

"She's downstairs, don't panic," he grumbles, shifting his weight.

Moving hurts more than I want to admit as I grit my teeth and drag myself up to rest against the headboard.

"There are more painkillers and water there," he says, gesturing to the side table.

Leaning over, I take them without question, hoping to at least take the edge off the fire that lances through my chest every time I breathe while my leg throbs ominously.

"Why didn't you just tell him she was here?"

Straight into it, then. Not that I'd expect any different from him.

"So he can throw her to The Sect? No, thank you."

"He's going to find her eventually."

No shit. I just haven't thought it through that far.

We sit in silence while I wait for the painkillers to kick in, adjusting uncomfortably as I peek at the mess that is the bottom half of my leg to the space a bullet was stuck in nothing more than a few hours ago. And for what? To keep Ruby my secret.

"What's going to stop the boss from shipping Ruby off to The Sect, then?" he asks, because he knows as well as I do that there's no way the boss is handing her over to the Five Families.

"Me."

"Yeah? And how did that work out for you last time?" He scoffs out an unamused laugh, shaking his head and scrubbing his hand down his face. "You scared the shit out of us."

"I know."

It wasn't my intention. I was only thinking about getting her safe and finding out what the Five Families knew. I never stopped to think through what the boss was going to say or do when he realised I had her safe but wouldn't tell him where.

"And for what?" he continues, clearly on a roll. "For some girl you think you owe a favour to? It wasn't your fault she was there that night, and it wasn't your fault she stuck her nose in with the Five Families. It certainly isn't your fault they're interested in knowing what she knows, and if anything, you being around her is making it worse."

"I hurt too much for this conversation," I grumble, wishing he could keep his fucking truths to himself.

"You didn't bother to talk to me about this first, so here we are, picking up the pieces, together."

As always.

We've always done things together, until recently. Now

he's off being trained as Leo's second-in-command, and it grates me that he's been left out of the decision-making process on this. He's got so used to having all the information at his fingertips, me knowing something he doesn't irritates the fuck out of him.

Not only that, but Ruby being here puts our house at risk, our family. I should have talked to him about it first, but there wasn't time. That's what I'm telling myself, anyway. Most of me knows I can't keep her and that I shouldn't even if I could, but it doesn't stop me wanting it, and, rightly or wrongly, instinctively acting on it.

"Okay, I get it. I fucked up. Someone tried to kidnap her and I just... I dunno, I just snapped," I admit. The panic that flooded through my system is unreasonable and unexplainable. Just the thought that someone was out there to hurt Ruby made me see red.

"Of all the people you could have grown an attachment to... her?"

He doesn't get it, but neither do I.

There was something in her panicked gaze way back on the very first night we met that called to me, and once I recognised who she was, there was no way I could have walked out of there. I'd have been signing my own death warrant as much as hers.

But there's been something growing between us over this year that's more than just the ease of companionship and friendship, but not the red-hot poker of lust, although that simmers there, too. I don't want her to get hurt, and I don't want her to be taken away. Seeing her with Nathaniel Peregrine on their *date* practically killed me, and I seriously considered the ramifications of ending him. Needless to say, they wouldn't be good, and he lived to see another day, but anyone else would have found themselves in a shallow grave.

Our connection is confusing but tangible, and I'm not sure she can explain it, either. Or maybe I'm just kidding myself and she sees me as nothing more than an unattainable shadow, the same way everyone else does.

"Ruby wants to meet with Ivy. I overheard her talking to mum," he tells me, picking a piece of fluff off his jumper, his irritation simmering back down. "You can't keep her safe from everyone, and I'm not sure why you want to."

"Neither am I," I admit. "But she's important to me, B. We can't let them have her."

"Who? The Five Families, or our boss?"

An awkward silence stretches out between us because he understands I mean both, and I have no answers as to how to do it. I wouldn't even if my head didn't feel like someone was playing drums inside it.

"What if she was your girl?" he eventually asks. "Officially. Sure, that would cause some problems with the boss, but it would explain why you're being so damn territorial about her, and it would explain why you're hovering about without tipping the Five Families off as to why…"

"I mean, it makes sense, but do you really think Ruby is going to accept that without an explanation?"

"Does she want to go back to school, finish her exams, and then move on with her life? Because there's only so long the boss is going to wait you out before he comes here looking for answers, and how long do you think the Five Families will give it before they come asking questions, too? You're already acting like a pissed off, jealous boyfriend. May as well make it official."

"And how would you like to spin that to her? *So, I know we sort of have this thing between us, but if you want to go back to your life, then you're gonna really need to lay it on thick with me to get everyone to back off. Oh, but I can't tell you why they're interested in you, or what they want, just that being with me will solve all your problems.* I can see that going down well."

"I can't say I honestly give a shit what she thinks," he clips out, leaning forward onto his elbows. "I want you safe, and I want our mother safe. Any more than that isn't my problem."

No, keeping Ruby safe has been my thing since the beginning.

"What are your other options? Die trying to keep her away from Vincent Windsor, or give the Five Families even more ammunition? Maybe even someone they could use to bargain with the boss? I'm quietly confident that neither of those options are going to end well for you."

"All right, I get it," I grumble, seeing his point. I don't have to like it, but I do understand what he's saying.

"It shouldn't be hard, anyway. She's as fucking sick for you as you are for her." He throws a lighter in my direction before making his way to the window and opening it a crack. "Just think about it, yeah?"

With a nod, I pull out one of my cigarillos, light it up, and drag the poison into my lungs. It's an awful habit, and something I should never have started, but I can't deny the comfort it gives me in those dark moments when I'm lost to my own thoughts.

"If she's going to be meeting up with Ivy anyway, then I'm going to give Leo the heads up. If anyone can make this girl see the sense in staying away from Pendleton fucking Prep, it's going to be them," he adds.

"So, uh, I'll just lay here and do nothing, then, shall I?"

"Probably for the best," he agrees with a nod and a smirk. "You're not much use right now, anyway."

"Ouch. You wound me." The chuckle that wants to rumble from my chest stalls as pain sears across my ribs with the movement. His words may hurt, but right now, they're the goddamn truth.

"I'm sure she'll be back up to tuck you in shortly."

He leaves the pack and lighter on the bedside table, putting the cigarette out in the ashtray for me because I can't reach it properly before heading out, hopefully to his own room to get some sleep.

But sleep doesn't come to me.

Instead, I lay there as my mind runs through everything that happened today and what I could have done differently, the decisions I could have changed and those I couldn't. The painkillers take the edge off, but getting up to close the window hurts more than I care to admit.

Getting back to the bed is more than enough movement as I rest my head back, barely managing to get my feet up before I'm falling into darkness again.

sixteen

Ruby

Blaise glowers at me as he plants his fists on the table no more than six inches from my breakfast bowl, seething.

"You're not going anywhere."

"You can't keep me here forever," I argue, not bothering to get up from the table.

It's been one hell of a night, day, twenty-four hours. At this point it's all starting to blur into one.

"Watch me." He grumbles the words under his breath, his intense gaze fixed on my face even as I do my best to ignore him and concentrate way too hard on my cereal. "He's not gone through all that," he continues, gesturing wildly to his brother upstairs, "just for you to walk right back into the shit."

"Erm, I didn't just walk into anything, thank you very much."

"You walked straight into two guys who attempted to slide you down an alleyway. If that is not the actual definition of *walked into it*, then I don't know what fucking is," he yells.

"Wow, so you're saying I'm to blame for people wanting to kidnap me? That is taking victim blaming to a whole other level."

The breakfast I've managed to get down churns in my stomach, considering its options on staying where it is or coming back as I abandon the spoon in the warming milk, not willing to risk any more whilst Blaise blames me for all this shit.

Who the hell does he think he is?

Why on earth does he think I want to be sitting here in my uniform?

And what the fuck is his damn problem? I didn't ask for any of this.

"There wasn't another route you could have taken to the carpark? Or you couldn't have left earlier and with other people? Hell, later and with other people would have done, too."

I mean, yes, I suppose, but that's not really the point, is it? I didn't know there were people out looking for me, waiting for me. It's not my fault this happened.

"But, oh, no. Little Miss Invincible here had to go walk out in the dark on her own past an alleyway where people were waiting for her, which got *him* thrown in the fucking shit," Blaise continues, his blue gaze piercing straight through my armour. "There's no way you're going to school today, so you may as well take that uniform off."

"I would if I could," I reply under my breath, refusing to look him in the eye.

Like this is a choice. I don't walk around with an

overnight bag, just school books.

I watched him work with his mother last night, holding Dex's leg in place whilst they did things I never thought I'd have to witness in my life, let alone to someone I care about. I watched the way Blaise moved and reacted, anticipating every move Dex was going to make while I noted the differences between them and the similarities, doing my best to avoid having to face the reality that screamed and writhed in front of me.

They may have similar blue eyes, but Dex's are lighter than his brothers. Although I think the irritation that flickers through Blaise's this morning was always going to make them darker. Even so, the strain of his biceps as his fists land against the table again is way too familiar. Have I ever seen either of them happy?

"What was that? Honestly, if you don't have something helpful to say, then I'm going to really lose my shit."

"Good to know this is you put together," I retort, fuming.

My mother hasn't so much as text me to find out why I never came home last night. I'm hoping she was out and assumed I was asleep when she got home, not that she checks. How sad is it that she potentially doesn't even know I'm not there? Some fucking mother.

"Children," Emmeline interrupts, tying her long hair up into a messy bun as she crosses the living room. "Can we all agree that it's a bit early for this volume? What on earth is going on?"

Standing, I head to the sink, disposing of the milk and rinsing the bowl out before adding it to the dishwasher without saying a word. If he wants to accuse me of something, *he* can damn well explain it.

"Well?" she asks again, looking between us.

"She's not going to school," Blaise starts again.

"I never said I was."

"You're eating breakfast at seven a.m. in your uniform. What else am I supposed to think?"

"That I haven't been home since yesterday morning, and contrary to what you apparently assume, I don't have spare clothes in my school bag."

"Oh."

"And if you had any clue whatsoever about me then you'd know that I don't sleep well, period. Even less so in a strange house with people I don't even know. Sure, Dex may have 'saved me' from whoever was trying to run off with me yesterday, but is holding me hostage here any different?"

I'm sure the intention is very different, but I'm trapped in some place I don't want to be with people I don't know for reasons I don't understand.

"Yes," Blaise grits out between his teeth.

"I've got exams and revision to do. How am I supposed to pass these exams if I'm not even there?"

"It's a few days. You'll live."

"Oh, that's all? Just a few days. Well, that's fine, then." Irritated, I storm across the open-plan space and into the living room, throwing myself back onto the sofa and dragging the blanket back around me.

But it's frustrating, and I'm aggravated. There's this buzzing need to move beneath my skin, so I'm back up and pacing the room like a caged lion before the blanket even touches me. I would happily spend days sitting in my bedroom ignoring the entire world, but there's something different about it when the choice is taken from your hands.

"You know that Scarlett has text me fourteen times overnight, right? That she's worried about me."

"And?" He crosses his arms over his chest, and I'm suddenly thrown back to being trapped in the car with Dex, his irritation swimming out and mingling with mine, the two of us at odds with each other over something we never should have been.

Once again, he saved me, and all I did was get upset that he didn't kiss me. That he erected those walls straight back up and shoved me out on my arse.

Not this time, though.

This time he saved me and brought me into his home, got himself into some trouble over it too, from what I can gather. Emmaline and I spent some time together before she went to bed, just talking about life and shit and why on earth my phone kept going off.

Luckily, she had a charger I could borrow, even if it was only to tell my friends that I'm fine and nothing more, but she seems like good people. Normal, down to earth, not interested in shouting her head off at me before eight in the morning about why I'm wearing the only clothes I've got with me.

Jackass.

"Okay, okay. Get the kettle on, will you?" Emmeline says, shooing Blaise away from me and towards the kitchen as she closes the distance between us, smoothing her hands down my arms until I shrug her off. I don't like people touching me on a good day, never mind when I'm feeling like this. The last thing I need is someone trying to placate me.

"I think it's safe to say that nothing these strapping boys own is going to fit your tiny frame. Blaise will go out and grab you something," she says.

"I'll—"

"Yep, you'll go and get the girl some damn pants to wear, and some shirts. If you say this is only for a couple of days, then some pyjamas and underwear is likely a must, too." She shoos him out the door with nothing more than the raise of her eyebrows and a wave of her fingers.

"You'll have to teach me how to do that."

"Mum perks. There aren't many of them, but this one I've earned," she replies, leaving me to go and pour herself a drink. "You want coffee?"

"No, I'm good thanks. I found juice and cereal. I hope that was okay."

"When I said help yourself to whatever, it's what I meant," she replies, dismissing me in favour of the dark brewed liquid.

"We didn't wake Dex up, did we?" I ask, looking at the staircase.

Dragging myself away from him had been harder than I expected, but lying with him in his mother's house didn't seem right, and he needed the space to get comfortable anyway. At least, that's what I'm telling myself. He was practically comatose when I went up to check on him, laid across the sheets in nothing but his shorts.

The bruising was already coming out across his back,

and I have no doubt that his leg is going to be some scary-looking colours by this morning, but seen as this is all my fault, it seemed like the least I could do was to leave him to sleep.

Unfortunately, that meant I laid down here with a pillow and a blanket whilst my mind ran through everything that happened, over and over again. Everything I could have done differently, should have done differently. How, if I'd just been quicker, thought faster...

It looks like I'm not the only one who blames me either though. Not that it matters. It's done, and I'm here. Closed up, trapped, unable to tell my friends where I am, or my family, if she was bothered.

"He was snoring when I came down, so I don't think so," she replies, snapping me out of my thoughts.

Folding up the blanket, I place it on top of the pillow and move them out of the way so there's space for both of us to sit, wishing I knew what to do.

"He didn't mean it."

"Who? Blaise. Oh, he definitely did."

And he was right.

I wasn't being sensible just walking around at the end of the day on my own thinking nothing bad was ever going to happen to me.

I wasn't asking for someone to kidnap me, that's on whoever they took away yesterday, but I wasn't doing myself any favours, either.

"He's all bark and no bite," she continues.

I've seen the darkness in Dex, and I'm not stupid enough to believe that for one fucking second.

"Don't think too hard on it. He's just very protective of his little brother. That's family, though, right?"

It may be this family, but it isn't mine.

I nod anyway, unsure what I can add to this conversation. I just need to get through the next few days here, help Dex get better, then go back to my life, keep my head down, and pretend nothing's happened. It will all be totally fine.

"Blaise took him some up last night, but he's gonna need some more painkillers shortly if you think you're up to it," Emmeline says, looking towards the staircase. "Coffee will probably help him too."

Of course. These things, I can do.

"Erm, I have no idea how he takes it," I comment, getting up.

"All those early mornings and late nights, and you don't know how the man has his coffee? Well, I never. Black, two sugars."

"Dark and sweet. Interesting."

"Let's not read too much into it. Mine is the same." She winks, a weary smile on her face. "They both spent way too many mornings stealing the coffee out of my cup whilst I got their shit ready for school, and I guess they got a taste for it."

At least she was getting their stuff ready with them or for them. She was at home packing their little lunches and brushing their hair out, making sure they had their PE kit and the stupid apron everyone forgets for food tech. It's more than my mother has ever felt able to give me on a consistent basis.

"There are worse things they could have been up to," I

reply with a smile, accepting the tablets she offers out.

"Very true. I'll be up in half an hour to get dressed myself and check his wounds over," she warns as I pass, mug in hand.

Nodding, my cheeks heat as I head up the stairs, noting her insinuation. He's broken and bleeding, so I think it's safe to say there's not going to be anything going on between us, closed door or not. The door is half open when I get to the top of the stairs, with Dex barely perched on the edge of the bed, pale and panting.

"Oh, shit. Are you okay?"

After placing the coffee on the side table, I reach out, doing nothing helpful to get him sitting back up against the headboard.

"Fine, fine. I'm fine. It turns out our bathroom moved about six miles overnight. At least, that's how it fucking feels," he grumbles, wincing as he leans down to adjust the pillow under his ankle. "But you have more magic pills and heaven juice because it's finally my turn to get an angel."

"I'm not sure I'd go that far."

Ignoring me, he reaches out for the coffee, throwing the tablets down, along with the burning liquid with a satisfied groan. "Now, if you can just bring me another bucketful of that, I would be most grateful."

"You're in a strangely good mood this morning."

Narrowing my eyes at him, I can't for the life of me work out what has caused this chipper demeaner. Until twelve hours ago, I think he'd managed a handful of grunts, words, or phrases, and none of them were particularly… sprightful. Not like this.

"What happened?"

"I guess someone finally knocked some sense into me." He grins.

"Uh-huh."

"Can you open the window for me?" he asks, reaching for the cigarillos I've never seen him smoke, but as he lights up and the smoke teams around us, it's as familiar as the uniform I'm wearing.

I open the window part way and pull the curtains open before dragging the lone chair over to the side of his bed and dropping into the seat.

"Well, this is odd. At night, it's usually you in the corner and me in bed, and in the day, it's usually you who's hiding in the shadows and around every corner whilst I go about my life unawares. And here we are with you in the bed overnight, and me watching you during the day. I'm not sure I like it."

"I'm not convinced it's my favourite, either."

"How you feeling?" It's probably the stupidest question in the entire world, but we don't normally sit and talk. He's typically quiet, distanced, doing his best to keep the walls up between us, but today, that all seems to be gone, so I'm making the most of it.

"Like I picked a fight with a bear. You?"

"You kinda look like it, too, if I'm being honest." I shrug, trying to work out how much to share. "I'm not a big fan of this hostage situation. I've got exams to pass."

And freedom to carve out.

I can't do that hidden behind these walls and missing the final pieces I need to get through these exams.

"Can Scarlett share her notes with you or something?" he asks. "I may have a solution on that for you too…"

The man has a solution to someone attempting to kidnap me and his brother keeping me hostage in their house. This is going to be good.

"Oh, do tell."

"Ruby, will you be my girlfriend?"

If I'd been drinking any of that coffee, he'd be wearing it.

"I'm sorry, what?"

He puts out his smoke, letting the acrid smell burn my lungs and my heartbeat pick back up before he continues, because this can't be real. He can't honestly be suggesting *that*.

"Look, I'm gonna be honest with you. What I found out yesterday isn't good news. There are people out there who have their sights set on you. People I'd much rather didn't get the opportunity to get near you. Do you follow?"

"Kind of. Is this because of what I saw at the warehouse?"

I spent way too many hours last night attempting to work out who would want me, and why, and that's the only thing I can come up with.

"Partly. There's no way you live where you do and go to the school you do without knowing about the Five Families."

I nod.

"Well, they've got questions. Questions that won't need answers if you're with me."

"But why?"

Why would being with him mean that their questions

just disappear.

Sure, Dex got me out of there before I could do something stupid like get caught, but if they have questions, doesn't that mean I got caught anyway? Who is he to these people that a relationship with me would suddenly be accepted?

"That's complicated."

Complicated? "Do you work for them? Are you part of them?" I ask, dreading the answer.

I've spent a long time keeping myself to myself, avoiding anyone who looked like trouble. Hell, I've reconsidered my friendship with Scarlett twenty-three trillion times over the last year because of her last name, and the fact that potentially part of their organisation has been sneaking into my bedroom night after night. Not just keeping an eye on me, but building something, creating something more than attraction or friendship. Something I can feel deep in my very bones. And the entire thing may have been a lie.

"I feel sick." Leaning over, I rest my elbows on my knees and drop my head into my hands.

This can't be happening.

I was free. Almost free.

seventeen

Dex

She's panicking. Hyperventilating. Losing her shit.

"Just breathe."

"Breathe? You're the fucking enemy." She continues her freak out, shaking her head and climbing from the chair as she storms around my room.

"Am not."

"You guys okay in here?" my mother asks chipperly, sticking her head around the door. "Need anything?"

"We're good. Great. Fine. Thanks, Mum."

"I'll just check—"

"Actually, can you give us two?" I ask as she moves towards my leg, my gaze focused on watching Ruby pacing. "I promise it'll still be there."

"Sure." She looks warily between the two of us, reading the tension in the room before slowly backing out.

How many arguments between Blaise and me has she had to intervene over the years? All siblings argue, even those of us that are practically joined at the hip. Being eleven months apart means we are way too similar in lots of ways, and completely different in others.

This isn't the same.

"Talk to me. What are you thinking?"

"You want me to be your *girlfriend* to get these people off my back, but you were the one throwing the phrase hookup down like it was a weapon less than a week ago," she practically hisses, glaring at the door before turning and pining me with an unconvinced stare.

"Yep."

She huffs an unimpressed snort in my direction, folding her arms over her chest before she shakes her head again.

I wish I could break it all down for her, tell her everything. Who I am, why I'm here, and how I got here in the first place, but all that's going to do is make her more of a target. So, I keep my mouth shut, let her attempt to put all the pieces together, and do my best to convince her that I'm not the bad guy in all of this.

"And how long, exactly, do you think this charade would be needed? I've got plans, you know."

"Oh. Plans? Do enlighten me."

"Don't be an arse."

"Why not? It's nothing new."

"I'm just gonna interrupt here," my mother says, banging the door back before either of us can add to the growing list of profanity. "Let's get this bruising checked over and then I'll leave you to it. You've probably got another ten minutes before Blaise is back with your clothes, sweetheart," she says, looking at Ruby with a fond smile.

"Clothes?"

"Yes, clothes. The clean things you usually cover your body with," my mother answers as she picks her way around the grim-looking wound on my leg. "Although it would appear you have forgone yours this morning, son."

"Extenuating circumstances."

As if Ruby hadn't realised that I've been laid here in my underwear all night, she suddenly goes very pink in the cheeks and turns away, finding something outside the window surprisingly interesting.

"I'd leave that open a little longer if you can, and get some more of that arnica on the rest of you, will you?" my mother asks, looking at me with concern. "Did the pills help?"

"I'm golden so long as I don't move," I reply.

It's not the entire truth. My ribs hurt like a fucker, and smoking is something akin to fire in my lungs. My leg... well, let's just say it's got its own heartbeat, and I'm *really* aware of it. Other than that, I'm fine. Totally fine.

"Headache? Ringing in your ears? Nausea?"

"Honestly, I'm fine."

Those things I can deal with. The pain lancing through my lower extremities less so.

"Ruby, are you okay with the gel?" she asks, more than aware I'm talking complete shit.

My mother never quite got to finish her medical training, but she knows enough to patch us up from time to time, and somehow managed to keep those friendships intact over the years. It's where she gets the sterile instruments and the good drugs from every now and again.

Nothing is guaranteed on this side of the law, so any and

all help that's offered, we take.

I miss Ruby's reply, too distracted with the conversation we were having and the blush on her cheeks, but I don't miss the sound of the door closing, then the air between us getting thick.

She's almost mine.

Not in any sensible or logical kind of a way. It would be a completely ridiculous move that would likely get me shot again, but it's tangible, and I can almost taste the desire on her tongue. The way her body melted into mine as she surrendered on the side of the car was nothing short of sublime, and I can't wait to show her exactly how high she can fly, if only she'll let me.

"So, where were we?" I ask.

Somewhere between her plans for the future and my lack of clothes.

"Do you want some clean clothes getting out to wear? I can... erm... I can help you," Ruby offers awkwardly, apparently done with her concern over me being the enemy, not willing to touch on the connection evident between us.

"There should be some shorts in the bottom drawer and shirts are in the one above, if you don't mind?" I ask, giving up on pushing her.

I could probably get them myself. Bending down whilst holding my weight on one leg is not going to be the easiest task I've ever undertaken whilst potentially dealing with a concussion but whatever.

She rummages around in the drawers long enough for Blaise to turn up, grunting and dropping two carrier bags in the doorway before walking back out again.

"Thanks!" I call, but his steps are already receding down the stairs.

"He's such a dick," Ruby grumbles, dropping my clothes on the edge of the bed before risking a peek inside the bags he brought. "But at least this lot isn't pink."

"I guess the shops open at this time in the morning are likely to be pretty limited, and his shopping prowess is not exactly famous. The best we can hope for is that they're drawstring, and you can get them fastened."

"I am never leaving the house in these." She grimaces as she drags a pair of navy joggers and some tiny half top from the bag.

"Absolutely not," I agree.

That thing would barely cover her tits, and there is no way in hell any recovering is going to be done whilst I'm sporting a semi all day, every day, looking out for the curve of her boob popping out.

"I guess he really got with the *keep you here* programme on that one," I deflect, grabbing the shorts and doing my best to cover the growing erection that's about to make this really fucking uncomfortable.

She pulls out a pack of underwear before quickly shoving them back in the bag. "Erm, I'll sort this lot out in a minute. Let me help get you with that gel and then you can get changed."

I'll take whatever olive branch she's willing to offer, hoping this diffused tension lasts longer than the five minutes of her smoothing gel on my bruises and helping me to get a shirt and shorts on.

I'm black and blue, and it's really starting to show by

the time she's finished smoothing gel all over each of the massive patches of bruises I'm currently sporting. Sexy as fuck. All too soon, she picks up her bags and disappears off to the bathroom to get cleaned up and sorted herself.

I do my best to get the shirt and shorts on unassisted, making a mess of it and then having to start all over again with the damn top like it's the trickiest bit of clothing I've ever met. I'm sweating and reaching for another smoke when the door opens and Ruby strides in, muttering under her breath, but it's not the words coming out of her mouth that catches my attention.

The leggings caress every dip and curve of her body, not covered in any way by the skin tight strappy top that graces her upper half. Fuck. She's completely covered, yet she may as well be naked.

"I'm borrowing a top. I can't walk around like this. It's ridiculous."

Remind me to thank my brother. I think this is the best thing he has ever done in his entire life.

"Looks fine to me." I cough to cover up the crack in the end of my sentence, really glad I managed to get the shorts on before she sees exactly what those luscious curves do to me.

She's gorgeous. Not that I didn't know that already. Obviously, she's stunning, but seeing all the things she hides underneath oversized jumpers and loose Demin has me reevaluating if I've ever really seen her before.

"Yeah, no," she argues, pulling the first T-shirt she can find out of the drawer and sliding it over her body.

If I thought there was something special about seeing

her in my hoodie, then my shirt takes it to a whole other level. The fact that the neckline is too wide and one of her perfect, pale shoulders peeks out is icing on the Ruby slice of cake.

"Wow."

"Shut up. Your arse of a brother managed to get the sizes just about right, but G-strings are not on my preferred list of underwear."

"Noted, but I'll let you tell him that."

I can almost imagine how that conversation will go and picture the mortification on her face. Not his. He wouldn't give a shit. He probably picked them out intentionally thinking they'd be the most uncomfortable underwear on the planet, anyway. He can be like that sometimes. But it's yet another image I don't need in my head.

"Fun. Do you need me to open the window again?" she asks, looking at the pack in my hands, my smoke completely forgotten in the wake of those legs.

"Yes, please." If I didn't need one before, I do now.

The shirt hits her mid-thigh and keeps most of her covered, but now that I've seen her, I can't unsee it, like an X-ray of the shape of her. She waits until I've lit up before pulling her seat back up against the side of the bed and asking, "So, who really are you?"

Isn't that the question of the day. Unfortunately, that isn't even the worst of it. It's who *she* is that's the biggest stumbling block, and I should have never forgotten that.

"You know exactly who I am."

"And who do you work for?"

"Someone you don't want to argue with." *And closer to*

you than you think.

"God, you're infuriating," she grumbles, watching me light up.

"What are these plans you have?"

"Oh, I dunno. Just pass these exams and go to the college that offered me a place. Find out if I'm really good enough to do the art degree I want to do. Find a million pounds and then go to university somewhere far, far away from my mother."

"That bad, is she?"

I know she is, but Ruby does nothing more than roll her eyes, then watches the smoke pull towards the open window.

"How am I going to be able to run off into the sunset if I'm with you?" she asks meekly, suddenly seeming way to small and innocent for this conversation.

"You can't."

She was never going to get out of this life, she just didn't realise it.

"You're wrong."

I'm not, and we both know it.

These stupid statements are nothing but the hopes and dreams she once had—ones she never should have been allowed because they were never going to happen. If only she knew the truth of her precarious situation.

"I've been accepted, and I've got a place. All I need to do is get the grades and then I'm on my way to college. To freedom."

She's a caged moth reaching for the sun. She just doesn't realise the only sun she can see is the other side of a mesh wall. Visible but unreachable.

"And that's why you want to get back to school, to secure your freedom?"

She nods, adjusting my shirt on her tiny frame.

"I wish that could happen for you, baby girl, but it was never on the cards."

"It is. I will," she argues, her nostrils flaring as irritation floods her system. "You can't stop me. Nobody can."

She's wrong. So very wrong.

"You know what? I can tell you exactly what you can do with your plans. You call roll 'em up and shove 'em somewhere I don't have to see them or hear them, because if you ever thought, even for a single moment, that you were getting away from me, you were wrong. You're mine."

We're nothing more than six inches apart, our bodies crawling nearer and nearer to each other the more this argument goes on. I can see the hazel flecks in her otherwise brown eyes, the hint of pink that blushes across her collarbone as agitation runs rampant through her veins, and the way her nostrils flare in irritation. And that's where we stay with one second dragging on in to two. Our gazes are locked and we're breathing each other's air. My smoke is all but forgotten, because all I need is her, and all she wants is to be free.

I don't know who breaks first, who moves, but before I realise it, her lips are on mine, and my fingers are threaded through her hair. She tastes like hope, but I'm the bitterness holding her back in the darkness, and I don't care for one fucking second.

Breaking apart for only a moment, I drop my smoke

into the ashtray, and she climbs over my lap, finding her place over my thighs before bringing her lips to mine again tentatively.

"Does this hurt?" she whispers across my lips in the sweetest torture.

"No." I lie.

Everything hurts, but it's worth every second of pain to have her here and in my arms, as temporarily as that may be.

"When did our paths cross in the daylight?" I ask, knowing I need to make this right before we go any further.

Sure, I've been around since the night that changed everything—strike one on her card with the Five Families—but there's a very key point where things moved into the light, the moment I was given her as a charge by the boss. When her life became useful to him.

"When I started going to the stupid Little Sister programme," she admits, pulling back and looking into my eyes.

Hers are peppered with the same desire she no doubt sees in mine, but she needs to know this.

"And what else happened around that time?" *Come on, Ruby. Put the pieces together for me.*

She narrows her eyes, pursing her lips together.

"Vincent Windsor threatened your mother's life if you didn't report back on…" I lead her.

"Leo."

"Leo," I agree.

It was bad enough that Blaise and I were locked out of the whole Pendleton Prep thing. We were dragged away and forced into the darkest shit we've ever had to deal with.

Sure, we were purveyors of death before that, but to be plunged into it day in and day out was a whole other kind of anguish.

We lived torture, breathed pain. Dished it. Doled it out. We made the biggest, scariest men you've ever met in your life beg for mercy, and then we did it all over again and revelled in it. At least I did.

Blaise was released from his torture camp stint earlier than I was so they could move him onto more strategic plans, but I'm sure they were just trying to keep us busy and away from Leo. Luckily for him, we've got contacts everywhere, and even when I was in the thick of the dirt, I could get messages out to him, sending help in the form of the codes we've perfected over the years.

A mark on a tree here, a seemingly unrelated gift there, a book that might turn up on a shelf. Whatever it was, he managed to put the pieces together eventually, but it was a mission. And it was interrupted only by the moments I made it to Ruby's house in the dead of night, breathing in her light and pushing away the darkness that threatened to consume me.

She was my light at the end of the tunnel, and she doesn't even know that she saved me, helping me retain what little sanity I have left. And then the boss was gifting her to me, pulling me out of the torture chamber and delivering me to her.

Okay, so sitting around and doing no more than watching and waiting was slow, boring, and hard, especially after everything I'd been doing in the months up until that moment. Who can blame me for wanting to get back into the thick of things?

This isn't exactly what I had in mind, though.

"He's family, and I'm not the enemy you think I am. Let me keep you safe."

eighteen
Ruby

His words hang heavily in the air, bringing a weight to them I wasn't expecting.

His boss is the same man who threatened my mother, the one who wanted information on Leo, and now he's watching over me? But... why? And does it matter?

Dex wants me; I can feel it. Does it matter the hows and whys and what fors of the situation?

Right now, he's willing to help keep me safe, and the way to do that is to give me the one thing I thought was always going to be outside of my reach: him.

So, I walk away from the questions and sink into the moment, hoping and praying this works out for the best. I'm not sure if he realises how precarious the trust is that he holds in his hands, or how tentative the hope is, but neither of them are anything compared to the desire that wraps around us both.

His large hands cradle my face, waiting for an answer I'm scared to give him. Taking the leap, I nod twice, closing the distance between us and bringing my lips to his.

The growl that rumbles from his chest touches me in places it really shouldn't, especially as he's not promising me the world. He's not even guaranteeing me next week, just that he'll keep me safe for as long he can.

It's enough. It's got to be.

I pour all my frustrations into him, let him take my confusion and the hurt ricocheting around my insides. I let him smooth the cracks in my heart, heal over the wounds he's created over the last year, and gloss over the pain.

He pulls me against his body, grinding me down on him as tingles spread across my shoulder blades and all the way down to my fingertips. It's too much and not enough all at once, tongues, fingers, the brush of the back of his hand against my breast before it glides lower and lower, sliding up the outside of my thigh.

He's everywhere and nowhere, and I need more.

Dragging his shirt off my overheated skin does nothing to quell the fire that rushes through my blood, especially when I feel his thickening length beneath me. Dex reaches up, pushing the strap off my shoulder to let my breast tumble free from the fabric.

Then he's there, with his lips wrapped around the sensitive nub, and his tongue flicking gently against my nipple as my fingers anchor into his hair, hoping and praying to keep me here in this moment and not let me float off on the ecstasy that wraps around me.

Incoherent words tumble from my lips as his other hand slides inside my leggings, gripping my arse and rubbing me up and down his length. I'm so close, teetering on the edge of oblivion, chasing a high I know is going to feel so good, and when his hand dips lower, pressing against my entrance, I crumble and fall.

Nothing more than his wicked lips and the threat of more has stars bursting behind my eyelids as an orgasm crashes over me. He holds me in his firm grip, safe and warm as the feeling fades, laying words of encouragement across my skin, peppered with his kisses.

"Condom?" I ask.

That might have been amazing, but I'm not done yet.

If he says we're together, then I want all of him, and I want him to have all of me. This is more than just the release of the sexual tension we've been dancing around for weeks and months. This is the coming together of two bodies that have craved each other with an intensity I've never understood. I don't even want to, but I need to meld my soul with his, combine the two of us in a way that's more permanent that anything I've ever felt.

"Drawer," he grits out, continuing to massage my breast as his hand moves away from my leggings.

Once I carefully climb off his lap, I shimmy the leggings and G-string off my body, abandoning them behind the door, and reach for a condom in the bedside drawer. Dex shuffles his shorts down, his hard cock popping free.

I've never wanted to worship at the altar of a man before.

Never wanted to take a piece of them and lathe my tongue along it, paint their skin with my saliva, watch them shiver and shake, tasting the salt at the tip and knowing deep in my bones that this is because of me. I've never seen their vulnerabilities laid out before me and understood the power that comes with that, but that's where I am as I watch Dex roll the piece of latex over himself.

I want to make him feel just as good as he made me feel, if not more.

I peel the vest top off, letting the cool air in the room pebble my nipples, once again, as I climb back over his lap. Some other time, I'll peel every piece of clothing off his body and learn every inch of it. I'll find out what makes him gasp and moan, what he likes and what he loves, but right now, I just need him. All of him.

Pulling my face to his again, he kisses me deeply, the two of us getting lost in each other as he teases the seam of my lips and presses against my entrance. The hot tip of his dick is different to the fingers he teased me with, and as he pushes in slowly, I can't help tensing, the briefest moment of worry filtering in.

I'm sure this is supposed to hurt, but when he grips my hips and guides me up and down, gently letting my body stretch and accommodate him, it's nothing more than a mix of pain and pleasure that makes my toes curl, and my nails dig into his skin.

Rocking in time with his movements, I'm sliding farther down onto him with every thrust, my legs trembling as something more powerful builds between us. Our tongues duel, and my hair curtains us from the rest of the world. It's just Dex and me in this bubble of never-ending pleasure.

I moan, and he swears as my hands press against his bruised chest to hold myself up when his wicked fingers come to my clit, and I clamp down around him. The first one was fleeting, but this pressure bursts over me like a torrent of pure bliss, and he follows me over, his hips stuttering to stillness.

When I slide off him, he removes the condom before tying it and dropping it into the bin while I grab his discarded T-shirt and slide it on before tucking into his side, our breathing heavy.

"That was…" he starts, the sentence trailing off as he struggles to find the right words.

"Amazing?" I offer.

"Life changing."

With a smile, I rest my hand over his chest.

"You know I've agreed to meet up with Ivy later, right?" I ask, with his heartbeat ticking away beneath my hand.

"I didn't, but that's not a good idea, baby girl. I can't go with you like this."

He can't, but his brother can.

This may not be the moment to bring it up. We could just lie here and enjoy this feeling a little longer, but I need to be honest with him, too.

"When was the last time Blaise got to spend half an hour with Leo?"

I know it's a low blow, because there's clearly something there between the three of them—a friendship that runs deep. If I remember rightly, it was Dex's car picking me up at Christmas that blew the little cover I had over at Pendleton Prep, so offering this moment to Blaise when Dex can't take it seems unfair, but I need to get out of here, and Ivy can help.

If I'm going to get back to school and get the grades I

need, I'll have to pull in every favour I've got. The list isn't long. In fact, this is the entire list, but I'm running with it.

"It's got to be safer than meeting up with Scarlett to get my notes, right?"

He cuts an unimpressed look in my direction, but I know he's thinking about it. "He can't just drop everything and go with you."

"Should I just get them to come here, then? I'm sure Leo knows where it is…" I push.

"No," he clips out.

"Look, if you really think us being together is going to make being back in the real world safe, then what are we waiting for?"

He was the one who said this would help, that I'd be able to go back to life as normal.

"You literally agreed to this no more than ten minutes ago."

"Well, I'm not convinced I've agreed, as such…" I hedge.

He's hot and scary, and he has this way of making me feel completely safe even though I absolutely, one hundred percent, am not. And whilst the idea of holing up inside his bedroom for a week or more sounds like it would be absolutely fucking mind blowing, it's also not going to get me where I want to go.

"You didn't agree?" he asks, running the edge of his tongue along his lower lip.

"Fine, fine. I totally did. I want you, I trust you, I just… I don't know. She wants to see me, and I need to get out of this house," I admit.

"You've been here for all of one day. Not even that if you look at the time," he argues. "Just give me chance to heal up a little bit and then we can get back to life. Maybe laying the groundwork with your friend might be a better start?"

"Huh?"

"If you were seeing someone, and that someone rescued you and ran off, that may be something you'd mention to your best friend, right?" he asks, raising an eyebrow.

"Ah, yeah. I suppose so. I'm not sure how I'm going to work that around Nate, though." I ponder. "We did literally just go out at the start of the week."

"Exploring your options." He shrugs.

"And where were you on Friday night whilst I was out with her?"

"Working. I'm busy a lot."

"But not too busy to be waiting outside school for me just days later?"

"The hours are unusual."

"And what exactly do I tell her you do? Where did we meet? How do I know you? These are things she's going to want to know," I continue, attempting to picture how the conversation might go.

"Just stick with something close to the truth and you'll be fine. I'm sure you'll figure it out." He places a quick kiss to my forehead before tucking me safely under his arm again. "I'm just gonna rest for a bit. Stay with me?"

"Of course."

The sofa was comfortable, fine. It's just that it's not my bed, and Dex wasn't leaning up against the wall watching me. As much as his things are casually strewn around this house, and his face is plastered all over in the framed pictures and mix and match postcards, it wasn't the same.

With everything else that's happened over the last week, I'm emotionally exhausted, and finally safe, in his arms. The one place I've wanted to be more than I'm willing to admit.

So, I close my eyes, too, and I rest, safe in the knowledge that he'll be here when I wake.

He's still sleeping soundly when I stir and unlock my phone to pick through all the messages to formulate a plan. I could stay here, warm and safe, or I could step out and forge my own path, take back the freedom I'm teetering so precariously on the edge of. One wrong step, and I could be stuck here, trapped in the cage of my indecision.

A shower starts running somewhere, with music playing or someone singing, and I make a snap decision to send some messages out, hoping and praying it all comes together in time, and, most importantly, that Blaise is out working for the day. This could all come crumbling down around me if he happens to be sitting downstairs.

I slide out from beneath the comfort of Dex's arm, trusting that this is the right thing to do as I pull down the edge of the shirt I'm wearing, slide on the underwear and leggings, and tiptoe out of his bedroom. He's beautifully at peace for now, and that's the memory I hold onto as I sneak down the stairs and find my boots beside the sofa.

While slipping them on, I thank every god I can think of that there's no one downstairs, watching the minutes slide past on my phone as I fidget by the window nervously. There are so many things that could still go wrong, not least me turning around and heading back upstairs, wishing I could just hide in this moment a little longer, but there's no time for that when I see Leo's Lexus finally pull up outside.

I quickly move to the bottom of the stairs and listen, crossing my fingers for the all clear. The shower has stopped running and a hairdryer now drowns out the music, meaning Emmeline is busy for the next ten minutes at least. Now I just have to get out of here in one piece.

Leo is out of the car and striding down the driveway, running a hand through his hair as he looks at the window upstairs. I can't remember who sleeps where, and if Blaise is in that front bedroom waving down at him then I am seriously fucked. Ivy must be in the car, so there's a good chance he's not planning on coming in, but the second the code is in the door and he's pushing it open, I walk through it, shoving past him.

"Hey," he calls, his head turning as he follows my direction right past him and down the driveway.

I don't watch and wait, instead going straight to the car and hoping like hell he follows me, confused or not. If he goes inside for a quick chat, then this is all over before it even starts. Luckily, he jogs to catch up with me, reaching out for my arm as I get to the car door.

"Later. I'll explain it all later," I say quietly before diving into the back seat, Ivy barely looking up from whatever's going on in her phone.

I probably won't explain, but if he goes in there looking for answers then I'm really up shit creek.

"Hey, chick," Ivy says brightly from the front seat.

"Hey," I reply, praying Leo gets the hint and jumps in

quickly.

With a shake of his head, he climbs into the front seat and starts the engine while I keep watch at the windows above, hoping and praying nobody sees me or recognises the car as he turns around and heads back down the road.

It's only when we're pulling out of the end of the street that I start to come down from the adrenaline rush and realise exactly what I've just done.

"So, who did you say we're meeting?" Ivy eventually asks.

"My friend Scarlett. I need to get some school work from her."

I didn't want to meet her on my own in case the Five Families are after me and following her to get to me.

"And Dex or B didn't bring you because…?" Leo leads.

"Blaise is out… working? And Dex can't drive at the minute," I reply hastily.

"Ooh, is this the guy you've been tripping up over?" Ivy asks excitedly, either not picking up on or ignoring the question in the middle of my statement. "Which one? Or is it both? Are you in the middle of some scandalous love triangle with two brothers?"

"Erm, you mean like you are?" I ask, deflecting.

She and Leo share a look and a smile, something I might never get again on the back of this stunt. If Blaise finds me… yeah, I don't want to think about that, but it would probably be worse when Dex realises I'm gone regardless. Instead, I tuck the what if's into my back pocket and concentrate on what I set out to do.

Get the work. Get the grades. Buy the freedom. Stay

away from the Five Families.

Simple.

"I think it's a little more complicated than that," Leo comments, sliding her hand into his.

"So is this," I tell him.

"How did you say you know them?" he asks, risking a look at me in the mirror before signalling to turn and looking back at the road.

"Oh, erm. Dex and I crossed paths last summer at a thing…" *What was it he said? Keep it close to the truth?* "It was a chance encounter and we've just become friends since."

"Friends?"

"Yeah, just friends."

The word is bitter on my tongue, especially considering everything I've just given him and the hell I'm going to face when he finds out I've gone. Maybe we'll never be friends again after this, but my freedom is worth it, isn't it?

nineteen

Dex

A cool breeze whips over my arms, the bitter edge rousing me from the slumber that dragged me under a handful of hours ago. Ruby is nowhere to be seen—probably downstairs watching shit TV with mum while I reach for my hoodie and the cigarillos on the side table.

Throwing the jumper on stretches out a whole bunch of muscles that could have really done with being left alone, least of all my ribs, but when her perfume wraps around me, I can't say I care. Part of me really doesn't want to light up, just hoping to sit and revel in the fact that this same fabric caressed her skin a few hours ago, but the other itch under my skin won't have it.

So, I light one up and drop the Zippo back on the table, swapping it out for my phone to find a whole bunch of texts:

L: *Are you even gonna reply??*

L: *I don't know what kind of shit you're into right now, but this isn't cool man.*

L: *Wait, why the fuck is Ruby at your house?*

L: *Codes are the same, right?*

"What the fuck?" I grumble, putting my smoke on the ashtray and hauling myself from the bed, dread sitting heavily on my shoulders as something cold slides down my spine.

What the hell has she done?

Taking one last drag, I put the smoke out and do my best to get to the doorway without yelling, hoping I'm wrong and she hasn't done exactly what I think she's done: left me. Pain lances through my leg as I make my way down the stairs, calling, "Ruby!" as I go.

The silence that echoes back at me is problematic but not unexpected. If I'm getting messages from Leo about her, then it's clear Ruby has Ivy on side, and she isn't going to be here. That doesn't stop me from shouting again, wishing she was still tucked up safely in the confines of the house.

"What on earth is going on?" my mother asks, pushing her headphones off.

"Ruby isn't here, is she?"

"I thought she was still sleeping with you?"

So did I.

"No. Blaise?"

"Dropped her clothes off and left hours ago."

Because of course, he did. He's not supposed to be on babysitting duty for me or her.

"Come and sit down before you fall," my mother says, standing and reaching out for me.

As much as I want to scream, shout, pace, and leave, I can't. Dropping onto the sofa has me reaching for my phone only to realise I've left it on the bed. Frustration wraps around every word as I ask Mum to go and get it for me, watching the seconds tick by as I wait.

Why would Ruby do this? She said we were in this together, that we'd *be* together, and then she waits until I'm asleep and slips out, with Leo of all people. Of course, the only other person with access to our house is the one wrapped around Ruby's friend's little finger.

"I'm sure she's fine, darling," my mother says, handing me the phone.

She has no idea.

I'm pulling his number up and pressing dial before Mum's even sitting back down on the sofa, shoving her headphones onto her head with a small smile.

Our phones have always been monitored, and when he went to Pendleton Prep we had to go radio silent, but now that Leo's lined up to take over from the boss, it doesn't matter. The person watching us and our movements reports back to Blaise, and Leo will be the one with the final say shortly.

So, as much as Vincent and Josiah currently hold the organisation in their hands, it's pulling our way faster than either of them anticipated, and the first thing we did was to reestablish the lines of communication. Leo text, B called, and I did both because it's been way too long since I heard from my brothers.

What we haven't managed yet is any time face-to-face, which is why I was so pissed off when Ruby suggested taking Blaise instead of me to meet up with them. I guess she took it out of both of our hands in the end.

"Where are you?" I clip out before Leo even has chance

to say hello.

"Diner, why?"

There are twenty million questions rattling around my brain, but only two of any importance.

"Is she there, and is she safe?"

"Ruby? Yeah, she's fine. What the fuck is going on, man?"

Those are answers I can't give him over the phone. The information may be directed back to Blaise, but how far will it travel between here and there, and who else will it be passed to? Just sharing their location is enough of a risk.

"Who else is there?"

"Ivy and some girl from her school, Scarlett?"

"Scarlett Loughty," I confirm.

"No..." He trails off. "It's not... she's not..."

"That Loughty? Yeah, she fucking is. Are you there by yourself? And who knows where she is?"

We need to get that place secured, and fast. If the Five Families know Scarlett is there and that she's meeting Ruby, not even Leo is going to be able to get them out of that shit.

"Fucked if I know," he grumbles.

"And I can't even get to you."

"What? Why not?"

Because there's a goddamn bullet hole in my leg that your father put there.

"I'm currently indisposed," I reply, not willing to get into it over the phone. There's a reason nobody else made it out of that warehouse, and it's not so that I can shout about this from the fucking rooftops.

"Funny that. Ruby said something similar," he says,

suspicion laced through his words. "Right, ladies. Get those drinks to go. We're on the move," he tells them.

"What?" Ivy asks, apparently unimpressed with their last-minute change of plans.

"Where can we meet?" he asks me, ignoring the girls and the chaos they're currently kicking up in the background.

"Treehouse."

He ends the call just as my mum slips the headphones off her head. "There's no way in hell you're climbing anywhere with that leg."

"Not *a* treehouse. *The* treehouse. Can you give me a lift?"

Blaise, Leo, and I have talked in code for way longer than I can remember, and nothing ever means what anyone thinks it means.

We have a treehouse here in the back garden. It's a tiny, pokey little thing that I'm not sure would even fit Blaise and me in it these days, but it's there. There's also one at Leo's place, the compound, but there's no way in hell I'd be walking Ruby and Scarlett through those doors and expecting them to come out the other side safely. That would be like walking the mice straight into the viper's den.

Our use of 'Treehouse' refers to a restaurant. It's a little place with wood panelling on the walls and old booths that have definitely seen better days, but when we sat in there one day, it reminded all of us of the treehouse in our back garden, so that became its nickname—one only the three of us understand.

"I'm supposed to be in a training call, but it's as boring as hell. So, why the fuck not?"

"Will you grab a pack of Leo's smokes from the drawer before we go, too?" I ask.

"Are yours still upstairs?" she asks, checking me over when I stand.

"Yep," I grit out.

With a nod, she disappears up the stairs, stuffing both mine and Leo's smokes with my Zippo into my hoodie pocket before grabbing her handbag and keys and ushering me out the door.

"I would have liked to get that covered before you went out in public, but I'm assuming this won't wait?"

"No."

With an exasperated sigh and a roll of her eyes, she pulls out of the driveway, following my directions and taking us to Ruby, the fear and anger simmering in my veins doing neither of us any favours.

"When you said restaurant, this isn't exactly what I pictured," Mum comments as she pulls into the carpark.

I know.

Climbing from the car is more painful than there are words for, and she knows it as she joins me, offering her arm out. "Just until we get inside," she whispers. "You can be the big, hard man we all know you are when you need to be, but just for this moment, let me look after you."

How can I say no to that?

Letting her help me means we make it to the front door. Leo is yanking it open just as we arrive and taking me from my mother. I'm pale and sweating buckets by the time I get to the dark back booth that's always been ours, but there isn't time for niceties and shit right now.

"Who knows you're here?" I ask, looking at Scarlett.

"Nobody. I'm supposed to be in class."

"And they're not gonna notice that you've just upped and left?"

"I told Nate I had to be somewhere. He's covering."

"Jesus," I grumble, running a hand through my hair and rubbing the sweat from my face. "Tell me your location is off."

"Come on. Do you think I've never slipped out before?" Scarlett asks, flicking her hair over her shoulder. "I'm not a complete novice."

"Is this third degree really necessary? After everything that happened the other day, you can't honestly think Scarlett is a danger to me?" Ruby clips, pining me with an unimpressed stare.

Unimpressed. Well, that makes fucking two of us.

"I'll deal with you later."

"Deal with me? I don't think—" Ruby starts, until Leo's hand comes down on the table between us, drawing my attention upwards.

"As lovely as it is to see you Emmie, what exactly is going on here?" he asks, looking at my mother and then to me, cutting off any other conversation as he takes a long moment to categorise the bruising and bleeding, looking twice at the hole in my leg while he waits for an answer.

"Would you give us five minutes?" I ask, looking at my mother.

I have never, not once, put her in the middle of something like this, and I'm not about to start now.

"It's nice to see you, Leo," Mum says with a smile,

running a hand fondly across his cheek. "You've got at least another hour before you need more painkillers. Do your best to not make that worse, will you?" she asks before heading to the counter and ordering herself something—probably a hot chocolate and a muffin.

"Ruby's got herself on the Five Families radar. They tried to take her after school the other day," I admit.

"And Scarlett jumped in to help me," Ruby adds.

"That doesn't change her parentage, or who requested the collection."

"Wait a fucking minute here. You think *I* had something to do with that?" Scarlett asks. Ivy is looking confused as fuck in the middle of the two of them.

"And what exactly do they want with her?" Leo asks, narrowing his eyes, ignoring the other conversations going on by the girls.

"Nothing good."

When do they ever?

"Who did that?" he asks, pointing to my leg.

There's no way I'd have ended up hurt in a one-on-one fight, weapon or not, and he knows it.

"It's complicated."

"Simplify it."

Clenching my jaw and waiting him out doesn't work, and as the girls finish filling Ivy in on who and what Scarlett's family ties are, the table goes silent.

"Who shot you, D?" Leo asks again.

"You know who." Your father.

"And why would he do that?"

Vincent and I have been at odds before, but I've never

come home like this.

"I wouldn't tell him where Ruby was."

"Wait, what?" Ruby intervenes, her hand reaching across the table to mine. "I thought that guy did all this…"

"You think one pissant who could barely get hold of you properly did all this?" Leo asks, way too calmly for the rage that burns in his eyes. "How many did he lose?" Leo asks me now, scoffing out an unimpressed sound from the back of his throat, because we both know I didn't go down easily.

"Four."

"Serves him fucking right."

The time will come for Leo to take vengeance for all the things he's lost over the years. His mother. His hopes and dreams. Hopefully, one day this will be added to the list.

"Why?" he asks, tapping his fingers on the table. "Why is he so interested in her?"

"Hey, I'm interesting," Ruby counters, interrupting the silent conversation Leo and I are having.

Don't ask that question, please.

"I'm sure you are, but why are you interesting to *him?*" Leo asks. "He put you in that school with the Five Families generational kids, then Josiah enrolled you in the Little Sister programme to get you close to Ivy and me. It seems… excessive. Wouldn't there have been some other girl already there they could have used?"

"Baby, I'm sure it's coincidental." Ivy tries reaching for him.

But it's the silence from both Scarlett and Ruby that concerns me most.

"What do you know?" I ask, looking into the blue eyes of the dark-haired best friend of my girl.

She's the key to all of this.

If the Five Families sent her to Ruby, then they've always had a suspicion—one they've finally decided to confirm. If not, maybe we can get through this without smashing any hopes Ruby was clinging to falling in to pieces at my feet.

"You know I love you, right?" Scarlett asks, reaching out for Ruby's hands, waiting for her to nod before continuing. "Our meeting wasn't accidental."

"What?" Ruby asks, tears suddenly clinging to her eyelashes.

Shit.

twenty
Ruby

I can't hear anything other than the ringing in my ears.

Our meeting wasn't accidental.

The words echo around my head, drowning out the tinnitus as I cling to the last vestige of hope.

The friendship I forged with Scarlett has been the template for everything—the standard I measured Ivy against once she started to break down the barriers between us—and it was all a lie. It started out that way at least.

"Tanner asked me to get close to you, to… keep an eye on you, but it wasn't like that—not really—and it's not like that now. It's just you and me against the world, babe," Scarlett explains.

"Yeah, sure," I reply numbly.

My best friend, my only friend, isn't mine at all. Or she wasn't.

"What am I missing here, bro?" Leo interrupts, drawing my attention to where he and Dex are sitting on the opposite side of the table, seemingly twenty-four trillion miles away.

"'Cos I'm sure as shit missing something."

Dex stalls, looking at me and then to Leo as he presses his lips together. There's something else. There's more.

"I thought he had you keeping an eye on Ruby because she'd been useful at Pendleton Prep, but that's not it, is it?" Leo pushes.

"No," Dex admits, adjusting in his seat.

"Come on then, what is it? Why is Ruby so important that my father is spending a small fortune on making sure that she's safe and protected?"

Dex hovers, and the entire table is silent as we wait on bated breath for the answer.

"She's your half-sister," Dex admits, swallowing thickly.

I blink twice, my mouth opening and closing, but no words come out, and nothing makes sense. Everything I thought I understood ten minutes ago was a complete lie.

"How is that possible? My mother killed herself." Leo spits the words out like the poison they are.

"Because of your father's infidelity," Dex admits.

My best friend was sent here to keep an eye on me, and the man who threatened and manipulated me into spying on someone who later became a friend works for a man I know to be dead: my father.

"Oh. My. God." Ivy breathes the words out on an exhale at the other side of Scarlett. "You have a sister."

Her gaze must be on Leo, but I don't see anything other than the blur of people around us, and it takes me longer than it should to realise it's because I'm crying.

"Baby girl," Dex placates, reaching out to wipe away

the silent tears.

"You knew."

He nods, making fresh pain pierce my chest.

"You knew this whole time that I wasn't going to get out and live a normal life, and you never told me."

Dex is silent as I shake out of his hold.

Of every person sat at this table, he knows me the best. He's seen me at my strongest *and* my weakest. He held me in the darkness and watched my steps in the light, and he knew the one thing I've been aiming for was never going to be within my reach, and he did nothing, said nothing.

"This is why Pendleton are sniffing about," Leo says, drawing my attention away from Dex and the hurt in his gaze. It's nothing compared to my heart right about now. "Because you're part of my bloodline."

"What does that mean?" Scarlett asks.

"That means she's at risk from a secret society, too," Ivy says.

"So, the Five Families want to confirm who she is and use her to... what? Bargain with Vincent?" Leo asks, the cogs practically turning behind his eyes. "The Sect already have me, so they have no further use for my bloodline."

"No, but he thinks they can keep her safe from the Five Families," Dex admits, the truth of situation far worse than I ever understood.

"And to keep her safe from both of them, you went up against him," Scarlett says, putting the pieces together.

"Alone?" Ivy asks, her concern for the man I care about more than I can contain.

The whole conversation happens around me like I'm

sitting in the corner watching it play out on the television. This can't be my life. It's not happening to me.

Trapped between a maniac that turns out to be my father and an underground consortium is not where I'm supposed to be. I'm finishing my exams and going to art college. I'm going to design great swathes of artwork for fancy homes, manipulate balls of clay and rolls of steel into something elegant and beautiful.

I am not a pawn to be fought over.

"No."

The conversations at the table continue, my word lost beneath the weight of the decisions waiting to be made.

"I said… no!" I repeat louder. "You knew the whole time that there was more going on, and you never told me. Our friendship may have grown out of Tanner's intervention, but you never even warned me I was in danger," I say, looking at Scarlett as the table falls silent.

"And you! You've known who I am and where I fit into this whole picture. Watching me and keeping me safe only goes so far when the person I've always been least safe with is you," I add, looking at Dex. "I don't want this knowledge, this series of betrayals. I don't want any of it."

"Welcome to the family." Leo smirks in my direction, clearly ready to add his two pence worth in. "You think she wanted to keep that knowledge?" he asks, gesturing to Scarlett and leaning closer. "Do you think Ivy or I wanted to be offered up to a fucking secret society?"

The table remains silent as he continues. "I'm not sure what kind of a life you've had up until this point. Maybe it's one where everyone is up front and honest, where you sit around the dining table every night and tell each other everything that happened that day and how it makes you feel, but that isn't the life any of *us* have lived. You do what you've got to do to keep yourself and those you love safe."

"Those you love? Oh, yeah I know all about family." He has no idea.

"*He's* my brother," Leo spits, gesturing to Dex. "My father broke me down and handed me over to The Sect, and my mother took her own life, apparently because of what he did with yours. I'm sorry if I'm not crying myself to sleep over someone or something I never knew existed."

"Fuck. Off. She told me my father was dead, then drank herself into a stupor. Spending night after night chasing after yours, the same man that sired me, apparently." I scoff out an unimpressed laugh. "Even after everything, she only wanted him."

"Yeah, well. Dex is family. Ivy is family. You're family," Leo declares, pointing at each of us in turn.

That's what it boils down to now, isn't it? We're family, tied together by blood.

The only problem is that the family I have by blood has done nothing for me. It's always been those I thought chose me who have turned up, and now it seems that was all a lie, too.

"Who's your mother?" Leo asks.

"Rita Sheridan."

"Of course." He nods like it makes perfect sense. How or why it would, I have no idea, and nothing to add to that.

"I always wanted a sister," Ivy comments breaking the tension.

"You're getting married?" Dex asks, looking between Ivy and Leo.

"Nah, that would be complicated as fuck." Leo laughs, the sound swallowing up some of the sickness in my stomach.

Ivy and Leo are in a poly relationship with Jacob, Nick, and Wyatt. I have no idea the ins and outs of the damn thing, but they make her happy, and as much as I tried my best not to care about her or them, somehow, I've found myself giving a shit.

"Sisters have got to better than brothers," Scarlett adds. "I've got three of the fuckers."

I can't help the way my insides twist knowing our friendship isn't built on the trust I thought it was.

"You know I'd have told you if I ever thought you were in any danger, right?" she asks, looking at me. "Tanner never said anything about it after we started becoming fiends, and quite honestly, I forgot about it. You're just my Ruby."

"I get it, I think. It's gonna take me a minute, that's all," I admit.

"And you still love me?" Ivy asks, winking as she presses her lips together in a kissy face that I really don't need right now.

"Oh, yeah. Totally."

"Great, so now we're all on the same page, can someone please tell me they've got a better plan than hiding you out at Dex's place?" Leo asks.

"Oh, yeah. This genius is sure that us being together is going to fix everything," I tell him, gesturing to Dex... not that I can even look too closely at him right now. I'm not sure If I'll burst into tears or hit him, teetering somewhere on the edge of a complete hysterical breakdown.

"Say what?" Leo asks.

"Hear me out," Dex starts. "The Five families won't wonder why I'm hanging around if they think we're together."

"Except that they had concerns about her before you started hanging around," Scarlett interrupts.

"And my father is going to blow a fucking gasket," Leo adds.

"But it does explain why I wouldn't hand her over, and why she can't go to Pendleton Prep."

"*Our* relationship didn't stop him sending me off. Do you really think this will stop him?" Leo asks, incredulity laced through every word.

"I said no. Nobody is sending me anywhere or demanding anything from me. I fucking refuse to accept it."

"Ruby." Dex tries reaching out for me, but I shake off his advances, angrily wiping at the tears on my cheeks before standing.

"No. You don't get to do that anymore."

He's lied to me, coddled me, protected me from everyone but himself, and at the end of the day, he's the only person close enough to me to actually hurt me. Or so I thought.

"I need a minute."

I find my way to the ladies' bathroom and run the cold water to drown out all the thoughts running around in my mind as I rest my hands either side of the sink.

"When I said let's get a coffee, this isn't exactly how

I saw it going," Ivy says, closing the door behind her and flicking the lock.

I'm not sure what I expected, either, but this isn't it.

"What are you thinking?" she asks, leaning against one of the stalls.

Everything.

Nothing.

"You don't want to know."

"Wouldn't have asked if I didn't," she says idly as I watch her checking her nails in the mirror. "I know this a lot to take in one go, I get it, but you have one thing going for you that I never did."

"What's that, then?" I ask.

"Family."

"Really?" I scoff out an unimpressed laugh. "You can't be serious right now."

"When Tamsin and I set off to Pendleton Prep it was at the *request* of my father. Neither of us wanted to be there. Well, I didn't. She was excited about the adventure, but we both know how well that worked out for her."

Ivy's best friend disappeared at some point this year— something to do with this secret society they're are wrapped up in—but I don't know all the details of it. Either way, she was a mess for ages over it, and she could barely say her best friend's name, so the fact that she's sharing this with me now mean it's important.

"My family wanted me wrapped up in all the shit that comes with Pendleton Prep, and it sounds like someone in yours wants the same for you. But you have someone I didn't: Leo."

"And what, exactly, can Leo do about all of this?" I ask, exasperated. He sounds to be just as much of a pawn in this as I am.

"I guess that depends on what you want."

"I'm not sure where what *I* want fits into all of this. Dex is only interested in keeping me away from Scarlett's family and away from Pendleton Prep. My *father* wants to ship me off to Pendleton Prep to keep me safe from the Five Families, and what they want from me, I don't even know. So much for art college. How the hell is this my life?"

After turning off the tap, I brace myself on the sink, finally getting her attention in the mirror and seeing the smile on her face.

"Have you seen the kind of power Leo wields?" she asks. "Now that's yours, too. I completely understand the damsel in distress moment you're having right now, but let's look at the big picture for a sec."

Turning, I rest against the edge of the sink, crossing my arms across my chest. There's no way in hell I'm getting out of here without hearing what she's got to say. May as well get it out of the way.

"You're the heiress to an underworld mob, mafia, syndicate thing. What's stopping you from doing whatever the hell you want? You want to accept your best friend's apology and start afresh with her, then fucking go for it. You want to go to college, then why the fuck not? You're Ruby Sheridan. When have you ever let someone else's limitations stop you?"

"Erm, when they threatened my mother's life or my own."

"That was before you knew your birthright and the control that comes with it."

"Yeah, right. I've watched Scarlett get passed up for her older brother time and time again. We all know that's not how it works for women in these situations."

"You don't think if Scarlett really wanted something that she wouldn't get it?" Ivy asks with the cock of her head. "Come on. We both know better than that. And it looks like Leo isn't your only ally in this, either."

"Scarlett can't help me here."

"I meant Dex."

"Oh."

Pain lances through my chest just thinking about how stupid I've been for all these months. I thought there was something there between us. All the firsts I've given him, the kind of trust I thought couldn't be shaken by anything, but I was wrong.

"I'm just a job to him." He's said it a million times. Why didn't I listen?

"Sure thing, chick. That's why there's a bullet hole in his leg because he went against one of the most powerful men I've ever met—and that's saying something—for you. But you're just a friend, a job, just... nothing."

I do my best to let her words penetrate, to soak in the possibility that there could be more for us than this.

"How can I ever trust someone who's lied to me the entire time I've known them?" I ask, and that goes two ways, because Scarlett did too.

"You lied to me."

"That was different. My mother's life was on the line,"

I argue, cutting her an unimpressed look as my stomach sinks, but she's right.

"Bigger picture? It's no different," she replies with a sad smile. "My family sent me off against my will, and someone I care about lied to me to build a friendship for their own goals. You have the opportunity to stand up and say *no*. To forge your own path with the help of a family you never knew existed and, sure, people who may have lied, but still give a shit about you. Can you do that?"

twenty-one
Dex

"They've been in there for a long time," I ponder aloud.

My heart sank when Ruby stormed off into the bathrooms, not helped much when Ivy went to join her just a few minutes later. I know I fucked up, but what choice did I have? At least she knows now. Better late than never, right?

"You don't trust my girl, D?" Leo asks with the cock of his eyebrow.

He's been surprisingly accepting of the whole situation, taking this much more in his stride than I anticipated. I'm not going to say I've spent a lot of time thinking about telling Leo about Ruby, but it was definitely more time than it should have been.

"Maybe I should go check on them," Scarlett says, pushing her chair back.

"Sit the fuck down," I growl, stopping her in her tracks.

Just because Ruby trusts her, it doesn't mean I do. I'm not sure even *she* does right now—not after all that.

"Why didn't you tell me?" Leo asks, ignoring the elephant in the room as Scarlett huffs, dropping back into the seat.

"You think if I'd told you this that you wouldn't have been straight in your father's face? It was part of a test, my loyalty to the family over you, and we both know if I'd so much as hinted that this was a possibility, you'd have had his balls in a jar within hours."

"You know me better than that. I'd have strung it out for days."

"Do we have to talk about balls in jars?" Scarlett asks, pushing the cake around her plate. "They're gross enough when they're attached."

"I'm sorry, man. Once you were out from under his influence, there just wasn't a moment, and it's not the kind of thing you just drop into conversation. I tried to tell you she was safe and on our side, even if she didn't know it at the time," I explain, thinking back to the conversation we had at Christmas.

"Half-sister... Fuck, man," Leo says, leaning against the table, his thoughts clearly whirring at a mile a minute.

"You should let her come back to school," Scarlett says quietly. "I can talk to Nate and my brother. She'll be safe with us."

"Except it was your *family* connections who wanted her in the first place. That's who attempted to take her outside the library the other night," I counter.

"What? No!"

Nodding, I cross my arms over my chest.

These exams are a waste of fucking time, anyway.

There's no way Vincent is going to let her drive off into the sunset. Especially not now she knows the truth.

"Can she stay with you for a few more days?" Leo asks, tapping the back of my hand. "I've got a few ideas, but I'm gonna need some time to sort through them all."

"You need to talk to the wife and the husband and all that?"

"Something like that. Can she stay?"

There are plenty of replies I'd like to give him: Of course. Always. Forever. Instead, I give him the only answer that matters: "If she wants to."

"Give her my number, yeah?" he asks, waiting for me to agree before turning to Scarlett. "And you'll keep on top of her revision notes and make sure she doesn't fall behind, won't you?"

"Of course," she agrees, her confusion as obvious as mine.

"Good, because here she comes."

"I've told Ruby she can stay with us for a bit," Ivy says, taking the seat opposite Leo.

"No can do, angel," Leo counters before quickly explaining our conversation while Ruby glowers at the coffee cup in front of her, clearly unimpressed by whatever plan Leo's concocting in his mind. "Text me, and we can talk. There are things we both need to know before we go into this, okay?"

He stands, waiting for Ivy and Scarlett to join him before reaching out to get hold of Ruby's shoulder and telling her he'll be in touch soon. Scarlett reminds Ruby to call Nate. Then it's just her, me, and the million things I should have said that she wouldn't have ever heard.

"Let's get out of here," she says quietly. "I can't believe I'm out in public dressed like this, anyway."

The car journey home is silent and wracked with tension, with Ruby disappearing upstairs and locking the bathroom door almost the second we're back inside the building. This is not how I wanted her time with me to be.

"I need to catch up on that seminar, but I'll be back in live training in like half an hour," my mother says, dropping her bag on the table while I engage the security system. "Go fix whatever the hell is going on, and rest that bloody leg, will you?"

She doesn't have to tell me twice.

Nodding, I head up the stairs and knock twice on the bathroom door, waiting for an answer, but nothing comes. So, I slide my back down the frame and sit on the floor. I can wait as long as she can.

The minutes pass, my mother's voice carrying up the stairs as she starts her afternoon session, but still, we sit, and we wait.

"Tell me you haven't locked me out and climbed out the window," I call out to her.

What if I'm sitting here waiting her out and she's fucked off again. There aren't many ways to get out of here, and that sure as fuck wouldn't be very safe, but she somehow already managed to escape once. What's to say she hasn't done it again?

"I'm still here," she replies from the other side of the door, closer than I thought.

"Why don't we go sit somewhere more comfortable and

talk about all this? It's got to be better than the cold tiles in there, right?"

"I'm fine."

"Mum is going to need the bathroom at some point."

"Well, I'll move then."

"Ruby, if I have to ask her to come up here, we're both gonna be in the shit. You may have seen nothing but the nice version of her so far, but trust me, you don't want to get on the wrong side of Emmeline Raymond."

"I can believe it," she grumbles, opening the door and walking past me. "She managed to raise you two, after all."

I think the darkness in Blaise and me has much more to do with the alcoholic bastard who fathered us, and all the shit we've done since the night we finally managed to ask for help, but if that gets her out of the damn bathroom, I'll take it.

Using the banister and the doorframe, I manage to haul myself up off the floor. It's not graceful, but it does the trick, and I hobble into my bedroom before dropping onto the edge of the bed we curled up in together less than twelve hours ago.

"Is that the reason you stopped to help me that night?" she asks meekly.

Because of course, that's where she starts, right back at the beginning.

"Yes and no," I admit. "When Lance dragged you out from the side of that bin, I knew it could go south. They are, well... they were, the worst kind of shit heads, and I'd like to think you know I'm not that kind of guy."

Despite all the blood on my hands.

Never women. Never children.

Blaise and I came into this as nothing more than children, thrown into an adult world with Leo and left to figure it out, but those are the rules we live by and, so far, have managed to uphold.

She doesn't reply, looking at me but not really seeing me as she remembers the night our paths crossed—strike one with the Five Families.

"The two of them worked for Gregory Wheeler, and whatever you saw, you saw too much. I was waiting to see how far the two of them were going to push it. When they got you in the light, I knew I couldn't walk away."

"So, our paths crossing that night was completely coincidental?"

"You stopped, not me."

I shouldn't be glad that she did, but I am.

"And the only reason you stayed that night, and all the other nights, is because you knew who I am." It should be a question, but it isn't. She's already decided that whatever this thing is between us was a setup—another deception on my part. The problem is that she's wrong.

"No."

"There's no point lying to me anymore, Dex. All this *you're mine* bullshit can stop. I'm here, I'm 'safe'. What more do you want from me?"

There's a defeat in her tone that guts me more than the pain I'm already battling because she thinks it's all been a lie. That everything between us means nothing.

"I'm not sure what the giveaway was at the races. Ben Osborne was the one who made the call on that, but it was probably your leisurely stroll with Nathaniel Peregrine that ended up being the final nail in your coffin with the Five Families. At least three incidents where you turned up in places you weren't supposed to. Once could have been an honest mistake, a coincidence."

"It was."

"I know, but twice is less likely, and three times is pretty much unheard of. They may not know who your father is, but they know you're more than just some charity case."

"Way to say it like it is." She shakes her head, standing and pacing around the room. "I don't care about them, and I get what Scarlett did. I don't like it, but I get it. You've known the entire time we've been... whatever this is. Every night you curled up in the corner of my room, you knew I should be somewhere else, somewhere different. He's got everything, and I had nothing," she admits.

"You never had nothing, and for the last year, you've had me. Do you really think Vincent Windsor is a better option? Because I can tell you for certain that Leo would argue that point until he's blue in the fucking face." She has no idea who her father is and what he's capable of.

"I never had you. You're mothing more than an errand boy watching over me because you had to." She spits the words out, all sense of melancholy gone in an instant. "I'm nothing more than a job, a friend, someone on the other side of that wall you erect between us every time we're alone."

Like now.

Only now I have nothing left to lose but her.

I stand, taking the weight on my bad leg as long as I can, and step towards her.

"You're not just a job."

She steps back, and I step forward again, my long strides eating up the space between us.

"And you're definitely not a friend." She proved that as much in this very room.

Again, she steps back, but she's out of room, colliding with the wall with a gentle thud as I limp another step closer, nothing but a breath away—her voice finally silent.

"And there aren't any walls now. Haven't been for a while."

Not since I crossed a line and pinned her against my car, tasting her sweet submission on my tongue.

"Liar," she hisses. Her eyes narrow, and her fists clench at her sides, but she's trapped as I rest my forearms against the wall, propping myself up and taking the weight off my leg. All it does is draw us closer, her breaths coming out short and sharp as her pupils dilate and the air around us shifts.

"I've been many things over the last year, but I'm not a liar. You were the light at the end of a very dark tunnel, the rainbow in my despair, and the reason I kept putting one foot in front of the other and forging forwards."

She grits her teeth, swallowing thickly as tears threaten to fall once again.

"Now you're so much more than that. You're the reason I get out of bed in the morning, and bringing joy to your life has done more for me than anything else I can think of."

Knowing that my father was never going to stumble back through our front door is the only other exception to that. She has no idea how important she's become to me.

"But I'm just the man who kept something from you, nothing more."

"Are you finished?" she asks, her words whispering across my lips.

Nodding, I wait for her now, mere inches from the fire burning in her eyes. Gone is the feeble little girl who stomped in here, the defeated child who didn't know who to trust or where to turn. In her place rises the fire starter I always knew her to be underneath. The girl who took a beating and then went to school. Who turned into a young woman managing death threats against a mother who hasn't been able to look after herself properly for years, never mind the daughter she was supposed to care for.

Now, here she stands blazing her full glory.

"Good."

Her movement takes me by surprise, but as her lips press against mine, there's no way I can stop the torrent that cascades between us. I press down, and she surges upwards, tangling one hand in my shirt as each soft curve and delicate line of her presses against me.

"Should we be doing this?" she asks as I take a step back, and she follows. "What about concussion?"

I nip along her jawline and take another step back, pushing the door closed as I go.

"And all the painkillers. Surely I'm taking advantage of you…"

"You take advantage as much as you fucking want."

Shuffling up the bed isn't exactly what I had in mind, but right now, she's here and I'm here, and I'd be fucking stupid not to make use of every second that we're on the same page.

"Ride my dick, my fingers, my face. Take it fucking all."

Pulling her down on top of me has her gasping and catching her weight on her hands either side of my head as she lands across my hips, straddling me—exactly where she was when she came like a queen, even if it does feel like a lifetime ago.

"I'm definitely taking advantage," she mumbles again. "But not until I've tried something."

She shimmies down my body, the soft fabric of the shorts she picked out doing nothing to hide the proof of my attraction to her. With nothing more than a handful of kisses she's got me harder than steel.

She shuffles them down over my hips, releasing my cock and staring at it in wonder for what feels like forever before her hand wraps around the base, squeezing and pulling from root to tip.

"You're mine, Dex Raymond, and it's about time you realised it."

twenty-two
Ruby

"**I**'m not buying this stomach bug bullshit Scarlett is plying. If you need a knight in shining armour, call me," Nate says cheerily, the voicemail ending.

"How many is that now, eleven?" Dex asks. "That boy's got it bad."

"It's not like that." Well, not for me.

"Looks like that."

Spinning the chair around, I pin him with an unimpressed look. I can't exactly call Nate up and explain what's going on when I barely understand it myself, and there are more than enough people in this stupid little circle as it is.

"What? I'm just saying," he counters with the shrug of his shoulders.

"Well, don't. I'm gonna have to talk to him eventually."

"Not if I have anything to do with it."

"I'll be going back to school at some point. This isn't a permanent solution, and we all know it."

He may not want to admit it, and I can totally agree

that completing the couple of hours' worth of revision notes Scarlett sends me back is a million times better than having to sit in the bloody classes—I'm actually getting something done for a start—but it's not going to last.

I can't get comfortable in his home, wrapped up in his scent and safety and protection. That's nothing more than a false sense of security, and it's temporary. When I go back to school it will be a free for all, unless Leo's plan works, and I can't hide behind the safety of these walls forever.

"Has your mum called?" Dex asks, making my stomach sink.

"Twice."

Not as many times as the guy who only noticed me a matter of weeks ago—the one I'm pretending is just fishing for information—but she finally figured out something's amiss.

"I'm sure Vincent has let her know you're safe."

"Yeah." About that… "Have you met her? My mother."

Dex, Blaise, and Leo are all part of this system I know nothing about, and somewhere, my mother fits into it all. I've been too scared to ask Leo about it after what he said about his mother, but I can't help the questions that have been running through my mind. I guess it's time for some answers.

"Rita? Yeah, I've met her," Dex admits, warily. "She's around the compound quite a bit."

"The compound?"

"Leo's place."

"I guess that makes sense if she's with his dad."

She's been living this whole other life with a partner

and friends, and I've just been left at home, the reminder of a life she wanted to leave behind. I can see her now, dancing around the living room with the man of her dreams, a glass of something in one hand and him in the other, a smile on her face. That's not something I see often, genuine emotion.

"She's not with Vincent," he says, pulling me back into the here and now. "I don't know much about their relationship—wouldn't want to—but he's the boss, and anyone he's seriously connected to is protected."

And she hasn't been.

It's there in all the words he isn't saying.

The boss's girlfriend would be lavished with money, power, protection. She'd be wrapped in silk and kept in an ivory tower... or maybe that's the romantic in me coming out to play.

My mother hasn't been wrapped up or protected. She's been kicked out at the end of the night, drunk or off her head on drugs, even though she had me to look after. And after everything he's used me for this year, he can't deny knowing about me. My *father* knows exactly who I am.

"You mean like Leo?" I ask, hoping that doesn't make my mother the *other woman* in this situation, but unwilling to ask the question.

"Kind of. Leo had Blaise and me watching his back. Until recently, anyway, but he's a force to be reckoned with all in his own right."

Ivy said as much. "And me?" The question was supposed to come out strong, but it doesn't, and I'm not sure I want the answer.

"As far as I can tell, you've been protected since he

realised you might be in danger. I can't speak for someone else, but I think he was hoping if he never acknowledged you, nobody else would, either."

Safety by denial is not quite the paternal instinct I was hoping for.

He's alive, and my mother is still flitting around him all these years later. I became useful to him, and that put me in danger because of a birthright I never even knew I had. Plus, I'd have never even known about it if I hadn't found myself friends with Scarlett.

My connection with her is what put in me in the path of Nate, Tanner, and Damien fucking Wheeler. They coordinated this friendship to keep an eye on me, and all that did was put a bigger target on my back.

If anyone is to blame for the situation I'm in, it's them. The Five Families. Not my best friend, who only did what she was asked by her brother, or the man who's done nothing but protect me from everything and everyone for the last year, even before he was supposed to.

Dex has protected me from the Five Families, from my father, and from the knowledge of who I am and what that would mean for my future.

It wasn't the right thing to do, but he did it for me, and now I get to put my life back together how I want it with the help of my family. The one I've been denied my entire life. The time for meek little Ruby Sheridan to sink into the background is over. Ivy and Leo are right. I have power here, and it's about time I acknowledged it.

Closing up my laptop, I push it to the side and grab my phone, pressing call on his number before I can overthink this.

"Hello?"

"Hey, Leo. It's Ruby. What did you have in mind?" I ask, putting it on speaker before dropping the phone on the bed as I climb up next to Dex, taking solace in his strength beside me.

An hour later, we have a plan, as rough as it might be.

"You need to talk to Blaise," Dex says resolutely. "We can't walk in there without him on board."

"Can't you do it?"

"I could, but he'd be doing it for me, and that's not going to work."

Great.

"You've got about twenty minutes to pluck up the courage," he adds, dropping his phone on the bedside table as he nudges my shoulder with his. "What do you want to do to kill the time?" He wiggles his eyebrows suggestively.

"I'm not sure that's going to help," I counter, even as his hand slides along my jaw. "Tell me everything you know about me, about my family. I think it's about time we evened the playing field a little bit, don't you?"

I don't know nearly enough about what I'm walking into, literally and figuratively, and if I'm going to get Blaise on board with this, I need to be as prepared as I can be.

"Ruby Sheridan, only child of Rita Sheridan. I'm not sure what help this is going to be."

"Humour me."

"From what I can gather, Leo's mother was the love of Vincent's life, but when one of his side pieces got pregnant, she decided she couldn't do it anymore, and she ended her own life. It broke him, and Leo, and the mean mother fucker got worse than ever. Rita dropped off the face of the earth for… fucking ages, then one day, she rocked up to one of the compound parties and has been a regular attendee ever since."

"So, she's nothing to him, just like me."

"I'm not sure I'd go that far," he admits, tucking a stray lock of hair behind my ear. "She's something to him—you both are—but he had Leo to raise, then later, me and B kicking around. Three boys are a lot, you know?"

"Sure." I shrug.

"It was hard to track down the financials, but he's been taking care of your home, the bills, and everything as far back as I can tell," Blaise admits from the doorway behind me.

Turning, I let Dex wrap me in the safety of his arms as we wait for Blaise to pull the chair up and join us, pushing the door closed behind him as he does.

"He's known about you for your entire life, and he's done the bare minimum to ensure you were fed and taken care of. He's led your mother along and strung her out on drugs that mean she's been nothing more than a shell of the person you should have had looking out for you, Then when he realised you might be of use to him, he dragged you into this sick circle of rebels, too," Blaise admits.

"Not quite the family ties I was hoping for."

"Family isn't just blood," Dex says, the sound vibrating through my back. "Leo is as much my brother as Blaise is, despite his blood being the same as yours, not ours."

Isn't that a weird thought.

"But we protect ours with everything, and if you're going to continue to be a danger to them, then we're going to have a problem," Blaise states.

"Me?"

"D is in literal pieces because he protected you, Leo is in emotional pieces because of you, and our mother was out there unprotected because of you. You didn't have all the information then, but you do now, and I won't let you do it again."

If Hollywood has taught me anything, it's what the bad guy sounds like, and Blaise preaches like the cold-blooded son of a mob boss if I've ever heard one, but I appreciate the sentiment differently to our loggerheads at breakfast the other morning.

This isn't him putting restrictions on me because he can and he wants to. Honestly, earlier wasn't, either. That was the fear of me putting more people he cares about in danger. I don't doubt he's done the kinds of things you'd see in a horror film, and that he'd make good on any warning he offered my way, but from what I've seen of this man, he cares deeply about those close to him. Hopefully, one day, that will include me.

Instead of offering him placations and words that mean nothing, I offer him action instead by asking, "Are you busy on Sunday?"

His eyes narrow and his head cocks to one side in the same way Dex's does when I say something that vexes him, and it causes a smile to pull at my lips. Pushing out of the safety of Dex's hold, I move to sit on the edge of the bed and fill him in on the plan Leo and I have laid out, waiting with bated breath for his take on it.

"Well, if that's what you want to do, I'll make someone available to you at the end of the week," he says, apparently accepting of our crazy plan.

"Yeah?" I honestly didn't expect that he'd be on our side, and my surprise is clear.

"I trust Leo, and if he thinks this is the way forward, then I'm on board."

"Just like that?"

"Just like that," he agrees. "What the boss says goes."

"Knew you'd get it, bro," Dex comments, reaching for his smokes.

"What *I* think doesn't matter, and you're not going anywhere fucking near this," Blaise adds, pointing at his brother. "You couldn't help yourself out of a paper bag today, tomorrow, or in three days' time, so you leave this one to me. Rob and Carl will be with you."

"Carl?" Dex scoffs out. "She'd be better with the damn paper bag."

"You need someone recognisable, and there's no way I'm sending Van into a building full of high school girls," Blaise argues.

I have no idea who these people are or what they're bickering about, but who cares? I get my freedom, kind of, or a way to start working towards it. It's a step in the right direction, of that I'm sure, and I can't help the excitement that starts to build in my stomach.

I'm doing it. I'm taking back control.

***

"Why the hell did I agree to this?" I grumble, walking down the corridor to my first lesson.

"I don't know, but it's fun," Scarlett replies, her arm locked through mine as she peeks over her shoulder, again.

"You're wrong. It's not fun."

"Did you see Marcia's face when the two of them strode in behind you? Priceless."

The looks continue as we get to the maths corridor, with Carl placing one hand on my shoulder as Rob strides down the corridor, checking out the intended classroom before waving us down.

"It's like being with the queen." Scarlett giggles.

"Don't start."

"Oh, oh. Not the queen, like the—"

"Princess, what's going on here?" Nate finishes, cutting Scarlett off and dropping an arm over my shoulder."

It's not that I've been avoiding him... much. I've been off school... sick, you know? I can't be replying to every call and text whilst I'm on my death bed.

Okay, I think we all know that's bullshit and that I've been ducking his calls. What can I say? I don't know what to tell the guy. I appreciate he was worried about me after what happened at the library, but I told him that I was fine, safe, and all that jazz. What more does he want?

"Excuse me. I'm going to need you to step back," Carl says, stepping towards Nate before I have time to address Nate's stupid nickname with either of them.

Carl waits expectantly as the passing titters turn into gawking, Nate's bestie joining our rag-tag group of four.

"He's joking, right?" Nate whispers, eying the man-mountain warily.

"I don't think so," Scarlett replies as I shrug out of his hold.

"Better safe than sorry," I add with an awkward smile, wishing the floor would open up and eat me.

"It's clear, miss," Rob states, pushing the corridor doors open and waiting for me to go down to my class.

"Hang on a minute. Don't I know you?" Nate asks, pointing at Rob while I do my best to get the hell out of here before all the pieces fall into place for him, then the rest of the school not so long after.

"You should do," Scarlett singsongs in response as she follows me down the corridor, an unexpectedly excited skip to her step. "This is so much fun!"

"Fun?"

"Yes, fun. I think you've forgotten what it looks like, or maybe you've never had it before because the look on his face right now is priceless, and you're missing it."

She hangs back in the doorway, watching the commotion in the corridor, until Carl and Rob both reappear and shove her into the class, finally allowing the rest of the students in.

"This isn't what I had in mind."

"Well, this is what we've got, so fucking enjoy it a little, will you?" she replies, dropping her bag into the seat beside mine before pulling out the books she needs.

"I promise they won't be in the way," I apologise to the teacher as she sits at her desk, mouth agape.

I know that the faculty were warned I'd be returning with staff, but I'm not sure they were expecting this. By the time we get to the end of second period and our break, it seems like everyone knows the truth—the one I wanted to share, to own.

Rob and Carl loiter on either side of our lockers, glowering at anyone and everyone, but I know there's trouble heading our way when they both stand a little straighter and step a little closer.

"So, it's true, then?" Everett asks, resting back against the railings opposite our lockers, arms wrapped over his chest.

"What is?" I ask, ready to get this over and done with.

"You're Vincent Windsor's daughter." He doesn't bother lowering his tone or keeping this private, throwing the words out there with all the venom he thinks they deserve.

"Apparently so."

"Scarlett," Tanner calls, jogging over. "You got a minute?"

"Erm, let me think about it. No," she replies, flicking her hair over her shoulder as she takes a step away from him.

"Come on. We need to talk," he pleads, looking from her to the two bodyguards surrounding us.

"Sorry, big bro. Things to do, people to piss off."

"Scarlett," Everett tries as Tanner joins him.

I take a step closer to her and wrap her arm in mine, Carl and Rob following me closely.

"Look, it's like this. You sent Scarlett to keep an eye on me, to find out who I am, and now you know, so she doesn't owe you shit. Plus, she's awesome, so you fucked right up because I think I'm going to keep her."

"Keep her?" Tanner squeaks out.

"Yep. Got to have myself a little Five Families bestie, right?" I ask, prodding the bear just a little. "Or would you rather I make that Nate instead?"

It's a low blow, and not something I would have thrown in either of their faces if he'd been standing here. There may not be anything relationship wise between Nate and me, but he's a nice guy, and he doesn't deserve to be used in this game, either.

The silence from Tanner and Everett says everything they don't, though: Nate is more important than Scarlett as far as the Five Families are concerned. It's probably not how either of *them* feel—definitely not if the irritated shuffle they both do is anything to go by—but they can't get into this argument with me.

"Thought not," I clip out. "Now, if you don't mind, I'd like to take five minutes outside with my girl."

The tension crackling as we step away is palpable, the whispers and the open stares irritating, but what worries me more is the silence from the fun-loving girl at my side.

The crowds disperse as we pass, but I wait until we're outside before asking, "You good?"

"Me?" she squeaks out. "Yeah, I'm good, but I thought they'd have put up more of a fight. Also, I'm your Five Families bestie. That's really what we're going with? And please tell me you wouldn't seriously trade me for Nate, would you?"

"Hell would have to freeze over first."

She barks out a laugh, shaking her head. "Then I guess

316   HEATHER PACKER

you and I better had get used to this kind of treatment," she comments, looking over at Carl and Rob. "This is a whole other kind of protection."

"Sure is."

twenty-three
Dex

"**G**et out of the car, Dex." Blaise holds the back passenger door open, waiting patiently, despite the exasperation wrapped around his words.

"Nah, I'm good."

"Don't make me haul your broken arse out of there. We both know I've done it before, and I'll do it again if I have to."

It wouldn't be hard considering the state I'm in right now, but I'm not going anywhere except with Ruby.

"Seriously, I'm fine right here."

He huffs an unimpressed breath out of his nose and quietly watches Ruby climb in on the other side. "You're not coming with us," he says, knowing he isn't going to get any support from Ruby on this one.

Ignoring him completely, I turn to her and ask, "You okay?"

With a nervous smile, she nods, smoothing her hands

down her jeans. Going home and picking up some of her clothes has made all the difference over the last few days, even if I was worried she wouldn't get in the car and come back to me. It turns out I shouldn't have been concerned, but it was definitely bothering me for a moment.

"You want me to come with you, right?"

"Absolutely," she says, grabbing my hand and threading her fingers through mine.

"You can't do this in there," Blaise says carefully. "If she's going to be accepted beyond those doors, it needs to be on her own merits."

"Yeah, yeah, we get it." Wrapping my other hand over hers, I stop Ruby's retreat and hold her close for as long as we can get away with it. "As far as the rest of the world is concerned, this is just protection."

"Just protection," Blaise repeats. "You think you can manage that?"

I'm not sure whether he means *can you keep your shit together* or *keep your hands to yourself.* Either way, I'm here for it. As long as I've got eyes on her, it'll be fine.

"Yep, you ready to roll?" I ask, buckling my seatbelt. "You know how patient Leo is."

With the shake of his head, Blaise slams the door closed, walks around the car and climbs into the front seat. "Some fucking protection," he grumbles.

The atmosphere in the car is tense as we pull away and head to meet Leo and Ivy, straight into the thick of it. This could be a huge mistake, but we're in it now so we may as well own it.

"Did you have any trouble at school?" Blaise asks,

catching Ruby's gaze in the rearview mirror.

To say I was nervous about her heading back into South Beach High is an understatement. I spent the entire day checking in with Rob and Carl, but she was fine. Totally fine. In fact, from what I heard, she rocked it.

"Nothing you don't already know about, I'm sure," she answers.

"It helps to hear it from the horse's mouth, but whatever."

"Tanner and Everett weren't happy about Scarlett sticking it out with me, and Nathaniel was confused as fuck, but I think we're good. If the aim of the day was to make a statement, I think we managed it."

"As far as I'm concerned, the aim was to get you back to school safely, but a statement at least means they should back off," I comment, squeezing her hand. "No awkward questions from Scarlett, then?"

I should leave them to it—girl gossip or whatever—but I'm not sure if she ever went ahead with the whole *we're together* thing outside of our house, and it bothers me knowing it may just be another plan that's fallen flat on its face.

"Oh, she wanted to know all about the, and I quote, 'hot man-mountain' who swooped in to rescue me, but we'd mostly covered that via text this week. She was pretty disappointed that you weren't there to keep an eye on us, though."

"Soon, baby girl."

Blaise raises an eyebrow, and he may as well have said: "You really think the boss is putting you back on ghost protection after this stunt?"

Not that it's going to be his decision soon, anyway. It'll be down to Leo.

Leo's Lexus is pulling up alongside our car sooner than I think any of us are ready for. Even faster than that, we're pulling up to the black gates which guard the compound. This is the place Leo has called home his entire life, and it's the one that holds the father Ruby never knew existed until recently.

There's no point asking her if she's ready—she's not—but she's strong enough to weather this. I know Leo has almost as many concerns as Blaise has, but I don't. I've already seen everything she's been through.

Ivy fluffs up her hair as we climb out, looking around almost as nervously as Ruby. Blaise greets Leo while I do my best to get out of the car without looking like the cripple I feel. Of all the places to look weak, this isn't it, and this sure as shit isn't the moment.

So, I suck in a breath, adjust the cuffs at my wrist, and step towards my brothers.

"Looking good, bro," Leo comments, slapping his hand against my shoulder.

I stutter air back through my lungs, the pain duller than it once was, but no less significant as I pray to God nobody else does that in greeting.

"Thanks. You, too."

With the pleasantries out of the way, the five of us walk towards the front of the house; security opening the door as we near.

"Remember what I said," Leo says quietly, chucking Ruby under the chin. "Fucking own it."

With a nod, she pulls her shoulders back, remembering exactly who she is and where she's going to fit in around here. She's walking into the lion's den with three of the most feared men around—absolutely nothing to be worried about. I may not be fighting fit right now, but my reputation goes a long way.

Theresa meets us in the doorway—the woman who was more of a parent to all three of us than our fathers—cooing over how long it's been since Leo's been home, until she spies Ruby and Ivy, and then all bets are off. She's twirling them around and showing off how beautiful they are, and the three of us men may as well not even be here, until Josiah clears his throat.

"I didn't know we were having company," he says.

"Good job Theresa did, then, huh?" Leo replies, closing the distance and shaking his hand.

If he's surprised to see us or the girls here, he doesn't show it, but a poker face has always been Josiah's best attribute. Nothing shocks him. At least that's what he'd have us believe. I don't doubt that the news of Ruby's return to school on Friday made it back to him, and if he didn't know where she was before that I'd be surprised. But us turning up here has only been discussed between the three of us, and I'm reasonably sure any monitoring of our calls stopped some time ago at Leo's request.

I can feel the nervous energy coming off Ruby in waves, but, sandwiched between Blaise and me, she comes to meet her father's second in command—the one who really pulls the strings, as Theresa disappears to put the finishing touches to the dinner she's lovingly prepared.

Without a hint of intimidation, Josiah offers a hand out to Ivy. "So lovely to finally meet you, your reputation precedes you."

"I can't say yours does, but it's nice to meet you all the same," Ivy replies, placating him with a smile, ever the politician's daughter.

Bringing her in here isn't a concern of mine. She's been parading through the wolves for years. They're just a different variety to those inside these walls. Ruby, however, has never had to hold her own in a situation like this, and I can't help the unease that creeps around the edges of my consciousness.

"Josiah," he introduces himself, moving towards Ruby and shaking her hand, too. "But I already know who you are."

Of course he does, because he sent her to the Big Sister Programme and forced her hand into spying for him. He thinks we don't all know the history, but we do. There are no secrets between us now.

Ruby smiles, shakes his hand, then steps back, carving space between them. The urge to pull her into my arms and protect her from the threat around every corner is strong, but she's Leo's half-sister, and she needs to know what that means in here.

"I'll give you both the full tour later on," Leo adds. "Shall we?"

He slides Ivy's hand into his and leads us through to the library before dropping into a sofa with her effortlessly while the rest of us follow. Blaise speaks quietly to Josiah, leaving me to concentrate on getting Ruby comfortable and easing the tension that coils through her shoulders.

Brushing up her arm, I attempt to reassure her that she's safe as I gesture to one of the chairs and take up a post behind it, waiting for her to sit before taking in the rest of the room. Luckily, we don't have to wait long before Vincent joins us. Before we know it, he's dropping into the other chair with a harumph as Blaise and Josiah loiter by the door.

"Well, isn't this just special. Ivy, Ruby, nice to finally meet you both," Vincent says, but it's clear from his tone that he couldn't care less. "Shouldn't you take the weight off that leg, Dex?"

I bristle, but I'm not the one who bites as Leo clips out, "Yeah, he should," as he looks pointedly at his father.

I don't move, not willing to leave Ruby exposed.

"Suit yourself. Do you want to tell me what this little stunt is about now, or do I have to wait until we're all fed?" he asks, looking from Leo to Ivy and then Ruby.

I'm not sure either of the girls are likely to eat a great deal, too wrapped up in their concerns to be able to stomach anything, but I guess time will tell.

"I just thought it would be nice to show my half-sister around the place. Ivy figured she may as well tag along, too." Leo drops the statement like he just asked a friend round for a drink, not like he's just blown all his father's careful considerations up in smoke.

"Well, it took you long enough. That girl's been under your nose for most of the last nine months," Vincent dismisses flippantly.

If we were expecting some kind of reaction from him, we don't get it.

"That's it, is it? Took us long enough to work it out? You were just waving me in his face and hoping he'd put two and two together, but what about me?" Ruby asks, no sign of her earlier concerns in the car.

"What about you? You served your purpose."

It's one thing for us to know he's a dick and to warn her of it, but it's another to see the crestfallen look on her face, to see her heartbreak. She had all this hope for a family that gives a shit about her, but Vincent Windsor only cares about himself. I guess it's best she finds that out now.

"I'm sure you mother is around here somewhere. Maybe we should find her and make this a family reunion. Wouldn't that be nice?" Vincent asks, but we all know it wouldn't be.

Not for Ruby, not for Leo, and not for him, though he's always been one to cut off his nose to spite his face. It's why Josiah has been kept so close for so long. He's the one who stops this stupidity, usually. The man in question, however, is as silent as a grave.

"Yeah, lovely, so you can ignore her the way you have done me," Ruby clips out.

"Oh, I don't ignore her, darling. She's fucking good at what she does." He rubs at a spot beside his mouth, probably thinking of all the salacious things they get up to. Gross.

None of this is getting us anywhere.

I cast a look at Leo, hoping he's going to make a move here. As much as watching Ruby stand up to her father makes me hard, watching her get shot down doesn't, and there are only so many times she's going to be able to take him doing that before it becomes personal.

I think the mantra she's rocking today is *fake it 'til you make it,* or something along those lines. Even so, I can already see the cracks in the façade she's wearing.

"The Five Families know who she is, and she's got full-time security in place. Is there any reason Ruby can't go on with her life like she wants to?" Leo asks.

Or are Pendleton Prep going to turn up and demand her presence at some point?

"And what, pray tell, has been discussed with the Five Families without my approval?" Vincent asks, his irritation flashing towards his only son.

"Nothing yet, but I made it very clear to everyone I crossed paths with exactly who I am," Ruby replies. "Any *negotiations* regarding my safety aren't my issue. I just want to be able to go about my life unimpeded."

Nodding, Vincent ponders his answer for a moment, looking over his youngest child with new eyes.

"Dinner is served," Theresa says brightly from the doorway, sticking her head through with a smile and interrupting the conversation.

Vincent doesn't wait for anyone else before he stands and storms out, leading the way. Leo winks at Ruby as I hold a hand out for her to join me, needing that brief moment of connection before we get any further. She's got this.

Josiah and Blaise go first, the rest of us following as Leo points out room after room to Ivy and Ruby, neither of them taking any of them in. If I could keep them both out of this house forever, I would, but I doubt it's going to be that easy.

Vincent sits at the head of the table, with Josiah and his

wife to his left while Leo takes his spot to his father's right. Ivy tucks in next to him, and Ruby slots herself carefully between Blaise and me, making the table as uneven as fuck, but who cares?

Food is served, conversations begin to flow, and the relief at getting sat down is unbelievable. They weren't wrong; I really shouldn't be standing on this leg, and I'm quietly confident that I've already bled through the bandage my mother put on before we left. I don't dare to look though. I couldn't do anything about it if I did, so why bother?

Josiah's wife Lynette asks Ruby and Ivy about their studies and their hopes for the future, and they answer as best as they can, but the entire meal is stilted and awkward. I'm still not sure what we ever expected from this, but having Ruby this close to Vincent is making me twitchy.

twenty-four
Ruby

L ynette seems nice, even if she is completely oblivious.

She asks the right questions and seems to be complicit in gathering information, but it doesn't feel to be intentional on her part. Luckily for us, Ivy is much better than I am at diverting the conversation back towards her and Josiah, attempting to glean as much as she can back. It's definitely something I'm going to need to work on if I'm going to be a part of this life.

But is that really what I want?

I've spent so much time hiding in the shadows, hoping everyone would just pass me by, that all of this standing in the limelight feels unnatural to me. Maybe that's what the time with Ivy and the Big Sister programme was supposed to be teaching me: how to function in society.

Ridiculous really that the only reason I was there was to gather information about Ivy and Leo, and now they're the ones here helping me, pushing me out into the world—with Dex, of course. His silent strength at my side bolsters me every time I start to feel myself waver, and right now, that's plenty.

The meal takes significantly longer than I expect and, as fabulous as I'm sure all the food is, I can barely taste it. Everything turns to ash in my mouth the longer this façade continues, and by the time coffee rolls around, and Vincent is suggesting a whiskey in his office, I'm more than ready to get this done.

"I'm going to get Lynette home if you don't need me?" Josiah says, looking to his boss for an answer, but he's dismissed with nothing more than the nod of his head.

"Well, then, boys. Shall we?" Vincent asks. "Dex, can you settle the girls in the den?"

He doesn't even bother to make eye contact with Ivy or me before standing and walking out.

"You knew he'd do this," Dex whispers by my side, reminding me of all the conversations we've had this week. "Leo's got this."

Just let him do the negotiating. He knows the stakes better than anyone, and after all the time he's spent asking me twenty-four trillion questions, he probably knows me as well as I know myself now.

So, trust the process, trust the man who's offering to give me everything I've ever asked for, almost. It's harder than it sounds, and it doesn't come naturally, so with a nervous nod and a deep breath, I risk one last glance at Leo and stand.

"Let's go see who's loitering about," Leo comments, threading Ivy's fingers through his.

While following them, I'm struck by how strange it

is seeing them so comfortably together. Sure, Leo's been around some of the time, but there's always been a weird tension between the two of them and the rest of their group that now seems to have dissipated. They're finally at ease with each other.

I guess it took them long enough to admit how they really feel for each other, and maybe that's all anyone needs: someone on their side no matter what. I guess I have that now, too.

The four of us make our way through the rabbit warren that is the place Leo called home. The building my mother knows as well as our own. It's strange to think that she's here somewhere, sitting in a drawing room with her friends and a glass of wine, laughing and joking, forgetting that I'm even an issue.

Leo grabs one of the guards as we pass and pulls the five of us into a sitting room. Plush sofa's line the room, and old movie posters hang from the walls, but it's the ease with which both he and Dex relax in here that makes this an instant safe space.

"James, can you and D keep an eye on these two for me? I've got to go to war," Leo says, looking at the black-clad guard as he kisses Ivy on the cheek. "I promise they'll be good."

"I make no such promise," I counter, even as nerves flutter in my stomach at the thought of being left alone in here.

"Me neither," Ivy adds with a wink.

Dex gestures for me to sit on one of the sofa's and makes himself comfortable in one of the chairs within perfect view of the doorway—ever the protector—while Leo continues a quiet conversation with his friend. All too soon, it's the four of us in the silent room, listening to Leo's footsteps echoing down the hallway.

"So, ladies. How are we enjoying our first trip to the compound?" James asks, his interest clear. "Did the boys show you around the gardens yet?"

"We've not really had the time," Ivy replies, but before we have time to delve any further into the conversation, we're interrupted.

"Heard you were in the building." Some guy winks as he crosses the room, shaking Dex's hand before looking around. "Is Leo around, too?" He's a slimy-looking man, with sharp features and beady eyes that take in far too much when they head towards Ivy and me.

"Yeah, office," Dex replies, disinterested. It's clear he doesn't like this guy. It's clear to me at least, because he barely spares him a second glance, his gaze trained on where James is sitting beside me.

I know Leo said we'd be okay in here with him, but what about everyone else loitering around the house?

"You must be the girlfriend. Ivy, is it?" the slimy, beady-eyed man asks, walking towards Ivy, his gaze running over her appreciatively before turning to me with a sneer on his face. "This one's far too young to be his type, but I'd take her for a spin."

"Just because you have no standards, Tony, doesn't mean the rest of us don't," James quips, cutting any retort I may have had off.

"Can't say I've got a thing for family. Gross," I add,

nudging Ivy's shoulder and winking conspiratorially at James. Fake it until you make it and all that.

"Family? You must be Rita's girl, then, huh? Better watch yourself there, James. She'll be looking to climb the ladder, too."

"Tony," James says with warning.

"Excuse me?" I interrupt.

I may be willing to let Leo lead the negotiations for my freedom, as if such a thing should be needed in the twenty-first century, and whilst I've been berated and dismissed by the man who's apparently nothing more than the donor of half my genetic material, I'm not going to be spoken to like that by this slick prick.

"I'm sure the apple doesn't fall far from the tree. You'll be trying to climb your way to the top on your back just like she is any minute," Tony replies, smirking.

"So, what you're telling me is that my mother is nothing more than a money-grabbing whore?" I ask, pocketing my rage and letting it simmer beneath the surface of my skin.

"Perhaps—" Ivy tries to intervene.

"That's not very nice," I add, cutting her off.

Leo said to own my position here, and letting these idiots walk all over me and talk shit about my mother isn't in my nature. I guess, considering his position in this building, it's not supposed to be.

"True, though." Tony shrugs, looking at James and Dex for some back up, but neither of them look impressed. In fact, Dex looks like he's half a second away from flattening him where he stands.

Scratching my ankle has me debating sliding the silver

knife from my boot and stabbing it somewhere soft, until I see the shake of Dex's head in my periphery. *Bad idea, then, huh?* Instead, I stand, cutting Tony off before he can get any closer to Ivy.

"You're a pretty little thing, though. Maybe I could help you with that climb," he offers.

Fucking idiot.

He certainly doesn't expect the fist that comes flying his way, and it may not be as effective as Dex's or Blaise's, but he stumbles back, surprise crossing his features before they harden.

He takes a step closer, and I suddenly realise that could have been a mistake. Just because Dex has been keeping me safe all this time doesn't mean there's a no hitting women policy in here, but I'm too incensed to care.

Who the fuck does he think he is?

Some overpaid door manager who can get away with calling my mum a whore? I don't think so. She may not have been the best mum in the world—the maternal instincts are not strong here—but she's turned up most of the time and done her best in her own way.

She's not be perfect, but she's done one hell of a better job than the sperm donor of a man that is mine and Leo's father.

"That was for my mum, and this one, is for me." I swing again, but he's ready for it this time and grabs my first as it nears his jaw, thinking he's got the upper hand. But I knew he would, so I'm already preparing for the next move. Peeling my foot back, I slam it into his kneecap, and he drops like a sack of shit, a strangled cry dragging from his lips.

"I'm not fucking anyone to the top, and I want absolutely nothing to do with any of this or any of you. Don't get me confused with any of those compliant girls you usually have coming through those doors, because I'm so far from that I'll give you whiplash." I hiss as James chuckles from behind me, clapping twice.

"Oh, and here I was thinking Leo wanted *me* to behave. Little did I know he was talking about you," James says as I step back and let him look over my hand.

I can tell that Dex wants to be the one doing it, and that having someone else's skin against mine burns him. It's in the twitch of his fingers on the arm of the chair and the way his jaw clenches in my periphery, but he lets me have this moment and own the win in front of his colleague.

"I think he was talking about me, actually," Ivy says with a cringe. "Apparently, having these guys behind me has given me a big mouth, but it looks like it comes to Ruby just naturally."

I can't help the amusement that bubbles up from beneath the surface as I bark out a laugh, even more confused when she peels one heeled-foot up and presses it against Tony's chest.

"I wouldn't recommend that," she adds, pushing him back onto his arse.

I hadn't even realised he'd moved, but I'm not alone here, and the realisation sinks warmth right into me. I'm not alone. They may not be the mother and father I was hoping for, but a couple of good friends, a half-brother, and the family he's created seem like all the family I need.

"Fuck off, Tony," Dex calls from his seat in the corner. "Nobody's interested in your shit here."

"You're gonna let her get away with that?" he splutters out, holding his knee as he looks from Dex to James for backup, but it's clear to everyone in this room it's not coming.

"Let her? You just pissed off Leo's half-sister. Do you really want to explain that shit to him?" James asks as he presses along my knuckles.

"And if that wasn't the nail in your coffin, irritating his girlfriend was," Dex adds. "Get the fuck out before one of us throws you out, and how bad is that going to look when it's one of the girls?"

"You two seriously suck," Tony grumbles as he picks himself up and limps out of the room.

"Remind me not to piss you two off," James comments. "Your hand will be fine, by the way."

"Thanks. On both counts."

The smile that crosses my face feels genuine for the first time today, and I can't help the look I flash towards Dex any more than he can stop the wink he returns, pride sitting well on his face.

"I'm not sure this is quite the 'keeping you out of trouble' I was tasked with, though, so maybe we should just find something to watch on TV?" James offers, holding the remote out to Ivy and me like a peace offering.

There's no way the two of us are going to agree on anything to watch, so I just hand it over to her and sink into the sofa, letting the conversations happening about my future behind closed doors that I don't get to be a part of fall to the wayside.

There are some things I can do something about, like mouthy idiots, and some things I can't. For now, I just need to sit, wait, and hope Leo is right.

twenty-five

Dex

Ruby rolls her eyes again at whatever Ivy picked on the TV, but she can't fool me. I see the sneaky smiles that slip free when she thinks nobody is looking. She fucking loves this cheesy shit. Luckily for us, James cares just enough about Leo to do anything for him, but not so much that he'd threaten his happiness, which means he was the perfect person to wrap these two up with for the last hour. An hour that has ticked away at a snail's pace whilst I watch the minute hand go around on the clock and do my best not to ponder too deeply on to the conversations going on right now, and where the two of us are going to end up following it.

If Leo manages to secure her safety, then she won't need me anymore. If she goes away to college like she wants to, I won't be able to slip into her room at night anymore. So, even though I want her to be safe from the threat of the Five Families and The Sect, I don't want her to be free from me.

I don't want her to ride off into the sunset with Scarlett,

Leo, and Ivy.

She means something to me, more than she was ever supposed to, and I don't know how to extricate myself from the pain that's going to come with her leaving, because there's no way I'm going to be able to follow. Vincent won't allow it.

Leo's jaw is tight when he makes it back to us, thanking James and greatly appreciating the suggestion of a walk around the grounds. At least that way we're not going to be overheard.

As the four of us make our way through the house, Leo explains that Blaise had a couple of things to finalise before heading home and would need half an hour or so. Works for us, I guess.

If I thought watching the minutes tick away on the clock was hard work, then the ones until we make it far enough away from the house are torture. I light up and pass Leo his smokes, even though I know he's been trying to quit. If Ivy doesn't appreciate it, she doesn't say anything, just wafts the cloud away from herself, and ducks under his arm like this is any other trip around the grounds.

If only.

My impatience makes me irritable, and so does the pain that comes from limping along behind them while doing my best to keep up and not reach for Ruby—another source of my foul mood. I want to wrap her up in my arms and whisper my truths in her hair, hoping they'd be enough to keep her here, but I know they won't.

"Welcome to the fountains," Leo declares as we turn the final corner.

This is not only somewhere which will muffle any listening devices around, but also somewhere I can get the weight off this leg. What a fucking star. And he knows it, if the smile he sends my way is anything to go by.

While perching myself on the edge of the nearest pond, I resist the urge to pull Ruby into my arms. She needs to hear this update without my interference, and if she still wants me around afterwards, so be it.

"Well…" Ivy prods, nudging Leo's side as she gestures to Ruby, the three of us waiting on tenterhooks.

"Well, what?"

"What was said?" she asks, catching the tick of his jaw.

"It wasn't good, was it?" Ruby asks, defeat pulling at her shoulders as she seems to shrink in on herself. "I knew it was a long shot, that you couldn't really barter this for me. I guess it was never going to be."

"I'm not sure I'd call it a complete bust," Leo says, stepping towards Ruby and taking her hands in his. "You're going to college."

"I'm… what? Shit. Fuck. No… I'm going to college!" Ruby exclaims excitedly as she jumps up and down on the spot.

It's the most excited I've ever seen her, but the disappointment I wish I didn't feel sours the moment. I wish she wasn't going. I wish she could be mine.

"You did it. We did it," she continues, letting go of his hands and coming to me. She rests her hands on my cheeks, looking deep into my soul and not finding the joy she expected when she whispers again, "We did it."

"Congratulations, baby girl. You're gonna be amazing."

"What's the catch?" she asks, keeping hold of me, but turning towards Leo, bracing herself for the other shoe to drop, knowing there's no way that she's being handed her freedom this easily.

"You'll be living off-campus with some security of my choosing. I'm assuming after that little debacle, we can take Tony off the list of potentials, right?" He smirks, catching her look. "And that's it. You are a member of this family, and you're going to be treated like it. Especially now all our enemies know who you are."

"Just like that?"

She's right to be wary, but she doesn't understand the height of the position Leo's in, and that she's about to be alongside. On the plus side, you can plan and prepare for the dangers you know about.

"Do I at least get a say in who comes with me?" she asks, looking back at me briefly.

"There's no way in hell our father is sending Dex out on bodyguard duty."

And that's what it boils down to in the end.

Leo's going to take over, Blaise is going to support him, and I'm going to be the one watching both their backs. We've always been a unit, a trifecta, and it's never been an issue... until the moment I wanted something for myself.

"What? Why?" Ivy asks, noting the excitement that rippled through Ruby just a moment ago is now pouring out of her like the water running through the fountains beside us.

"He's way too skilled for that," Leo replies tactfully.

I'm *the ghost*. Never seen, always acknowledged. I can

get in and get out, and the only people who see me are the ones who aren't going to live to tell the tale. It's a reputation that has served me well over the years. Sad, then, that it could be the reason I lose the one thing I've always wanted.

"Well, I'm not going without him." Ruby throws the challenge down like Leo hasn't just gone to war for her, pulled every string, and shot down every argument, but he has no jurisdiction over the associates. Not yet, anyway.

"Why?"

I can see the pieces lining up in Leo's mind as one second drags into two. I watch as he notices the placement of my hand on Ruby's thigh, hers on my face, the closeness he hadn't even registered because he was too wrapped up in the high of the news he was holding on to.

And I get it. There aren't many opportunities for men like us get to give good news to someone, so in the moments when we do, everything else is forgotten until reality snaps back into place.

"Because he saved me. Because he's kept me safe," Ruby answers.

"That was his job," Leo snaps, irritated that he's missed something so obvious.

I was intentionally vague with him when we walked these gardens together at Christmas and Leo asked me who and what she was to me. Partly because I honestly wasn't ready to admit how I felt even to myself, and partly because I couldn't tell him who she was, full stop.

He needed to finish his trials with The Sect and cement his position of power before he could do anything with that information. So, I held on to it, kept the secret I'd been tasked with like the ghost I'm supposed to be.

"And before then? What about that?" Ruby asks.

As much as we both know that this has been building between us a long time before I was tasked with keeping her safe, nobody else does. Hell, Leo didn't even know she was his blood a week ago. Throwing our extended *relationship* in his face is not going to stop the black eye I'm likely to walk away with.

"Go to college, Ruby. Go and live your life and be free. That's what you want," I tell her quietly.

She rears back, hurt rippling across her features as her hand drops from my skin, the reality of what comes next is a hell of a lot worse than I ever expected it to be, because I can practically feel the loss of her already.

"No." The slap of her skin against mine gets eaten up by the flow of the water, the heat blossoming on my cheek lasting nothing more than a moment before it dissipates. "You don't get to tell me who or what I can do with my life, either. I'm Ruby fucking Sheridan, and I'm going to art college, and you're coming with me."

"There's no place for me there."

"Your place is with me. It always has been," she replies quietly.

The logical part of me knows that Leo and Ivy are here, watching, but the rest of me doesn't care as I slide my hand through the hair at her nape and pull her down to press my lips against hers gently—a promise that this isn't over, but telling her that I can't hold her back, either.

"Always, baby girl, but this isn't my call or my decision. It would be up to Vincent whether I would be put

346   HEATHER PACKER

on rotation."

"Erm, is it not Leo's decision?" Ivy asks. "If he's the one picking your security detail, then isn't it down to him?"

Something warm twists in my stomach, and I dare to hope that there's a chance for us. That this might become something permanent.

"If he's too qualified for a bodyguard position, there's got to be something else he could do, right? Head of security? Or... I dunno, college liaison?" Ivy suggests, grasping at straws that we never even knew were there.

Leo's intense gaze finally catches mine, an understanding behind his eyes that wasn't there earlier on. "I'm going to ask you this again: what is she to you?"

I could lie and say she's a friend, a girlfriend, or that she's become something more over time, but there's only one answer that feels right in my bones. Only one word that explains everything she means to me and more.

"Mine. Ruby, is mine."

I'm not fully aware of how close we've become until she twists in my grip, turning to look at her brother, to plead, once again, her case. Only this time, it's for me.

"And Dex is mine. I'm not going without him," Ruby declares.

"Nick warned me that siblings were a pain in the arse," Leo grumbles. "Are you going to be able to keep a clear enough head about this shit if I make you head of security? And let's be clear: if there's something I need, then you're on my arse first."

"He's kept me safe so far, hasn't he?" Ruby replies, but it's my answer he wants because he knows I'll only give him the truth as best I can.

"I'm yours if you need me, but overseeing her security would be more than I ever considered," I admit, shoving the emotion this stirs up deep down inside.

I always thought this would be the end and that she'd be walking away from me. I never even entertained thoughts of going with her because I knew Vincent would never let me, even if it was just to keep Leo safe. Priorities and all that. His daughter has never been one before. Why should she be now?

"Fuck me, I can't believe I'm considering this. What if you change your mind in six months? What if he was nothing more than your saviour, and once you get out into the big wide world you see something else you want?" Leo asks Ruby.

"I won't."

"And you? What if you decide she's too much hard work and you should have stayed well away? You think you're going to be able to walk back into his arms and workforce? This is going to cause an absolute shit storm, and you know it. There's no strolling back through the doors here, heading to collections, and working your stress out on some poor fuck's face."

"I know," I admit. It's not like I never thought about it, I just didn't dare dwell on it too long. "She's mine, and that's never going to change."

"Honestly, you can coordinate the security and head it up, but if so much as a single hair is out of place on her head, we're gonna have problem."

"You seriously think I'm going to let anything happen

to her after all this?" I ask, gesturing to the state of my face, my chest, and my leg.

He can't see the bruises because they're all covered up by the suit, but he saw enough when it was all still fresh to know the hell I've walked through this week. At his father's hands. To keep his sister safe. *Not* because she's his half-sister, but because she's *mine*... my everything.

"Well, just because you say that now doesn't mean it won't change at some point."

"You changing your mind about Jacob?" I ask, irritated. "Or Nick. Ivy, maybe? I didn't think so. Let's not dismiss this out of hand, shall we?"

Leo clenches his jaw, his irritation matching my own, and I'm more than ready for this rollercoaster of a fucking day to be over.

Ruby's going to college, and I'm going with her. Breaking that news to my mother and Blaise is going to be a whole task in and of itself. Blaise is not going to take well to the news of me leaving, especially under the circumstances, but hopefully he sees the same sense in it that Leo clearly does, even if he's having a hard time reconciling the relationship neither of us intended on being in.

"So... he can come?" Ruby asks, her excitement seeping back into the conversation.

"Yeah, he can go."

Ruby does an excited little dance between my thighs, punching the air and wiggling her hips with her little victory. Gotta take them where you can, I suppose.

"So, this is the guy, huh?" Ivy asks Ruby, some kind of coded conversation happening between them as she catches her attention.

I wonder how much she knows about Ruby and me, about the quiet months before the shit hit the fan. I guess time will tell. Leo and Ivy may well already have a relationship built with Ruby, but that's going to change significantly now they all know the truth. Family ties are different.

"This is the guy," Ruby confirms, dropping her arms over my shoulders.

"Well, this guy is going to need to get back and get this dressing changed before he bleeds through his favourite dress pants."

"And this guy better get his girl home before everyone else starts to panic," Leo adds.

"Too late," Ivy adds with a smile, checking her phone. "The group chat is going crazy."

"Only you could need a group chat to keep up with your harem," I comment, barking out a laugh that cracks across my chest.

The only friends Leo had growing up were Blaise and me. The three of us were so tightly knit, it took a secret society to ply us apart. We've never needed anyone else, never wanted anyone else either, until he strolled into that place and fell in love with a girl, a guy, and a few others along the way.

"And only you could fall for the one girl so far off limits, it's not even funny," he counters.

Falling for anyone has never been on my radar. The only thing I've ever been interested in is keeping those I care about safe, until now.

"I'm right here, you know?" Ruby interjects.

"Yeah, yeah. Well, bring it in to your big brother, because I've got more good news."

Awkwardly, Ruby steps out of my embrace and heads to Leo, letting him drape an arm over her shoulder before he continues.

"Seen as your now officially a member of the family, your new bank account will be set up this week, and the matching credit card will be with you a few days after. Until then, you can use mine."

He hands her the shiny black card, and I watch as wonder mixed with concern flicks across her face. This is more money than she's ever had access to in her life. She could go on a serious spree and still barely hit the limit on that thing.

Money has never been an issue for Leo—Ivy, neither, if my research is anything to go by—but for Ruby... well, it's been there. She just never knew about or had access to it. Now, she's free to do what she wants with it.

"D will need to get you a driver sorted out for college, but Marcus is going to be looking after you until then. If you can cope with Carl and Rob as your temporary security, then I'm sure they'll be happy to stick around in the short term."

"A driver *and* security? So, this is a permanent thing, then? Not just a right now for show kinda deal."

"No, this is a for the duration thing. You're worth a lot to someone who wants to barter with Vincent or use you as blackmail. None of that shit is good, and none of it is going to come your way so long as we keep you safe."

"You don't have a driver and security," she argues,

looking up at him, even as he directs her towards the path and back towards the house.

"I can drive, and I'm more lethal than anyone interested in using me to barter with, and they know it, but that's not something I want for you."

The training we went through is not something I want Ruby anywhere fucking near, either.

"You can come to the gym with me and join me in the self-defence classes," Ivy intervenes before Ruby can delve any further into his statement.

"We're about to head a whole bunch of miles away, angel, but I suppose the two of you could get a couple of months basic training in if you wanted to?" Leo offers.

"Will that mean I don't need your security?" Ruby asks, her freedom clearly coming with concessions she wasn't planning on making.

"No," Leo and I reply together.

As if remembering I'm still here, Leo closes the distance between us, helping me up from the edge of the pool and shaking my hand, only to punch me squarely in the chest and knock all the air out of my lungs.

"That's for keeping fucking secrets. We'll talk about fucking my sister when you're all healed up."

I think it's safe to say that talk will be mostly with our fists.

"Wouldn't expect any less," I croak out, doing my best to breathe.

Ruby rushes over, slapping Leo around the back of the head before shoving him away and checking me over. If I ever thought there would be a moment where someone could hit him and walk away, I never pictured it like this.

The four of us make our way back to the house, the girls filling Leo in on the debacle with Tony while Ruby and I walk hand-in-hand. She's got everything she wanted, including me. Why not flaunt it now?

Blaise is waiting in the kitchen when we get back, one ankle kicked over the other as he types in his phone, his head rising as we join him.

"Ready?"

"Ready."

Now just to break the news to him...

twenty-six
Ruby

"So, you've got everything you ever wanted, and I've got sixth form with Nathaniel Peregrine breathing down my neck. Life is so unfair," Scarlett moans, dropping her head onto her forearms dramatically.

The table beside us give her a wary glance before noticing the way Carl's weight moves from one foot to the other behind me and turning quickly back to their revision books. Technically, we don't even have to be here because we've finally reached the holy grail that is study leave, except the only place either of us seem to be able to get any space to breathe is back at school, in the library. Go figure.

"Did you ever get a reply from the college?"

"No, but I was right. Someone intercepted my acceptance letter and did... I don't know what they did with it, but they never gave it to me."

"How did you work that one out?"

"I called and asked." She shrugs, looking at me like, *duh,* before dropping her head back against her hands. "It's so unfair."

"Sorry, chick. I wish there was something I could do."

"You can't use your newfound powers to talk my father into letting me out of his sights? Or maybe you could sweet talk Nate, seen as he still thinks you're his girl."

"He does not."

We totally talked about that… didn't we?

"He was bigging it up in the chat about how he survived a date with the daughter of Vincent Windsor and lived to tell the tale," she argues, peeking one eye open.

"Dramatic, much?"

"Totally."

"But I definitely talked to him… I think."

"You're not sounding so sure there, my friend. I can ask him to pop in if that helps?"

"How the fuck would that help?" I ask, trying my best not to draw any more attention to us, but I'm not sure how these guys would act if Nate were to waltz in here and join us.

Not that I want him to.

Not like that, anyway. He's a nice guy, as far as they go. Of course, it seems like the Five Families have been keeping a closer eye on me than I realised, but I'm sure that wasn't what our ice cream trip was about.

Either way, the possessive way Dex kissed me this morning before handing me off to my security detail did all the telling that needed to happen on any relationship Nate or anyone else thought I'd be having. Although, there wasn't the usual gaggle of girls loitering around to see it and spend the rest of the day breaking every second of it down to throw back in my face, which means even that may have missed his attention. Great.

"Do we really have to do this now?"

"No time like the present."

"Isn't he likely to be studying just like we're supposed to be?" I ask as she grabs her phone, fingers already flying across the keys

"Yes, but luckily for us, he's on site today, too. Something about the chem lab notes or, I dunno…" She trails off.

"Let's wrap this up. I'm not going to get anything done with this looming over my head. And what kind of chat group do you guys have going on? I never realised the two of you were close-close."

"Oh, we're not."

Except he was the one who introduced her to Jeremy, and he was the one who was chatting with us at the track night, not the guy she was supposed to be there with.

"Sure seems like it…"

I leave it open for her to fill in the gaps, but I know how annoying it is when people ask questions you aren't ready to answer. Ivy did it for months. So, when she does nothing more than shrug her shoulders, I leave it.

If or when something appears between them, I'll do my best to not say *I told you so.*

"Princess," Nate calls as the library door bangs closed.

Subtle as ever.

The librarian throws him a warning hush, and more than one table shushes him as he passes, whistling happily before he drops into the seat opposite me.

"Ask and you shall receive. What can I do for you lovely ladies this fine afternoon?"

"Why are you so chipper? Actually, scratch that. I don't want to know," I say, changing my mind once the words are out of my mouth. There are some things you just don't need to hear. "You know there's nothing going on between us, right?" I throw it out there.

"As wounded as that makes me, princess, we are on different sides of this line, and there's no way I could ever go there. Sorry."

"Good."

"And if that wasn't already enough, what was it you called him?" he asks, looking at Scarlett before clicking his fingers as he finally remembers. "Man-mountain. If that wasn't enough, then your man-mountain made a pit stop at my place and made it abundantly clear how unavailable you are."

"Of course, he did."

He's already been warned away, and that's why neither Carl nor Rob batted an eyelid at Nate joining us. I can just picture how that went down, too. Fucking men.

"So, I guess I was right, too. Princess is a perfectly apt nickname."

"Really?" I ask, just as Scarlett bursts out laughing.

"And here you were thinking it should have been my nickname when all along you were the one that should be wearing it. Welcome to the club, sis." Scarlett offers a fist out for me to bump, and I take it with a small smile and a shake of my head.

There's no point arguing with her. Especially not when

she's right, and we both know it.

"You're running with it, then?" Nate asks, gesturing to the two huge guys loitering not nearly as in the background as I would like.

"No choice if I want to get on with my life."

"Do you think Daddy would let me walk off into the sunset if I had a couple of man-mountains of my own?" Scarlett asks dreamily.

"No," I reply, just as Nate says, "Not in a million years."

"At least you two can agree on something. Shame it has to be my downfall."

"A couple more years keeping me company isn't exactly the end of the world, is it?" Nate asks, nudging her shoulder with his.

"No," she concedes.

"At least your brothers won't be here anymore. That's got to give you both more freedom, right?" I offer.

"Probably not," they reply in unison.

"Okay, this is getting weird. If you could, like, stop sharing a brain or whatever is going on right now, that would be great."

It was strange enough when they were friendlier than I expected. Now they're even starting to sound the same.

"We don't share a brain, but we do share a lifestyle," Scarlett admits.

"I mean, mine is a bit more involved than yours, but that's out of choice. I can one hundred percent guarantee that if you asked to help your brother at the races like I did you'd be shot down instantly," Nate argues.

"Like I want anything to do with that noisy, smelly

mess," she complains, tapping her pen against the notebook in front of her.

"It was an example, but the response would be the same no matter what you asked to be involved with on our side of the projects."

"I wonder if Brent and Damien are any less misogynistic?" she ponders, pursing her lips as if deep in thought, but we all know that's not a line she'd cross.

The divide between the two halves of the Five Families is deeply entrenched, and whilst I have no idea what started it, even I know there's no way the two sides will ever swap notes, never mind a person.

You'd have to pray hard for any person that might end up as an olive branch between those two sides, and there's no way in hell I'll be sitting by idly if they decide it's Scarlett. I've got power now, and influence—something I'm going to need to learn to wield better if I'm going to need to keep her safe, too.

"I think we can safely say they aren't," Nate clips out, folding his arms across his chest.

A blonde at the table over from us throws an unimpressed look in our direction before whispering, "*Hush,*" and going back to her books. This was probably not the best location for this conversation, but we're here now.

"Back on topic, mind-swappers. You two are going to be happy little campers next year, and I'm going to run away to college. Nate was never under any false impressions, and as fabulous as you both know I am, I'm taken. Are we all on the same page now?"

"Perfectly," Nate replies as Scarlett glowers at him,

stealing the words out of her mouth when she slams it shut again. "So, what now?"

"Now, I've got notes to go over. Don't you?"

"Yes," he grumbles, looking at the books spread out over the table. "Got space for another?"

"I guess we'll have to find space," I reply, piling a couple of my books together as Scarlett shuffles hers beneath an open notepad.

And that's how the three of us spend the next hour, going over notes and re-reading text books before eventually giving in and finding a side room to quiz each other on our crossover subjects before we get thrown out for being too noisy.

"Well, only a trillion more subjects to go," I comment with a sigh.

"At least some of yours are portfolio based. All of mine are academic and boil down to this exam and the assessments I've already got in," Nate replies with an unimpressed huff.

"Yeah, but I've been building that portfolio for two years. That's a whole shit-tonne of work right there."

"Don't doubt it. Not trying to argue. Just saying that I've got a little bit more riding on these results, that's all," he replies, holding his hands up in surrender. "Please don't sic the man-mountains on me."

His silliness breaks the tension that's been building in this small, enclosed room, our futures looming over us ominously, even though it feels like there's nothing we can do about them.

"We need to get out of here. All this stress isn't going to help any of us. We need to find something fun to do and shake the stress off," I muse.

"Ooh, there's a song right there, but I think I have the perfect place. Do your big fellas drive?" Nate asks. "I'm not up for a walk with all this lot."

I'm not sure if it's something Dex or Leo said to them, but both Carl and Rob have warmed to Scarlett over the last week or so. Once we're all packed up and ready to go on Nate's magical mystery tour, they take her bag of books and mine and follow the three of us down the corridor, out into the muggy, pre-summer air.

Nate raises an eyebrow when he's left to carry his own but gets on with it without complaint, no doubt tucking that bit of information into his back pocket for later. I hate that I question the motivation behind every conversation, but I'm doing my best to act like everyone is on my side until they prove otherwise.

Scarlett and I are ushered in to the back of the car whilst Nate has a quiet word with Rob, and I know for certain there's no way he's going to take us anywhere with any inherent danger. Still, when the three of them climb in and Rob starts the engine, I'm surprised.

"Do we get any clues on this mystery location?" Scarlett asks as I watch out of the window, squished between the two of them.

Nates arm presses up against mine, and Scarlett shuffles to one side to give me a little more room. Who knew the guy was so broad once you got him in a confined space? Scarlett, if this is anything to go by.

"It's cold, but also kind of not."

"Helpful."

As we make our way towards the sea front, it suddenly makes sense, though.

"You just want to know if you were right, don't you?" I ask, thinking of the place he brought me just a few weeks ago. A few weeks that feel like a lifetime.

"I can neither confirm nor deny," he argues, a mischievous twinkle in his eye.

"I love this place," Scarlett coos as the three of us pile out the back of the car and into the ice cream shop, Carl doing his obligatory walk around before anyone dares release me from the safety of the vehicle.

Nate raises an eyebrow at the lemon sorbet I choose but keeps his opinions to himself this time while he waits excitedly, watching Scarlett as she peers through the glass at the boxes of ice cream like a kid in a sweet shop.

She orders the raspberry ripple, like I knew she would—two scoops, in a tub, with extra sprinkles—and Nate opts for double chocolate in a waffle cone with a flake sticking out of the top this time. Matching big kids.

"I'm not interested in what my sorbet flavour tells you about me, and I definitely don't want to analyse that monstrosity of an ice cream for too long, either," I say as we walk out, Rob and Carl both adamantly refusing ice creams while mumbling something about professionalism under their breaths.

As much as they're turning down the offer, I'm quietly confident they're not going to refuse something I've bought them. Next time, I'll get them one and ask after.

"Can we walk on the sand?" Scarlett asks, but she's already handing Carl her tub and unlacing her sandals.

Where my black skinny jeans and heavy boots do not suggest summer has arrived, her sundress does, and once she swaps her shoes for her ice cream, leaving Carl looking very confused, she skips onto the sand.

With a shrug of his shoulders, Nate slips off his trainers and joins her, the two of them looking at me expectantly.

"Great. I'll be picking sand out of places it was never supposed to be for hours when I get back." Grumbling, I unlace the boots and stuff my socks inside, carefully moving the blade up my sleeve, hoping nobody notices as I do.

Rob takes the boots before I even manage to hook my fingers in them, gesturing with his head for the steps down. The two of them are huge, but their looming presence has seemed less and less obvious over our time together. Maybe I'm just getting used to them?

Whatever it is, walking across the beach with two of my friends as the sun does its best to warm the earth could only be made better by one other person being here. And, as if summoned by nothing more than my thoughts, he loiters at the next set of steps down, trainers in hand.

"Mind if I join?" he asks, sliding his fingers through mine.

I don't know where the butterflies come from, or how girly they suddenly feel, but the heat the look on his face causes to ripple through me is dangerous.

"How odd that you happen to be on this beach, at this time," Scarlett comments with a smirk. "It's almost like someone tipped you off."

"Don't know what you mean," Dex replies, offering a nod to Nate.

"Oh, it's like that, is it?" she asks, looking between the two of them. "I get to keep my frenemy, so you're going to make yourself one, too, huh?"

"Frenemy?"

"You're the enemy who became my friend…"

"I'm not sure I ever realised I was your enemy."

"Not in so many words, and not in any way I'd have let someone act on," she counters, seeing the spiral before I even head that far down it. "Okay, bad choice of words, but you know what I mean."

"I think so."

Dex squeezes my hand, reminding me of the strength I own and the woman I'm becoming. I don't need to let what other people used to think of me mean anything. Scarlett is my friend, and so is Nate. The hows and whys of that are no longer important, and I'm not going to give them any more time. They don't deserve it.

twenty-seven

Dex

The car door bangs with a finality I'm not ready for. As much as I knew this moment would come, I still feel unprepared. I'm not sure I ever would be, but having her here and in my space has finally made home feel complete.

"Are you sure this is the right thing to do? You know you can just stay here, right?"

We've gone through this conversation at least a dozen times already, and it always ends the same, just like this.

"It's not forever. It's only a couple of months until we move into the new place."

"Do you think we could get the keys early? That way I can get everything set up ahead of your schedule starting in September. I'm sure the boys would appreciate the extra time to scout everything out and get used to the routes for your classes."

"I'm reasonably sure that Blaise will have a fucking heart attack if you leave any earlier than you need to," she replies, rounding the car and leaning against the boot, arms crossed against her chest.

She's right, of course, but still, this place is going to feel weird without her here. I've got used to waking up with her hair draped over my arm, my face, absolutely everywhere, and now it's not going to be there.

"Don't worry, you can sneak in whenever you want to. I'll even give you a key if you want one."

I close the distance between us, needing to be close as much as she does when she wraps her arms around my waist and rests her face against my chest, breathing me in before kissing me gently.

"It's not forever," she repeats, telling herself as much as she's telling me, probably more. Maybe if she says it another twenty-four trillion times it will feel like the truth.

"A key sounds great."

The first thing she did after we left the compound with Leo's credit card was get the doors and windows replaced on the house. Her mother had a fit when she got home two days later and couldn't get in, but I'm quietly confident that Ruby didn't feel an ounce of guilt over it. I know I didn't. I only wish we'd been there to see the look on her face.

After that came the new bedroom furniture and the flooring she wanted, and she spent way more time than I think either of us anticipated looking at kitchens, only to change her mind and decide it wasn't worth it for the couple of months she was going to be there.

The priority was to get the house secure and safe, and to make her space comfortable until she could escape to pastures new, with me, and the rest of the team, but we'll not worry about that too much just yet.

Ivy and Scarlett gave her a whole two days before booking in a shopping trip that I'm not going to relish tagging along to, but I guess this is the start of something new for all of us. She's finally got friends that want to open her eyes to all the things she's missed out on. And I get the opportunity to be there, so it's not something I'm willing to dismiss offhand.

"Shall we get this party on the road, then?" she asks, pulling me back in to the moment. "I've already said goodbye to your mum, and Blaise left his number on the bedside table this morning. I'm assuming that's his moving out gift, seen as you probably have it already."

"Sounds about right," I agree. "He's never been one for goodbyes, and with both of us leaving shortly, at least this way you can keep in touch with him if you need anything."

"I thought it was just so that I had someone to complain to about you." She smirks, looking up at me through dark lashes.

"Nah, you'd need to bitch at Leo about that, and I'd assume that Blaise has taken your number too, just in case you get a random text."

"Good to know."

Pulling back, I move towards the passenger side, open her door and let her in before I jump in the driver's seat and start her up. It still hurts like a fucker, but I'm not dying, and my leg is not at any risk of breaking, so that's progress.

Progress I'll take.

I know Leo still wants someone else to drive Ruby, and Carl and Rob are not going anywhere, but this one is on me. She links her phone to the car and picks a playlist, watching out the window as we wind through the streets, heading back to the place she's called home until recently, her fingers linked through mine.

It barely looks the same when we pull up, the dark-grey trim and modern doorframe giving it an updated look that it desperately needed. There are new curtains over the windows, and fresh flowers on her bedroom windowsill.

I guess that means I'm not the only one who knows she's heading home today.

"Ready?" I ask.

"Nope, but let's do this anyway."

She peels one of the keys off and drops it into my hand before climbing out to reach for one of the bags in the back. Together, we manage to get everything to the house, opening the door to the smell of fresh paint.

The flooring I had put down now sits pretty against clean, painted walls, and repaired lighting. The banister no longer hangs off, and it looks like a house that someone actually cares about, unlike before.

She's finally got the freedom to choose what she wants, and she's embracing it if the smile on her face is anything to go by. We don't bother peeking in the rooms downstairs, instead making our way straight up to her bedroom and the new things she's picked out there.

The walls are steeped in charcoal and burgundy, with the copper accents and wall lights giving it a classy finish, but the thing my eye is drawn to is the huge, four-poster bed sitting in the middle of the room. No longer is her bed a mattress on a floor. Now it's a space fit for a queen.

It's about time.

"Who put these here?" she asks, plucking a card from the flowers as she balances a box on her hip. "Hope you don't mind me letting myself in. Glad to see you're finally helping yourself first, but you've barely broken a sweat on that card. Keep going."

"Leo," we both say at the same time.

The only other person with a key is her mother, and I'm quietly confident she isn't leaving flowers in her room.

"I think you're gonna need a new wardrobe, too, if the girls have anything to do with it," I muse.

I know how little is stashed in hers currently, and I don't think I'm the only one. There's a reason Blaise bought her enough clothes to stay with us for weeks on end, and I'm reasonably sure it's not because he enjoys her company.

He may have acted like a protective arsehole at first, but the two of them have formed some kind of truce and even managed to smile and laugh together on one occasion. It's not bestie status, but it's something.

"Oh, I'm sure they've got all kind of plans for skirts and shoes and handbags made by people with names I can't even pronounce," she replies, dropping the card on the desk and putting the box on the new computer chair. "But I have something else we need to test out first."

"Yeah? What's that?" I ask, closing the wardrobe.

She wraps her arms around my stomach, nestling her face against my shoulder blade when she whispers, "The bed."

"And what, exactly, needs testing out on this bed?" I ask, smiling as I let her lead me towards the oversized thing.

"Just the usual. What if it's lumpy and uncomfortable?"

She pushes me down on to it, waiting until I've shuffled up to the pillow before joining me, her hair tickling my arm as she gets comfortable on the pillow beside me.

"Considering what you paid, I'd be surprised if it was."

It's interesting what you pick when money becomes no object.

"Squeaky?"

I give the mattress a testing push with my hands, but there are no squeaks.

"Well, then. Seen as we're here, we may as well just…" She turns towards me and wraps one leg over mine as her hands skate across my chest, and before I've consciously thought about it, my body is moving towards hers like we're two magnets drawn together.

Her soft lips meet mine in a lazy kiss, tongues tangling as we take our time and enjoy the moment, until the front door bangs shut.

"I don't know who you think you are sending someone to change the locks on my house, but you've got some explaining to do, young lady," Ruby's mother yells, seething as she stamps up the stairs.

Rearing back, Ruby is on high alert before her bedroom door flies open and her mother is planted in the doorway.

"It's lovely to see you to, Mother."

"Well? What do you have to say for yourself?" she demands, crossing her arms over her chest.

I may as well not be here as far as she's concerned. She probably spends way more hours than any of us know ignoring and avoiding the rest of the associates around the compound, so I'm probably nothing more than background noise.

"What do *I* have to say? Well, did you notice the doors and windows have changed, too? It's not just the locks." Ruby peels her leg from mine, preparing for whatever battle this is going to be, and I get to be here for the ride. Great.

"Don't be a smart arse. You know exactly what I mean."

"You've got a key now. What's the problem? Do you want me to change them back to the ones that barely closed and wouldn't have stopped anyone getting in if they needed to?"

She's not wrong. They didn't stop me, and I didn't even try very hard. The only reason I left the front door was because I was doing my best to be unobtrusive, and she never even noticed it was broken.

"It's not about that, and you know it."

"What is it about, then? The new paintwork? The flooring? The fact that I actually have a bed to sleep on now? Go on, tell me. What is it about?" Ruby throws back.

"You came to my workplace, you assaulted my colleague, and then you locked me out of my own home. What on earth kind of a daughter does that?"

Colleague? I think that's pushing the boundaries of the truth.

"What kind of..." Ruby replies, then suddenly speechless for a moment. "What kind of mother leaves her teenage daughter home alone, night after night, so she can go out drinking and fucking at parties? Fuck that, it's been going on much longer than that, hasn't it, *Mother*? You were out doing that and forgetting about me long before I was a teenager."

"That's not fair—"

"Fair? You must be out of your mind to walk in here and talk to me about what's fair. I've done some awful things to keep you safe over the last year, and for what? For you to deny my existence, turning up day after day at the home of the man you want, who doesn't give a shit about you. You know that, though, don't you? That he couldn't care less. That he used you to keep me in line the same way he used Dex and his brother to keep Leo in line. Oh, yeah, my half-brother. The one I never knew existed."

Ruby is breathing hard when she gets to the end of her tirade, but all of her truths are now out there.

"Half-brother. That's what he's going with, is it?" her mother huffs out. "Way to step in and be the big man, now."

Her tone gets my back up. Not that she notices when she continues.

"That boy has had everything handed to him, but finally, Vincent is paying some attention to us. Haven't you noticed the house has been getting better recently? That things are looking up. That's because he's taking care of us. And then you turn up, kicking off and sending his son in to vouch for you so that you can swan off to college and leave me here. You're being a silly little girl, and I thought I raised you better than this."

"Raised me?" Ruby's voice reaches fever pitch, and she's practically vibrating with anger, but I step in, placing a calm hand on her leg before turning to address the poison that is Rita Sheridan.

"Now, let's get a few things cleared up, shall we? The house has been getting better because *I've* been making repairs, and now *your* daughter is paying for them with money that she should have always had access to. You are very lucky she's even bothering and hasn't just walked out of here completely as far as I'm concerned," I intervene.

"I don't know who –"

"Leo has been through hell and back, and you better not utter his name in my presence again," I continue, cutting her off. "And if there is one more negative thing to come from your tongue about the woman I love, I'll cut the fucking thing off and hand it to Vincent Windsor myself. We'll see just what interest he has in you when you can no longer suck his dick."

You could hear a pin drop in the house next door, it's that silent when I stop, but I can still feel the rage vibrating beneath Ruby's skin, and my intervention hasn't sated her in the slightest.

"You don't get to bring his attack dog in here and let him speak to me like that, either," Rita continues, waving her finger, until I stand, and then her mouth snaps closed very quickly.

She's been around that compound long enough to know exactly who I am and the reputation that precedes me. Pissing me off any further is not going to end well for anyone in this room, and she knows it.

"He's here because I asked him to be, because he's the one who's been keeping me safe from you and that dickhead you're obsessed with," Ruby says from behind my shoulder.

"Now, you're going to walk back out of this house and be any-fucking-where else until Ruby and I leave for dinner, and the next time you have something to say to her, it will be thank you," I warn her, making it abundantly clear where the two of us stand right now.

Ruby's mother stands agape. Her mouth opens and closes but no words tumble from between her lips. Then, as if brought out of her stupor, she stamps her foot and walks out, a growl turning into a screech as she stomps down the stairs. Neither Ruby or I breathe or move until the front door slams, then we both tumble to the bed laughing.

"Did she really just storm out of here like a toddler because you told her to?" Ruby asks once she eventually catches her breath.

"I think she did."

"And what was that about dinner?"

"We'll need to go out and get food eventually. I didn't actually specify whether that was going to be today or not."

She smiles, wrapping her arms around my neck, and it warms something deep inside I'd once thought was lost long ago. Ruby Sheridan has been putting back the pieces of my soul a lot longer than she realises.

"I love you, too, by the way."

twenty-eight
Ruby

The hostess smiles when I enter, looking way more interested than I wish she would once she notices Dex following me into the diner. She barely spares me a second glance but offers him her hand out the second he's within reaching distance.

"It's so nice to see you again," she purrs, and for the briefest second, I wonder if they have history together.

She's taller than me, curvy in all the places women are supposed to be curvy, blonde, smiley, and she's older than me. Not by much, but enough to be on his radar more than I am. I know nothing about his past or his dating history. Maybe she's hoping for a second chance, or a third. Except, he does nothing to acknowledge the flirty interest she directs his way, simply shaking her hand and pulling me into his side.

"Sure, we've got a table booked," he dismisses.

You can practically see the wind escape the sails she was just floating high on right in front of us as his familiar aftershave wraps around me, once again the safety blanket I didn't even realise I was used to.

"For two?" she asks, looking on her tablet.

"Ten," I correct, just as Nate and Scarlett come barrelling through the doorway behind us.

"Found you. This way, please."

The waitress swings her hips a little more than necessary and reaches out to touch Dex's arm as he takes a seat, until I check her with my shoulder, turning to speak to Scarlett. She doesn't reach for him again, but she doesn't openly acknowledge it either, instead taking our drink orders and disappearing.

I know he's a good-looking guy, but people need to learn to keep their damn hands off.

Before long, Ivy, Leo, Nick, Jacob, and Wyatt tumble through the doorway, laughing and giggling as they join us, the table filling faster than I expected when Blaise arrives. Everyone meets and greets, hair is complimented, new shirts shown off, and Ivy even notices the bracelet she picked out for me wrapped around my wrist.

As the meal goes on, I look around the table, and my heart is fuller than I ever expected it could be. Ivy wormed her way in there, even though I had been sent to spy on her, and once she'd found a hold, there was no way she was letting go.

Then there's Scarlett, and even though she was sent to keep an eye on me by her brother, we're two of a kind, and I'm not willing to give that up, either. It seems like Nate is along for the ride with her though, and he does pay for decent ice cream, so that's an exception I'll allow.

And the guys? Well, Blaise comes as a package deal with Dex, and the truce we're manoeuvring at the minute is holding. Jacob comes with Leo and Nick, and Wyatt comes with Ivy, and all five of them come together, so that's a whole lot of complicated I don't have time to unravel right now.

Even though my mother stormed out of our house upset that I wasn't being the dutiful daughter she expected me to be by cleaning up the home we live in and preparing myself for the life I'm going to create for myself, I know I'm better off without her.

She's done the best she was able to, as short as it fell, but I don't have to settle for less anymore because I have a table full of friends and family here to care for and support me. People who have lifted me up and kept me safe. That have cared about me even when I didn't deserve it.

And that's what I hold onto when the waitress looks longingly at our table, knowing that this is a circle she'll never be invited to.

These people ae the family that chose me, and I'm choosing them, too.

epilogue
Ruby

S omething shuffles in the back seat, but not far because it is crammed full of boxes and bags and things and stuff. Who knew you could accumulate so much stuff in such a few short months? I swear you could have put my entire belongings into two boxes before I met Leo, and now it's taking up the back of two cars.

"We're almost there. Are you ready?" Dex asks from the driver's seat, checking the second car follows when he indicates and turns.

"As ready as I'll ever be."

"And you're happy with the house?"

Ivy was sneaky.

We went for a drive around. Just to look, of course. We drove through the different neighbourhoods around the college campus and took a tour of the dorms. She even made sure to ask me about whether I wanted a big place or a small place, and if I was hoping for roommates or a single space.

Then she took all the information she'd gathered up

straight back to Leo, who found and bought two semi-detached houses from the people who were living in them —they weren't even up for sale. Then they colluded with Dex, who took all my kitchen and bathroom shopping ideas to them and had the whole damn thing remodelled.

There are five bedrooms, a security room, an office, two living rooms, a craft room, and the kitchen of my dreams. And when I asked them who on earth was going to look after all that square footage, he informed me that the housekeeper and gardener would be there weekly.

I'm not sure which world I woke up in, but it's one hell of a leap from the one I lived in six months ago.

"I'm over the moon with the house, and the people living in it with me," I reply, squeezing Dex's hand.

An engine roars from somewhere nearby, and a motorbike comes flying down the road behind us, pulling up alongside and flipping his visor up before tapping on the window.

"Is that Tanner?"

"Yes," Dex replies through grit teeth. "What on earth does he want?"

After pulling over, Tanner parks up in front of us, then both the guys in the car behind us are out and moving towards ours before the engine is even turned off.

Tanner isn't alone either, and before I'm out of the car to ask what's going on, both Hugo and Everett are pulling up behind us, too.

"What's up?" I ask warily, watching Rob move to my left as Dex rounds the car towards me, my little protective bubble in full force.

"Jesus, I thought we'd sorted all this shit out and were cool now?" Tanner asks, stepping closer.

"You just pulled me off the road with no reason, and your buddies are here. I'm not sure I'm feeling very forgiving today," Dex tells him "What do you want?"

"You're moving into that big house near college today, right?" Everett asks as the three of them come together, our cars pinned in.

"Why?" I ask, looking between the three of them for some kind of reasoning.

"You've got security there?" Tanner asks.

"Obviously," Dex replies, gesturing to Rob and Carl, who loiter ominously around us.

"And you'll be staying, too. You're not leaving Ruby alone in that house, are you?" Hugo asks.

Warning bells ring in my head.

Something has happened, another war is breaking lose and I'm about to be in the middle of it, again. Only, instead of being trapped between the Five Families and a secret society, I'm going to be at risk from the family of my best friend.

Every worst-case scenario flickers through my mind quicker than I can keep hold of them, but there's only one way to get to the bottom of it, and that's by asking the question.

"What the hell kind of a question is that?" I bite back. "All I want to do it go to college. Is that really too much to ask? What on earth is going on now?" I complain, already picturing the lockdown they'll have me in.

I won't be able to breathe for them.

"No, no. Nothing has happened," Tanner intervenes, offering his hands out in surrender. "Scarlett wants to go with you. If you can guarantee her safety, I think I could talk our father into letting her go."

"What? Really?"

Suddenly, a lockdown doesn't seem that bad. If I'm being locked down with Dex and Scarlett, I think I could probably survive for a little while.

"What's in it for us?" Dex asks, crossing his arms. "We'd be taking on a lot of risk by adding her into the house, and I can't guarantee there will be someone with her all the time."

I'm on pins and needles waiting to see how this plays out while knowing better than to interrupt them when they're in work mode. This isn't about me and my best friend being able to live and learn together or being able to barter for our freedom together. This is them negotiating that freedom.

"Oh, she doesn't need *this* kind of security," Hugo bushes off, gesturing to Rob and Carl. "But we're the overprotective brothers and we need to know she's not sneaking off to some little boyfriend or getting herself knocked up at fresher's week."

Yes. Yes. Yes.

"Gotcha." Dex nods, clicking his fingers.

He's the head of the security team, so it's down to him who he's letting inside the safety of the house we share, but I can't help but cross my fingers at my sides.

"She knows where the house is, and there's a spare room. I'm sure if she were to turn up, we'd be able to accommodate, but make sure she's not any crazier than this one." Dex wraps an arm around me. "And we'll call a favour or two in at some point. I'm expecting a favourable answer when that day comes."

"Absolutely, thanks man." Tanner offers his hand out, and Dex shakes it, the two of them finally coming to some kind of truce too.

The man I care about and the brother of my best friend. Two people who have been on almost opposite sides of a line for a long time, now settling on something akin to a truce.

Two of the daughters of the underworld tackling life, love, and freedom together.

Watch out world. You're not ready.

***

Thank you for reading Perilous Desire. I hope you enjoyed it.
Catch up with what happened at Pendleton Prep with Her Devil: Books2read.com/HerDevil
And get ready for more with the Five Families series.

Why not keep in touch with me here:
https://authorhlpacker.com/keep-in-touch/

Find out what happened at Pendleton Prep with Ivy, Leo, Nick, Jacob, and Wyatt.

DEVIL

I should have known that this was coming...

I'd done the right things, chosen the right friends, kept my grades up, primped and primed and smiled when I was supposed to, and then I escaped the clutches of the man they'd chosen for me. What. An. Idiot.

If I spend the year at Pendleton Prep, I can go back on my merry way. The problem is that life here is not exactly what I expected.

I'm not just another student, here to serve her time and get out. Oh no, that would never do. I've been wrapped up and served on a platter for the Devils of Pendleton Prep.

They're hot, stupidly hot, and involved in something I want nothing to do with.

More than one of them has me set in their sights, but I'm already entangled in the world of the elite, they just don't realise it yet. Where ten begin, only three will end... how far will they go to secure their place?

This secret society, dark academia, poly romance starts off with Ivy and Tamsin arriving at Pendleton Prep, clouded in secrets and wrapped up in lies. Can they untangle this web, or will they be left to die?

THE FIVE FAMILIES OF SOUTH BEACH.

Loughty. Osborne. Peregrine. Milligan. Wheeler.

Once upon a time, they were at war, fighting each other and everyone else for tiny pieces of a large pie. They battled and warred, gained an inch against one just to turn around and lose it to another, until the day someone else turned up to fight.

With more money and experience, Gerard Windsor walked into South Beach and decimated the existing structures, laying waste to anyone and everyone in his path. All except these five families folded, handing over their spoils and walking away.

The ones who didn't cave banded together to find safety and security in their unity. They fought their corner, sniping away at shipments and disrupting sales, making a nuisance of themselves until Mr Windsor could no longer ignore their influence.

Instead of crushing them beneath the heel of his boot, he appreciated their ingenuity, granting each of the Five Families a piece of the pie on the condition that they remain separate, individual entities, and paid forth their dues, of course.

But as each father passed down this legacy to his son, and

his son in turn, the stories changed. No longer a tale of unity and the underdog claiming his prize, it became twisted and fraught with miscommunications and misunderstandings, until five boys at the same primary school hated each other, with no real reason as to why.

So, when Tomasz Novak proposed the question: "Is the enemy of your enemy your friend?" it changed the course of their lives.

One became two, and two became three, but three could never become four, and the five would never be reunited. The Five Families would remain divided and at odds with each other. They had to, if only the youngest generation knew why.

Milligan and Wheeler. Loughty, Osborne, and Peregrine. Separate and safe.

But in the dark, secrets are shared, and what happens when those secrets threaten to topple everything?

acknowledgements

Thank you so much for being here and reading Dex and Ruby's story, I hope you enjoyed it!

I want to say a massive thank you to my husband for telling me all those years ago that one day I'd write a book. I guess you were right ;) I know I wouldn't have been able to do it without you though.

Thanks also has to go to Hannah for keeping me on the straight and narrow and all the writing springs, to Donna, Stephanie and Karen for their beta feedback and support, and to all the bloggers that have liked, shared, created, and generally fallen in love with this story as much as I have.

About the Author

H.L. Packer is, quite frankly, a busy bee.
An avid reader as a child, her love for all things written waned into adulthood, the excitement of real life things taking over. But when her life slowed down as she finished her office job for maternity leave, her husband purchased her an e-reader, and that obsession was rekindled.

Quickly she went from reader to reviewer, and then from reviewer to blogger; street teams and promo tours galore. When she began collating her own book boxes over at Romance Readers Book Box UK and had the opportunity to include her own words and worlds, the characters began talking.

Those cheeky characters quickly found themselves written down on the page, and her first series was in progress.

When she is not coordinating her worlds, you can find her running around after her free-spirited three children, and husband, or tending to the dogs, bearded dragons, and snakes that also reside with them.

A break can be found soaking in a bubble bath or enjoying a glass of wine, often still with a book in her hand.

Newsletter: https://bit.ly/3rdYAny

Also by H.L. Packer

Fated Series

Home

Within Reach

Within Hope

The Shadow

Amore

La Familglia

The Ties that Bind

The Bonds That Break

Pendleton Prep

The Sect

Her Devil

IIis Angel

Their Hell

Standalones

Sinister Protector

Perilous Desire